FADE TO
BLACK

ALSO BY DAVID ROSENFELT

ANDY CARPENTER NOVELS

Collared

The Twelve Dogs of Christmas

Outfoxed

Who Let the Dog Out?

Hounded

Unleashed

Leader of the Pack

One Dog Night

Dog Tags

New Tricks

Play Dead

Dead Center

Sudden Death

Bury the Lead

First Degree

Open and Shut

THRILLERS

Blackout

Without Warning

Airtight

Heart of a Killer

On Borrowed Time

Down to the Wire

Don't Tell a Soul

NONFICTION

Lessons from Tara: Life Advice from the World's Most Brilliant Dog

Dogtripping: 25 Rescues, 11 Volunteers, and 3 RVs on Our Canine Cross-Country Adventure

FADE TO BLACK

DAVID ROSENFELT

MINOTAUR BOOKS

NEW YORK

FADE TO BLACK. Copyright © 2018 by Tara Productions, Inc. All rights reserved. Printed in the United States of America. For information, address St. Martin's Press, 175 Fifth Avenue, New York, N.Y. 10010.

www.minotaurbooks.com

Designed by Omar Chapa

Library of Congress Cataloging-in-Publication Data

Names: Rosenfelt, David, author.
Title: Fade to black / David Rosenfelt.
Description: First edition. | New York : Minotaur Books, 2018.
Identifiers: LCCN 2017050901 | ISBN 9781250133120 (hardcover) |
    ISBN 9781250133137 (ebook)
Subjects: LCSH: Police—New Jersey—Fiction. | Murder—
    Investigation—Fiction. | Amnesia—Fiction. | GSAFD:
    Suspense fiction. | Mystery fiction.
Classification: LCC PS3618.O838 F33 2018 | DDC 813/.6—dc23
LC record available at https://lccn.loc.gov/2017050901

Our books may be purchased in bulk for promotional, educational, or business use. Please contact your local bookseller or the Macmillan Corporate and Premium Sales Department at 1-800-221-7945, extension 5442, or by email at MacmillanSpecialMarkets@macmillan.com.

First Edition: March 2018

10 9 8 7 6 5 4 3 2 1

FADE TO BLACK

His name was William Simmons, but no one he knew really cared about that.

SOCIAL WORKERS ASKED HIM FOR HIS NAME WHEN THEY GAVE him a meal, or if he checked in for a cot on a particularly cold night, but they wrote it down without paying much attention. He could have said "Adolf Hitler" or "Kim Kardashian" and they probably would have dutifully made the notation without so much as looking up. He was a number, a placeholder, so his identity was of no consequence.

On the rare occasions when they spoke to him or referred to him by name, they called him Willie. It was as if they felt William carried a dignity he did not deserve, and they neither knew nor cared that he had never been called Willie in his entire life.

He didn't think of them as bad people; on the contrary, he recognized that they were performing selfless and much-needed work. But they were so consumed with the task of helping people that they didn't have time to really see the people they were helping.

William had been on the streets for almost sixteen months, but he probably didn't really know, at least not exactly. One day just went into the next, and into the next. He measured time in seasons, and he measured seasons by the weather. And he never looked back; that was much too painful.

The vast majority of the people on the street hated winter the most, but not William. He couldn't stand summer; in his mind that was the worst. He could guard against the cold by covering up with cloth and paper, or by getting into unlocked hallways in some buildings. When it got really bad he could go to a shelter; all he had to do was give them his name. Or any name.

But when it was hot, and the streets of Hackensack, New Jersey, could get really hot, there was no escape. The shelters weren't air-conditioned and thus provided no relief at all. So he spent the summers anxiously waiting for the fall, for football weather, which unfortunately reminded him of his high school playing days.

Complicating every day of William's life was the fact that his eyesight was maybe 20 percent of normal. He had suffered from macular degeneration for almost fifteen years, and was no longer able to get treatment of any kind for it.

This particular November night the temperature was in the mid-forties, no problem at all for William. He was lying in the alley behind the Italian restaurant, where it was quiet and he could snack on the discarded food. They threw everything away in containers and plastic bags, so it was clean and safe to eat.

At night, William liked to be off the beaten path like this, where it was peaceful and pedestrians wouldn't be coming by making noise. In the morning, he'd be out front, trying to get money from the people heading to work.

He sometimes thought about one day getting enough money to get a place to live, but he was fooling himself, and down deep he was smart enough to know it. He also thought about getting a job, but he didn't think he could face the real world again. And besides, listing your address as "behind the Italian restaurant" was unlikely to motivate potential employers.

But the night was for resting and sleeping, and that was what

William was doing when the man came by. He woke William up; not with his foot, like most people would, but by leaning over and shaking his shoulder. Not aggressive at all, almost like they were on a train and he was telling his fellow passenger that they had reached their stop.

"Wake up, fella. Come on."

It took William a little while to get his bearings and focus on what was happening. He looked up, but in the darkness, and with his very limited eyesight, he couldn't tell what the man looked like. He also couldn't tell how big he was; from his prone position every-one would look big. "What do you want?" he asked.

"I got some stuff for you," the man said. "Drugs. Whatever you need. Free."

In his groggy state, it didn't make sense to William. It wouldn't even have made sense if he was clearheaded and totally awake; people didn't come along and offer him free drugs.

"I don't do no drugs," William said, because it was true. He never had and never would. By then he was thinking that maybe the man was a dealer looking to get him hooked so he would have to pay for the stuff down the road. Which was ridiculous on its face; how could a man sleeping in an alley be considered a future source of profit?

"Come on, of course you do," the man said.

"Leave me alone, will ya? I don't do drugs. Let me sleep."

"Sure. My mistake. No problem," the man said, smiling at his good fortune. "Go back to sleep."

William laid his head back down on the little towel he used as a makeshift pillow. The man suddenly and swiftly pulled the towel away and brought his foot down on William's head. The entire two hundred and ten pounds of the man's weight came down, crushing William's head into the pavement.

The man reached down and expertly felt William's neck, searching for a pulse. He found a weak one; William was still alive.

Rather than finish the job, the man calmly walked away. William's injury would no doubt be fatal, and the man knew he would die later, at the hospital.

With his gloved hand, he took a cell phone out of his pocket and dialed 911. It was a phone he had purchased for cash that day, the kind there is no contract for.

He told the 911 operator about having discovered a body behind the restaurant, and when asked, said that he had no idea if the man was alive, but at the very least he was hurt badly.

The man promised to wait there until the police arrived. Then he hung up and just walked away into the night, dropping the phone in a trash can. He wiped it clean, even though he was wearing gloves and could not have left any fingerprints. He was very careful about things like that.

Behind him he could hear the sirens, and he allowed himself another smile.

"I don't really want to be here," I say.

I DON'T MEAN TO OFFEND HER BY SAYING THAT, AND HER SMILE indicates she understands.

"That's as good a place to start as any, Doug," Pamela says. "If you feel that way, then why are you here?"

"My girlfriend . . . my fiancée . . . Jessie Allen . . . suggested it. She thinks it might help."

"But you don't?"

I shake my head. "Not really."

"Why do you feel that way?"

"How much do you know about me?" I ask, hoping that I don't have to tell the story from scratch. I'm tired of telling my story, and thinking about my story, and worrying about my story, and living my story.

"Maybe a lot, maybe very little," she says. "I've seen your story in the media, of course. It was rather impossible to avoid; you're something of a celebrity. So based on that, I would say you're a state police officer who is considered a hero for preventing a huge terrorist attack on many buildings in New York City. I know that you were shot, and that you've had some memory issues."

"Memory issues," I repeat. "Yeah, you could say that."

"But all of that is from media reports. I usually find that I don't really know anything about a person until I hear from them directly."

"What you heard is all true, especially the part about me being 'considered' a hero," I say, emphasizing "considered."

"That's not how you see it?" she asks.

"A lot of people did a lot of good things. I was one of them. I was doing my job."

"Why don't you tell me about it from your perspective?"

So that's what I do; I tell her about it. I don't talk much about the nuts and bolts of what happened on the police side of things, since the media reported it pretty accurately. I helped stop a terrorist attack, and I killed an organized crime figure named Nicholas Bennett in the process.

I got much more praise than I deserved, but I've stopped saying that publicly, since people just frown and say I'm being too modest.

But I do tell her about my being shot and falling off that balcony and sustaining the head injury that caused me to lose ten years of my memory. And I tell her that I've learned that losing ten years of my memory is the same as losing ten years of my life.

Of course, I remember nothing whatsoever about the shooting itself; that's one of the periods I have been completely unable to recall. But I've been taken through how it happened, and even visited the scene.

"I had, or I should say I have, what they call 'retrograde amnesia.' Are you familiar with it?"

Pamela nods. "I am, Doug. Although it can take a number of forms. Are you still experiencing symptoms?"

I nod. "They're getting better, but at the same time they're getting worse."

"What do you mean?"

"I got quite a bit of my memory back; it's hard to say how much, since I don't know what I don't know . . . but probably a third of it.

There's no rhyme or reason to it. I remember some older things but not some that are more recent. Some important stuff and some meaningless events. And I'm very slowly remembering more all the time, so that's good."

"You said it's also getting worse."

"Yeah. I'm also experiencing more memory loss from that period. Some of the things I've remembered, I'm losing them again. It's a weird feeling; I *remember* remembering something, but not when it actually happened. Am I making sense?"

"You are," she says, but I'm not sure I believe her.

"Are you forgetting current things? Or just things that happened before you were shot?"

"Nothing current," I say. "I remember everything that has happened since then. I'm able to form new memories."

"Good. So what is your goal in coming to see me?" she asks.

"Jessie thinks that all of this is affecting me emotionally, that it's a strain. She thinks you can help with that . . . getting me to deal with it better."

Pamela smiles. "So now I know what Jessie thinks. What do you think?"

"I think it's probably a waste of time," I say. "Sorry about that."

She smiles. "No problem; I appreciate the honesty. Have you ever been in therapy before?"

"I don't think so." Now it's my turn to force a smile. "But I can't be sure, you know?"

"Do you think you're under an emotional strain?" she asks.

I shrug. "I guess so; it's certainly on my mind all the time. But the problem will exist, no matter how long we talk about it. So if I know that's the bottom line, I just have to deal with it and accept it. No one can do that for me but me. Not you, not Jessie, nobody."

"So that's what you think you'll get out of coming here. Now tell me what you would hope to get out of it in a perfect world."

"I know you can't help me get my memories back. I just don't want to be a basket case when I go back on the job."

"You haven't been working?"

"No. I took some time off. With all the publicity and stuff, and with all I went through, it seemed like a good idea. And believe it or not, I actually earned much more money. Groups and companies paid me to come talk to them, which is about as ridiculous as it gets."

She smiles. "Nice work if you can get it."

I return the smile. "And I got to throw out the first pitch at a Mets game, which was very cool."

"What have you been doing to help yourself?" she asks.

"I've been going to an amnesia recovery group," I say. "Another one of Jessie's ideas; she's pretty much desperate to help me. I'm going there later; a lot of talking going on today."

"How is the group working out?"

I shrug. "It's an okay way to waste time. Nobody seems to be recovering in the recovery group. We just talk about not recovering, and wanting to recover."

She nods as if she knows what I mean; for all I know she runs a group just like it. Then, "So you've told me you don't want to be a basket case when you get back to work. What other goals do you have? Personal ones."

I think for a few moments, trying to decide if I should go where I'm about to go. "I guess I'd like to find out who I am" is what I finally say.

"What do you mean?"

"People, like Jessie and my partner, Nate, tell me that I've changed a lot. For example, I used to be much more of a risk taker, especially on the job. I was hard to control; I would sometimes act too quickly, before I thought things through. 'Impulsive in the extreme' is the way Jessie describes it, and Nate nods when she says it."

"And now your actions and behavior have changed?"

I nod. "Yes, or so I'm told. But I don't care so much about that. What I care about is that I don't remember being like that. And I'm not talking about events; it's like I have no internal connection to the person they are describing. Yet the person they are describing is me."

"That must be disconcerting," she says.

"You got that right. So I don't know whether I've changed because I've changed, or because of my injury."

"People can undergo change as the result of a number of factors, certainly including a catastrophic physical or emotional event," she says. "It's quite natural and normal for that to happen. And you and the people around you would notice some of the changes, and not others."

"Right now I feel like I'm standing outside my body, watching my behavior. That is also pretty damn disconcerting. So, bottom line, there's one thing I want to know when it comes to me."

"And that is?"

"What's real and what isn't?"

"Doug, my name is Sean Connor. Can I talk to you about something?"

IT'S ONE OF THE OTHER MEMBERS OF THE AMNESIA RECOVERY group, coming up to me after our meeting. I've seen him here a couple of times, but he's been quiet.

I'm not thrilled with the request. I'm sort of talked out right now when it comes to memory loss, and I'm sure that's what this is about. My hero status in the media has made me something of a celebrity in the group, when I'd much rather be anonymous. I've been thinking of bailing out of the group entirely; I feel worse when I leave a session than when I went in. I don't think it's supposed to work that way.

"You mean now?" I ask. "Because I really need to get home."

"No, not now. There's something I have to show you, and I don't have it with me."

"Okay. Maybe before the next meeting?"

"I was hoping that maybe we could meet somewhere away from here. It's pretty important, and I want to keep it private."

He seems nervous about making the request, and I'm feeling a little bad for him. "What's it about, Sean?"

"I really can't say right now; you need to see what I have. But I wouldn't be asking unless . . ."

I finish the sentence for him. ". . . it was important."

He smiles a nervous smile. "Yeah. I promise I'm not going to waste your time, although in a way I hope I am."

That's a little cryptic, but I don't really want an explanation right now. "Okay, Sean, but I don't know any more about this stuff than you do. I'm just taking it one day at a time, trying to figure it out."

He shakes his head again. "It's not about memory loss. Well, it is, in a way, but that's not why I'm coming to you." He pauses for a moment, as if trying to decide whether to go on. Finally, "I'm talking to you because you're a police officer."

I don't feel like I should be asking more questions; it seems like he's going to let the information dribble out when and where he wants to. I'm also not all that interested. "When would you like to talk, Sean?"

"I was thinking tomorrow, maybe eight in the morning?"

I tell him that's fine with me, and we make a plan to meet at a small coffee shop that he says is near his house in Clifton. "I can't tell you how much I appreciate this," he says, "no matter how it turns out."

Nate Alvarez is waiting for me across
the street when I come out.

HE IS STILL PARKED IN HIS UNMARKED POLICE CAR, IN FRONT OF
the Dunkin' Donuts, just where he was when I went in. He is fin-
ishing off a cup of coffee as I get in the car.

"You been talking all this time?" Nate asks.

"It seemed longer in there, believe me. But mostly I've been listening. You didn't have to drive me here and wait like this."

"I got nothing else to do; I'm off today." He points to the
Dunkin' Donuts. "You want some coffee?"

"No."

"I'm gonna get another cup."

"There are a lot of donuts in there," I point out. "It's a danger
zone. Might be safer to use the drive-through." Nate is six foot three
and two hundred and eighty pounds, and is always claiming to be
on a diet. If that's true, it has been the least successful diet in history.

"No problem," Nate says. "I was in there before. Just coffee all
the way; no donuts for me. It's a mind-over-matter situation."

"I think matter might have won the last round. You've got
powdered sugar on your face."

Nate is caught in the act, and the fact that he quickly wipes his face cannot erase his guilt. Instead, he angrily goes on the offensive. "It's goddamn entrapment in there. They advertise coffee, and then they practically shove those donuts in your face when you walk in. We should shut them down."

"It's called Dunkin' *Donuts*, Nate."

"I know what it's called."

"I was just pointing out that you're on a diet."

"*That* you remember?" he asks. "Everything else you forget, but when it comes to my diet, you've got total recall? My diet is going fine; you don't have to worry about it."

"I know. You're looking great. How much have you lost?"

"You mean on a scale?" Nate asks, obviously scoffing at the idea. "I don't worry about scales; they don't mean anything, and those digital ones are the worst. I don't let scales run my life; they're up and down. I go by distance from the wheel."

"What does that mean?"

Nate points to his stomach. "You see that? Last month my stomach was right up against the steering wheel; now look how far away it is. You can drive a truck through that space."

"Did you push the seat back?"

"You know, I liked the old you a lot better. How was the loony group today?"

"They are not loony. We are all having memory issues."

"Well, excuse me. Then how was the shrink this morning?"

"It's personal."

"I wait out here for almost an hour and you give me 'it's personal'?"

"That's right."

He shakes his head. "Shrink in the morning, loony group in the afternoon. What's on tap for tonight? Yoga? Meditation?"

"I'm going to watch a basketball game, but thanks for asking."

"You coming back to work?"

I nod. "I am. Tomorrow. After breakfast."

"It's about time." Then, "Where am I dropping you?"

"Jessie's."

"What the hell does she see in you?" he asks.

I shrug. "To tell you the truth, I don't remember."

"Let me know if you find out." Then, "Although you must have something going for you; I wouldn't risk going into a Dunkin' Donuts for anyone else."

Jessie's not home from work yet when I get there, but I have a key, so I let myself in. Her work and office are the same as mine used to be, and will be again starting tomorrow. She's a state police lieutenant, in charge of the cyber division, and she supervises all electronic surveillance as well.

It's not an assignment that thrills her. She used to be a regular cop, out on the street, but had the smarts and misfortune to show an aptitude for computers and technology. Since we were not exactly an operation full of officers with that or a similar talent, she just naturally eased into the job. She'd rather be back out in the action, but I think down deep recognizes her value where she is.

We're not officially living together; she's still in this house, and I have my apartment in Hackensack. But I'm spending more and more nights here, especially since we got engaged, and this is probably where we'll live once we're married.

Of course, I don't know when that will be; Jessie hasn't had the guts to agree on a date yet, so I'm not sure it's even an official engagement. We're sort of engaged to be engaged; we have a commitment to make a commitment.

Even though I've been spending so much time here, I still enter warily. That's because Jessie's dog, Bobo, doesn't seem thrilled by my being around. He's never been aggressive toward me; he just stares at me with a barely concealed disdain.

I like dogs very much, so ordinarily Bobo's attitude would be something I would just take in stride and gradually overcome. But the thing about Bobo is that he's enormous. Jessie says that he's a

Newfie mix, and while I'm sure that's true, he must be mixed with brontosaurus. He looks like a refrigerator with hair.

He grudgingly agrees to let me take him for a walk, which I do pretty regularly when Jessie is not home. I never know whether to use a leash or a saddle, because I think there's a decent chance Bobo could win the third race at Santa Anita.

When we get back, I feed him, in a vain attempt to get on his good side. Then he goes to sleep, only awakening when he hears Jessie come to the door. He loves Jessie, which is the one thing Bobo and I have in common.

Jessie is all smiles, and we chat about meaningless stuff while she avoids asking me the question she most wants to ask. Finally, as we're getting ready to go to bed, she blurts it out, while trying to sound casual.

"How did it go with Pamela?"

"Fantastic. I'm completely cured."

"Doug . . ."

"I talked, she listened. Then she talked and I listened. We had a blast."

"Don't expect too much too soon," she says.

I laugh. "Believe me, there's no danger of that."

"Do you still remember that you love me?"

"Absolutely. But I'm having trouble remembering why."

"Maybe I should show you," she says.

"Maybe you should."

So she does.

And another great new memory is created.

Sean Connor is waiting for me when I arrive
at the coffee shop.

HE'S SITTING AT A TABLE NEAR THE BACK, WHILE THE HALF dozen other diners in the place are up near the front. That will give us some privacy, which is what I think Sean wants. He looks even more nervous than he did yesterday; what he has to say may turn out to not be a big deal to me, but it certainly is to him.

"Hey, thanks for coming," he says, standing slightly and then sitting back down when I get there.

"No problem." I take the chair across from him and pick up the menu. "What's good here?"

"What?" he asks, as if surprised by the question. I have a feeling he never actually considered the possibility that we might be eating breakfast at our breakfast meeting.

"What's good to eat? Have you been here before?"

"Oh . . . sure. Everything's good." Then, "Get the pancakes."

I don't ever have to be convinced to get pancakes, so I don't even bother to look at the menu. The waitress comes over with some much-needed coffee, and I order blueberry pancakes.

"Short stack or full?" she asks.

"I don't know; I haven't fully thought it through."

She takes a step back and looks at my body, focusing on my stomach. "You look like you can handle the full."

I laugh. "Okay, thanks. That's the best compliment I'll have all day. Go for it. But sugar-free syrup."

Sean says he's good with just coffee, and she frowns slightly but goes off to put in the order.

"So what's on your mind, Sean?"

"I know you're doing me a favor by coming here, and I appreciate it more than you could know...but I need some assurance first."

"Assurance of what?" I ask.

"Confidentiality. I need you to promise that my name will not be attached to this, that you will not mention my involvement to anyone."

"Sean, if you're confessing to a crime, I can't give that to you. I'm not your priest or your lawyer. So if that's the case, you might want to reconsider."

"I understand that. I'm not confessing to a crime, and if you find out that I committed one, you're free to do with it whatever you want. But until that point, my name stays out of it. Please."

I can't imagine where he's going with this, but it's getting interesting. "Fair enough."

"Thank you. Does the name Rita Carlisle mean anything to you?"

I think for a moment. I have that disconcerting feeling again, the one where it feels like something is familiar, and I should know it, but I don't.

"Not at the moment, no."

"She went missing three years ago, and was never found. It was a big case around here."

I'm searching my memory bank, which in terms of size is not exactly Goldman Sachs. I come up with nothing. "It must be in one of my blank periods," I say. Since it happened three years ago, and my memory loss covers the last ten years, I'm not surprised.

He smiles a humorless smile. "Believe me, I understand." He pulls a briefcase from near his feet up onto the table. I hadn't noticed it was there. He opens it and takes out what seems to be a newspaper clipping, and puts it in front of me. "Here's a picture of her."

It's a story about the kidnapping, and the photo is of a young, pretty woman. It looks like it could be a college graduation photo, or maybe one that was originally part of a marriage announcement.

I look at it and don't say anything, and he starts taking out other clippings. "Here's another . . . and another . . . and another." They're all stories about the kidnapping.

"What about her?" I ask, looking through them.

"I'm hoping you can tell me, that you can find out what's going on. But I'm getting ahead of myself," he says.

"Yes, I think you are."

"If there are levels of memory loss, I have it worse than you," he continues. "I remember almost nothing about the last four years of my life. It's a clean slate. I've pieced a lot together, of course. I had a very good job; I was a financial counselor, and I made a lot of money. I lived in Westchester."

"Why did you move here?"

He points to the briefcase. "I'm getting there. After my accident—I was in a car accident and suffered a head injury, that's how I lost my memory. Once I came to terms with my condition, I spent a lot of time and effort learning as much as I could about myself. I'm sure you know how that is."

I nod, because I certainly know how that is, and he continues.

"I actually searched my own house to look for clues, and at one point I went into the attic. There was a lot of junk up there, but I went through it all. Eventually I found this; it was in a plastic bag, tucked under some things. Almost like it was hidden. Sorry . . . exactly like it was hidden."

He takes what looks like a scrapbook out of the briefcase and puts it in front of me. I slowly turn the pages, but I already know what I am going to find. Every page is another media story about the Rita Carlisle kidnapping; whoever put this together, and I have to assume it was Sean, was obsessed with the case.

"Did you know her?" I ask.

"I don't know. I have no memory of it."

"You want me to take this?" I ask, meaning the scrapbook.

He shakes his head. "I'd rather hold on to it for now, if you don't mind."

"Is this all you have that connects yourself to this woman?"

He shakes his head. "There's one more thing. Apparently she was at a bar in Paramus with her boyfriend the night she disappeared. They had a fight, and she stormed off."

"So?"

"I went back over my credit card records; I was there that night. The bill is a small one, probably just two drinks, or a drink and an appetizer, so I was probably alone. But obviously I can't know that for sure."

"Maybe that's why you became obsessed with the case."

"Maybe," he says, obviously doubtful about it. "Or maybe I had a more direct involvement."

"That's unlikely, Sean. You were there, you saw her, then you read about what happened and it hit you really hard that she went missing. So you followed it closely, you clipped out articles. These kind of things happen all the time."

"I clipped the articles and then hid them in my attic? Why would I do that? I wish I could believe you."

"Why are you telling me all this?" I ask, although I already know the answer.

"You're a cop, and you also understand what I'm going through with my memory loss. I want you to find out if I kidnapped that poor woman. And if I did, I want to pay the price for it."

Nate says he wants to be there when I get to work.

I ASK WHY, AND HE SAYS IT'S BECAUSE I DON'T ALWAYS SEE EYE to eye with Captain Bradley, and he doesn't want me to get fired before I actually return to work. Apparently that would have a negative impact on my pension.

It feels good to be back at the precinct. I haven't been here in a few months, and I only remember isolated parts of my time here before that. But it's comfortable; when I walk in it feels like I'm among friends. There's a camaraderie that I've missed and that I'm glad to get back.

I say hello and talk briefly to everyone I see, some of whom I actually remember, and some of whom I only know from meeting them after my injury, during the terrorist investigation. The greetings take a while, and Nate finally interrupts and says, "Unless you're going to have tea and get a bridge game going, maybe we should go see the captain. He's waiting."

Captain Jeremy Bradley seems to be a decent guy. He also quite obviously has had problems with me in the past, and both of those assessments are supported by things that Nate and Jessie have told me. It's not that he doesn't consider me a good cop; he's apparently grudgingly admitted as much on occasion. It's more that I've supposedly been difficult to control.

I know my actions in the terrorist investigation that came after my injury weren't always in line with his orders, but I was at the point where I didn't care, and I told him straight out that his only option was to fire me.

I had reached the decision that I had to do it my way; I had been shot and had my memory taken from me, and I was going to see to it that the people responsible did not get away with it. Since I was integral to the operation, he had to give in. Especially since he was being forced to take a backseat to the Feds at the time.

It worked out, and there was enough glory that he was able to get his share, but I still don't believe he was happy with my attitude. If I were him, I'd have been pissed as hell, and I probably still would be.

When Nate and I walk into his office, he doesn't get up from his desk. "Well, if it isn't the Lone Ranger and Fat Tonto" is his greeting.

"Reporting for duty," I say.

"It's about time. You sure you're finished with your media tour? I haven't seen you on *Regis and Kelly* yet."

"Regis isn't with Kelly anymore," Nate says. "Neither is Strahan."

Captain Bradley gives Nate a look and a sneer. "Thanks for sharing that, Nate." Then, to me, "You feeling okay?"

I nod. "Physically I'm fine."

"And the memory?"

"Some of it's back; some not. Doctor says it may stay that way, or not."

He nods with some sympathy. "Tough way to live. You want to start on desk duty, work your way back in slowly?"

"Actually, I was hoping you'd put me on cold cases."

Nate turns to me in surprise. "Where the hell did that come from?"

"I've been reading about a case that interests me. A kidnapping, about three years ago. Woman named Rita Carlisle."

"Then you're not reading that well, because that's not a cold case," Captain Bradley says. "The boyfriend was tried and convicted."

I'm a little embarrassed to hear this; I didn't see any mention of it in the scrapbook that Sean Connor showed me, but I had skimmed through it only briefly. I'm surprised that Sean didn't mention it to me, since the existence of a proven guilty party would make his own guilt less likely.

In any event, I should have researched all of this much more deeply before I brought it up with the captain.

"I guess that part wasn't in my memory bank," I say. "Forget I mentioned it. I'm ready to go back to doing what I used to do. No restrictions."

He nods. "Okay, starting tomorrow you're back in the rotation. I'll reassign Perez." He's talking about Artie Perez, who has functioned as Nate's partner in my absence.

"I was thinking I'd start next week, Captain."

Bradley does a double take. "Next week? Why not tomorrow?"

"There are some things I need to do."

He looks like he's about to argue, but then just shakes his head and thinks better of it. "Next week. That'll give me time to order rose petals for the guys to sprinkle when you walk in."

"Thanks, Captain; I'm partial to yellow ones."

"Get the hell out of here."

We leave the office, and Nate immediately asks, "What was that all about?"

"What?"

"Now you're not going to start until next week? And all of a sudden you want to work on cold cases? Did I miss a memo?"

"Sounds like it might be appealing."

"And the Carlisle kidnapping? Where did you come up with that?"

"I've been interested in it," I say.

"Interested in it? You don't even remember it."

"Do you?"

"Of course I do. We worked overtime for a month on it."

"Including me?" I ask.

"You sure you've been reading about it? Because if you have, then your reading skills seem to have taken a major hit."

"I have. Not everything, obviously, but my plan is to dig into it further."

"You do that," he says, shaking his head in what seems like disbelief. "You can spend the whole weekend digging."

"Do you think the boyfriend did it?"

He laughs a short laugh. "Why don't you ask the arresting officer?"

"Who is that?"

"You."

"Do you remember the Rita Carlisle case?"

"OF COURSE," JESSIE SAYS QUICKLY, AND THEN SEEMS TO REAL-ize I might not remember it. Knowing how sensitive I am about this stuff, she smiles and adds, "Vaguely. Very vaguely. Barely and vaguely."

"I don't."

"Why do you ask?"

"Can I tell you something privately? Off the record?"

"Doug, we're engaged . . . in a manner of speaking. We're going to be married . . . at some point."

"You're really going way out on a limb there," I say.

She nods. "I'm a risk taker. Anyway, semi-engaged, engaged, married . . . those are by definition private, off-the-record relationships. You can tell me anything. And I'll keep it a secret, unless we split up, and then all bets are off."

"That's so beautiful. Anyway, a guy came up to me after the meeting yesterday." I tell her the entire story, including his obvious fear that he might be the guilty party.

"What is his name?"

"I can't tell you that, at least not yet. I promised him; that was his only condition for sharing this with me. I'm not positive, but I think a solemn promise supersedes the almost-engaged-someday-possibly-to-be married-if-we-don't-split-up relationship rule."

"And you don't remember anything at all about the case?"

"Not a thing, but I've been reading about it this afternoon, and Nate has been filling me in, so it's going into that gray area."

Jessie nods; she knows what I'm talking about. When I research and learn a lot about past events that I had been a part of, then the line between actually recalling those events, and just thinking I recall them, starts to blur.

"So what are you going to do with this?"

"I told him I would check it out, so I guess I will."

"You think he could be the killer?"

Like everyone else, including me, Jessie is assuming that Rita Carlisle is dead, even though her body has not been found. "I doubt it. I think the fact that he was in the bar that night, so close to the victim, probably shook him up enough that he followed the case. Maybe he heard the argument between her and her boyfriend, and the next day, when he learned what had happened, felt guilty that he didn't somehow intervene. But he's worried it's much more than that."

"Hiding the scrapbook in the attic might change the calculation a bit."

"That's something he pointed out as well."

"There's someone in prison for this, Doug," she says. "You helped put him there."

"So I've been told. Hopefully he's in there for good reason, and that whatever I learn manages to ease the mind of the man whose name must not be spoken."

She laughs. "For a second I thought it was going to slip out." Then, "You want me to get you some more reading material?" Jessie is a Google maestro; she will get more background information in ten minutes than I would in three hours. If I was ever good on a computer, it's among the things and skills that I have lost touch with.

"That would be great. You know, you're pretty handy to have around."

"And you are some sweet talker."

I take Bobo for a walk; I bring a large plastic bag with me, because everything Bobo does is large. While we're gone, Jessie somehow manages to make a great dinner and print out what seems like the Library of Congress. I'm up until almost midnight reading about the case.

Rita Carlisle was thirty-one years old when she disappeared. She was in a management position at Bergen Hospital, the largest in North Jersey. She had married at twenty-one, and that apparent mistake lasted for two years. At thirty she met John Nicholson, a real estate agent who was three years her senior.

All their friends said it seemed to be a happy courtship and relationship, but that's what they always say after things go horribly wrong. It's like the neighbors of a terrorist or serial killer; no one ever admits to having had the slightest inkling that anything could have been amiss. The alternative to that denial is saying, "I thought that guy was going to do a mass shooting, but I decided it wasn't any of my business."

On the night of Rita's disappearance, she went with Nicholson to The Grill, a Paramus restaurant with a bar area that seems to have been one of the hotter spots in Northern New Jersey.

I've been to The Grill—just three weeks ago, in fact—and it's not a dive at all; a light beer cost me eight bucks. I'm not bitter about it, but in my mind prices for everything immediately jumped from where they were ten years ago to where they are now, so there's a bit of ongoing sticker shock involved.

Other patrons at the bar said that all was calm until an argument broke out between Rita and Nicholson. It got increasingly loud, and finally Nicholson yelled, "When the hell were you going to tell me this?"

Rita seemed to look around in some embarrassment at the scene they were making. She got up abruptly and left the bar. Nicholson, after a few moments of hesitation, threw money on the table and angrily stormed off after her.

There's no indication in the press reports that anyone knows what it was that provoked Nicholson's anger, or Rita's departure. But there were rumors that Rita had ended her relationship with him, with the trashier publications speculating that she was having an affair with an unnamed person at her office. Most reports assumed that the breakup, and the possible affair, were the reasons for the anger, and then the murder.

Technically, at least in the eyes of the law, there was no murder. No body was ever found, and in fact, Rita seemed to vanish cleanly from the face of the Earth. The last anyone saw of her was in a video taken from a street camera. The footage was damning; it was of Nicholson catching up to her and grabbing her arm, and her pushing him away.

I don't see any explanation on Nicholson's part as to his side of it, nor any alibi he might have claimed. He didn't testify at trial, probably a smart move by his lawyer. But he might have told his story to the detectives investigating the case, and in fact he might have told it to me. I just have no recollection of it.

When I get back to work, I can go through the case records, and they will probably include notes that I can't recall taking. But I really want to get this behind me, do what I told Sean I would do, and be done with it.

So I might as well talk to Nicholson.

> "What are you looking to nail me on now,
> the Kennedy assassination?"

JOHN NICHOLSON IS VERY SURPRISED TO SEE ME, AND NOT ALL that pleased. I think the fact that I helped put him in prison has something to do with it. Of course, I'm only assuming this is John Nicholson, since that is who I told the prison officials I wanted to meet with. He does not look remotely familiar to me.

"Hello, John," I say, giving him the opportunity to correct me.

He doesn't. Instead he says, "You are the last person I expected to see, and the last person I want to see."

"I'm sorry about that."

"What do you want?"

"I'm not really sure. Look, John, I'm going to be straight with you. I was shot a while ago, and . . ."

"I read about it. I can't say I was pulling for you."

"I understand. The thing is, I lost a good deal of my memory. It's called retrograde amnesia."

He nods. "I read about that, too."

"Right. So I'm trying to re-create a lot of it. To piece together some things, including much of the Rita Carlisle case. Your case. And I could use your help in that effort."

"You don't remember what happened?" he asks. "None of it?"

"I don't."

"You don't even remember me?"

"I'm sorry; I don't."

"So you want me to take you down memory lane and tell you how you put me here? No thanks; living through it once was bad enough. Ask your buddies on the force to tell you about it; maybe they can read it to you as a bedtime story. Or Google it. All I care about is that you get the hell out of here."

I shake my head. "I understand how you feel, but that's not it at all."

"Then what is it?"

"Someone has come to me with some information about your case. I want you to know that it may be nothing of any significance; in fact, it probably won't. But I thought it was worth looking into."

"What kind of information?" he asks.

"I can't tell you that, at least not at this point. And I can't tell you who came to me. It's a promise I made in order to get the information."

"So how does it affect me?"

I shrug. "Maybe it doesn't; I won't know until I know."

"Then why should I talk to you?"

Coming here was probably a mistake; this guy is bugging me. "You're in prison and your arm is handcuffed to that table," I say. "You see much to lose here?"

He thinks for a moment, and actually looks at his cuffed arm. "Okay, that's a decent point. What do you want to know?"

"Let's start with what you and Rita Carlisle were fighting about that night."

Another pause; clearly the idea of talking openly to a person he has long considered his mortal enemy is not coming naturally to him. "Rita broke up with me. She didn't say so, but I think she was having an affair with a guy in her office."

"You have a name?"

"No; if I did I'd probably be in here for murdering him."

"So she was breaking off your engagement?"

He shakes his head. "First of all, we weren't actually engaged, although I had bought a ring and was planning to ask her. She was telling me there was something going on in her life, and she might be leaving town."

"She didn't say what it was?"

"She said she couldn't; that's why I thought it was an affair. She was asking for my forgiveness, and said that if I knew what was happening, I'd understand."

"Did you press her on it?"

"As best I could, but I got nowhere. Then I asked her what would happen to her job if she left town, and she said she didn't have a job anymore. Then she ran out. She seemed upset and scared, like she was having trouble holding it all together."

"And then you got angry?"

He nods. "Damn straight I got angry. I'm angry now just thinking about it; the fact that she felt she couldn't trust me upset me more than anything. The whole thing came out of left field. But I wouldn't kill her . . . I wouldn't hurt her. I loved her."

"Why did she run out?"

"Because I was saying things that weren't particularly pleasing for her to hear. I guess I wasn't handling the news the way she thought I would. I wasn't being supportive enough." He laughs. "She was dumping me and I wasn't being supportive enough. She said she had to leave."

"So you followed her out of the bar."

"Yeah. I kept calling to her, but she wouldn't stop. I had driven there, and I didn't know where she could go on foot, so I wanted to get her to stop so I could take her home. I grabbed her from behind; that's the part the video cameras caught. She pushed me away, and ran off across the street."

"What did you do then?"

"Went back to my car and drove around looking for her. When I couldn't find her, I went to her house. I assumed she got in a cab or something. But she wasn't there, and she never came home." Then, "Even now, after being in here so long, I still can't believe it."

"I know you've said that you're innocent—"

He interrupts. "I am innocent."

"So did you then, or do you now, have any idea who might have done it?"

"The only thing I can think of is whoever she was having an affair with. Maybe she told him that she was going to work it out with me, and he followed her that night. Maybe her fear came from being worried about what he might do. But I don't even know who he is, or if there is such a person at all, and my lawyer was never able to find out."

"Let me ask you this; did you know anyone else at the bar that night?"

He shakes his head. "It was just the two of us."

"I don't mean with you. I mean elsewhere in the bar. Did Rita say hello to anyone, or indicate she might have known someone that was there?"

"Why?" he asks.

"John, we're still in the phase where I ask the questions and you answer them. When and if I have meaningful answers, I promise I will tell you. It has to be that way for now."

He frowns, but doesn't push it. When you're in prison hand-cuffed to a table, you don't have that much leverage. "I don't recall that we knew anyone else there, and I don't remember her saying anything to anyone. But it's possible that she did; she was pretty sociable, and knew a lot of people. Way more than me."

"Is it a bar you went to a lot?"

"No, maybe a couple of times before that . . . I think once with Rita. But it wasn't a favorite place, or anything like that."

"Did you make a reservation that night? Or was it a spur of the moment thing?"

"I don't remember. But the place was crowded, so we probably had a reservation. If we did, Rita would have made it; she handled that stuff."

I make a mental note to see if there is video footage inside the restaurant that night. If there is, it would have been introduced at trial.

"Thanks, John. You've been helpful."

"Will you let me know what you come up with?"

"Yes. But don't focus on this too much; we're talking about a major long shot."

"Okay, thanks for that. I've got a job in the prison laundry; I'll focus on that. And I'll focus on decorating my cell."

He's clearly bitter, and I can't say I blame him. "I'll get back to you, John."

"What if you come up with nothing?" he asks. "Will you tell me that also?"

I nod. "That I can promise."

I'm not happy with myself,
or the situation I've created.

TO EVEN ATTEMPT TO GET ANYWHERE ON THE RITA CARLISLE kidnapping would require a full-scale investigation. But even that likely wouldn't accomplish anything new, since it's been done before.

And the most ridiculous thing of all is that I was apparently a key member of the group who conducted this exact investigation back when the case was fresh. I just have my head too far up my memory-free ass to remember it.

In any event, I don't have the inclination to devote the kind of effort that a full reopening would require, and since I'm starting my job on Monday, I wouldn't have the time to do so if I wanted to.

So there is no conceivable way for me to get anywhere, and the consequences of that are twofold. For one thing, the pressing personal question that Sean Connor needs an answer to is not going to get answered. I feel bad about that, but I'll get over it. For another, I've unnecessarily raised the hopes of John Nicholson, which bothers me less, because the guy is a convicted murderer and almost definitely an actual murderer.

But there is no sense in prolonging this by going through some motions that don't get me anywhere. It's ridiculous for me to conduct some perfunctory interviews with witnesses, especially since I don't know what the hell I'm even asking.

I'll look through the case files when I get into the office, to see if anything obvious jumps out at me. It won't, and then I'll break the news to Sean at the next meeting. I'll also go back to the prison to give the same message to Nicholson. He deserves that much.

I call Captain Bradley. "What is it now?" he asks when he picks up the phone. "You want a signing bonus to come back to work?"

I ignore the jab and say, "I changed my mind. I want to start tomorrow."

"My eyes are filling with tears," he says. "Nine A.M. There'll be some paperwork to fill out, and then your shift starts at ten."

Click.

I call Nate to give him the news as well, and he responds with, "You're a little bit nuts, you know?"

"I'm aware of that."

"You want me to pick you up?" he asks.

"No, I'll drive in with Jessie."

"She starts at seven."

"That's okay," I say. "I want to look through some files first."

"They're locked in my desk."

"What are?"

"The Carlisle files," he says.

"How did you know I wanted to look at them?"

"The thinner I get, the smarter I get. I'll meet you at the office at seven." Then, "Seven? What the hell are we, dairy farmers?"

"See you then, skinny."

Jessie isn't home from work yet, so I decide to surprise her and make dinner. I look at some recipes, and that causes me to reconsider my decision. Instead I will surprise her by taking her out to dinner. Cooking is really not my thing. I can't remember exactly, but I don't think it ever was.

She's fine with going out to eat; we go to a local Paterson restaurant called The Bonfire. It's been there forever; my father used to tell me about going there after dates in high school.

I am very glad I remember my father.

Once we're seated, I update Jessie on what I learned, or more accurately didn't learn, about the Rita Carlisle kidnapping. "There's just nowhere for me to go with this," I say. "So I called Captain Bradley and said I'm coming in tomorrow."

She raises her glass of wine and clinks a toast with my light beer. "To a new start," she says, "and a perfect segue."

"What do you mean?"

"There's something I want to talk to you about. I think it's time we gave some thought to you getting rid of your apartment and moving into my place permanently."

"I thought we've already been thinking about it?" I ask.

She nods. "Yes, but that was casual thought." Then, "This is more serious; the second stage of thought."

It's taken Jessie a while to completely trust our relationship and my feelings for her. That makes perfect sense; I had broken up with her before the shooting. A teenager that I cared deeply about had been killed, and I sunk into a depression that caused me to withdraw from a great deal of life, Jessie included.

With my memory wiped clean, I met her for what to me was the first time, and fell in love all over again. But her memory is not quite as barren as mine, and she still remembers well the hurt she felt when I broke up with her. So asking me to move in permanently, even though we are sort of, partially engaged, will be a big step when she does so.

"How many stages of thought are there?" I ask

"I don't know," she says, taking my hand. "I'll have to give that some thought."

"Good idea."

"And just to be clear, I'm not sure about the 'you giving up your apartment' part."

"I think we're moving too fast," I say. "It's like a whirlwind."

She laughs. "We're going to be married, Doug . . . eventually. Living together seems somehow appropriate. Besides, you're not the old Doug. You're more mature, and centered."

"You make that sound depressing."

She shakes her head. "Not at all; it's why we've moved into the second thought stage."

We leave the restaurant and head for Jessie's house in Engle-wood. There's construction on Route 20, so instead we work our way through the east side of Paterson toward Route 4.

We stop at a streetlight at the corner of 18th and Vreeland, and I hear some kind of commotion to the left of us. I look over there, and it's hard to make out, but it seems like a man and a woman, standing next to a parked car, having a loud argument.

I turn back to see if the light has changed, and Jessie says, "He's pushing her against the car."

"Park it," I say, and I jump out of our car, still standing at the light.

I run across the street, and sure enough, the guy is pushing the woman, and she is withdrawing in fear.

"Police officer!" I yell. "Get your hands off of her!"

He looks at me and says, "Bullshit. You ain't no cop."

"I said leave her alone and step away. You've been warned."

"This is my wife," he snarls. "And you better get your ass away from me, or you'll get worse than she's getting."

Suddenly, our car comes screeching to a halt behind me. Jessie has made a U-turn and pulled right up to us, and she has the brights on, shining into the guy's eyes.

"Shit!" he yells, and turns to the woman. "Get in the damn car."

He opens the door and tries to push her in roughly. She's resist-ing, and hits her head against the door and falls to the ground. She screams in pain and fear.

I've seen and heard more than enough. I move forward and

grab the guy, swinging him around and throwing him facedown onto the hood of the car. I throw him harder than I need to, but not as hard as I want to.

The sound that his face and nose make as they hit the hood, and the blood that starts to spread, makes me satisfied that it was hard enough. He yells in pain, but it's garbled, so maybe I've dislodged some teeth in the process. I'm okay with that.

I can hear Jessie calling 911 for the Paterson police, and then moments later she comes over and hands me a pair of handcuffs, which I use on the guy.

The Paterson cops appear moments later, three black-and-whites worth. I identify myself to one of them, but he says that he recognizes me. Fame has its privileges.

Jessie and I both describe what happened, versions that are contradicted in the moment by the woman screaming that her husband didn't do anything wrong. It's depressing and might well mean that the guy won't get charged for this, but Jessie and I both say that we'll testify. At the very least the asshole won't be anxious to look in the mirror for a while.

We get back in the car, and I can feel the adrenaline starting to wear off. Jessie asks, "That felt good, didn't it? I mean your part in it."

I think for a moment, and then nod. "It did. I wasn't thinking about what I was doing; I was just doing it. It felt natural. What does that say about me?"

She smiles. "That maybe you're the old Doug after all. Which isn't all that bad."

"You slammed a guy's face into a car?"
Nate asks when he walks in.

"I MOVED THE GENTLEMAN OUT OF POSSIBLE ONGOING TRAF-
fic into a position where the car happened to be standing. It was for
his own safety. When he turned to thank me, he slipped and fell
into the car."

"That was quite a slip. He broke his nose and lost four teeth."

"Boy, that really puts things into perspective. How do you
know about this?"

"You mean other than the fact that it's on the news? The Paterson cops have already called here, looking for your written statement."

"I'll call them later. Let me have the files."

"I'm not sure if I can find the key to my desk," he lies. "Maybe
if you told me what was going on, it would jog my memory. You
know about memory jogging, don't you?"

I shake my head. "Confidential."

"We're partners. Do you know what that means? Or did you
forget that, too?"

Nate has a point, so I decide to tell him about Sean's story and
his scrapbook. As when I told Jessie, I leave out Sean's name, since
that's the only actual promise of confidentiality that I made to him.

When I'm done, he says, "That's it? I came in at seven o'clock for that? You're wasting your time."

I nod. "I know. The guy must have been spooked that he was in the bar with a woman who got snatched and probably killed a few minutes later. So he followed the case carefully; he felt connected to it."

"Exactly. You're not as dumb as you look."

I spend the next couple of hours looking through the files. It's weird to read my own notes, knowing it's my handwriting but having no recollection of writing any of it.

I was the arresting officer but not the lead detective on the case. That was Hector Davila, the ranking detective in the department. He's a terrific cop who has been around forever; that much I remember.

Not surprisingly, nothing I see causes me to have any question that the arrest was legitimate and John Nicholson is the likely perpetrator. The evidence is circumstantial, but compelling, and at the very least I can say to Sean that I did my due diligence, and that I've found nothing to make me think he was involved.

"You satisfied?" Nate asks when I'm done.

"Satisfied."

He puts the file back where it was, and I head to administration to do the paperwork necessary to get back on the job. It seems like a lot, but I plow through it a page at a time, and I'm done in forty-five minutes.

I also have to sit through two re-entry interviews, which are uneventful until they start asking me things about my life that I can't answer. Fortunately the interviewers are aware of my issues, so they gloss over the gaps.

I'm wrapping up the last of the interviews when Nate sticks his head in the door. "You almost finished?"

I look at the interviewer, who nods.

"Almost," I say.

"Then you're finished. We've got to move; a jogger found a murder victim in Eastside Park."

"Was the body buried?" I ask.

"No. And it's not exactly a body."

During the ten-minute drive to the park, Nate updates me on the little we know so far. "It's a severed head. No trace of the torso, at least not yet."

"And a jogger found it?" I ask.

"Yeah. How come joggers always seem to be the ones to find bodies? Makes me glad I don't exercise."

As soon as we get to the park, the location we're looking for is obvious. There are a bunch of cop cars, a coroner's van, and two police forensic teams.

The action is about a hundred yards from the tennis courts, not far from a runner's path. It's not the kind of place you'd want to leave a severed head if you didn't want it discovered. It's definitely a place you'd leave it if you wanted to send a message.

We are the ranking detectives on the scene; it will be our case. As soon as we get there, the cops who were here first update us on what they know, which isn't much. The unlucky jogger is in a nearby car, waiting to be interviewed, and the coroner is here and is awaiting our okay to remove the head.

Forensics people are also here, doing their jobs and searching for evidence, trace and otherwise. No identification has been made yet, which makes sense, since the deceased probably wouldn't be carrying a wallet with ID in his mouth. Fingerprints are obviously going to be a bit difficult to get as well.

Once we've consulted with everyone, I say, "Okay, let's get a look at our victim."

One of the officers leads us over, and everyone parts to let us through. Because of Nate's size, they have to make a wide path.

Within moments we're in the front, looking down at the severed head, which almost seems contorted in a smile.

What I'm looking at stuns me. "I can make the identification," I say.

Nate turns to me in surprise. "Who is it?"

"Sean Connor."

I call Nate to the side, where no
one else can hear us.

"WHO IS SEAN CONNOR?" HE ASKS, ONCE WE'RE OUT OF EARSHOT.

"He's the guy who had the scrapbook on the Rita Carlisle kidnapping. The guy I told I would look into it."

"This ain't no coincidence."

"That's for sure."

We go over to talk to the jogger, who can't be more than eighteen years old. Her name is Donna Wagner, and it's no surprise that she is very shaken by the experience. While we are talking to her, she waves shakily to her parents, who have just arrived on the scene.

Ms. Wagner has very little to offer, other than the circumstance by which she happened on the severed head. The track was muddy from a recent rain, so she veered off a bit to find more solid ground. That led her right to the head. It is a moment that she will remember with fear and revulsion for the rest of her life.

"What did you do when you saw it?" Nate asks.

"I screamed and then I threw up," she says, a little sheepishly.

"Exactly what I would have done," I say.

We take down all her information and say that we will be

contacting her, but the truth is she probably won't hear from anyone again unless the case goes to trial and the prosecutor needs her to set the scene. It's clear that she has no involvement in the crime, nor any special insight into it.

By the time we leave there are six media trucks on the scene, having made their way from Manhattan. Dead bodies attract attention; heads without the dead bodies attached create a media firestorm. Therefore, it is no surprise that Captain Bradley has left word that he wants to see us the moment we get back into the office.

"Well, welcome back to the job," he says when we walk in. "You still want to work on cold cases? Or maybe spend your time reopening the Carlisle kidnapping?"

"Actually, yes."

"What the hell does that mean?"

"I knew the park victim; he approached me and we had breakfast the other day. His name is Sean Connor; he was part of my amnesia group."

"What's an amnesia group?" he asks.

"People with amnesia get together to talk about their amnesia."

"Sounds like a blast. Go on."

"He told me he was afraid that he was responsible for the Carlisle kidnapping, but had no recollection of it."

"Then why did he think he was responsible?" Bradley asked.

"Because he found a scrapbook filled with newspaper articles about the crime hidden in his attic, and he uncovered a credit card receipt that showed he was in the bar that night."

"You have the scrapbook?"

"No, he wanted to keep it."

"And this is why you came in the other day with that bullshit story about wanting to work on cold cases?"

"It is."

"Good to know you're not totally nuts, but you might want to share things like that in the future. In case you've forgotten, we're a team here."

"Got it, Captain," I lie.

He nods. "Okay. The media shit has already hit the fan. I want to be kept in the loop on your progress."

"You got it," Nate says.

"And keep in mind that this is a murder case, the victim being Sean Connor. This is not the Rita Carlisle kidnapping case, part two."

I understand where Bradley is coming from; his department, with yours truly in one of the main roles, put John Nicholson in prison for the kidnapping of Rita Carlisle. It would not be a positive if Nicholson was innocent. But Bradley knows we'll follow the facts wherever they go; he's just telling us not to push it too hard toward Carlisle until and unless we are forced to.

From what I understand, the old me would have ignored him, and there's a very good chance that the new me will do the same. There is simply no way a financial consultant from Westchester moves to New Jersey, reveals his belief that he might have something to do with the Rita Carlisle case, and then gets his head chopped off without it having something to do with that case.

Nate and I leave Bradley and head for Jessie's office. She's heard about the severed head, and knows it's our case, but isn't aware that the victim is Sean Connor. I had told her about the situation, but not Sean's name.

When we tell her, she says what I've been thinking: "It's got to be tied to Carlisle."

"Bradley doesn't think so," I say. "Or at least he doesn't want to think so."

"He's just protecting the conviction. The last thing he wants is for Nicholson to be innocent."

"Well, I'm pretty sure Nicholson didn't chop off Sean's head."

"You two almost done chitchatting?" Nate asks.

"Almost," I say. "You can go get us some coffee while we finish up."

Nate ignores me and says, "Jess, Memory Boy and I need to know whatever you can find out about Connor."

She nods. "What do we know so far?"

I shrug. "Not too much, beyond the name and the fact that he went to the amnesia group meetings thanks to a head injury he got in a car accident. You can get his contact information from them. Oh, and he said that he lives in Clifton, near the coffee shop we went to, and that he used to live in Westchester. He also said at one point that he was a financial consultant, or counselor, or something. Apparently he did pretty well."

"Okay," she says. "I'm on it."

We head back to our office. The preliminary forensics report is in and it's of little value to us. The perpetrator left no apparent trace evidence for us to use. It certainly appears as if the murder did not take place where the head was discovered, since there was very little blood. But there is nothing that would lead us to the actual site of the murder.

Nate calls the coroner's office to see if they have learned anything that could be helpful to us. They haven't. They are able to set a time of death as anywhere from six to ten hours before the jogger found the head, but they can't even accurately determine a cause of death.

All they can say is that there were no new brain or skull injuries. While the severing of the head would obviously be sufficient to cause death, it is possible that it took place postmortem. At this point there is just no way to know.

Based on the time of death, it's probable that the head was left there under cover of darkness. Officers are canvassing the area to see if anyone saw anything suspicious, but I doubt they'll come up with anything. Someone probably would have come forward already.

We're not going to be able to really get into investigating Connor's murder until we learn more about him, and that process is going to begin with Jessie. In the meantime, despite Bradley's view, the only lead we have to go on is the fact that he thought he might somehow be involved in the Carlisle kidnapping.

To that end, we requisition the videotapes that were submitted as evidence in the trial. There is a tape from inside the bar that night, though it was not of great value at trial. It shows Rita Carlisle leaving, quickly and in apparent anger, and Nicholson following about twenty seconds later. It does not capture the argument that they were having at the table, and in any event there is no audio.

But that's not why we're looking at it; we're trying to see if Sean Connor was actually there, as he stated he was, and if he took any action that might concern us. For example, if he followed Rita out as well, that would be suspicious and tend to confirm his feeling that he might have been involved.

Despite the fact that Nate has seen the severed head, I am the only one who knows what the living Sean Connor looked like, and I don't see him. There is no guarantee that the video recorded everyone in the place; very likely it didn't. But if Sean Connor was there, he went unphotographed.

So at this point, we don't know who Sean Connor is, whether he was at the bar, whether he was involved in the Rita Carlisle kidnapping, or whether he was telling me the truth.

The only thing we know for sure is that his head was in Eastside Park this morning.

"I don't know who he was, but he wasn't Sean Connor," Jessie says the next morning.

SHE DIDN'T MENTION ANYTHING ABOUT THIS LAST NIGHT AT home, just that she was still working on it. I think she waited until she could get more information, but mainly because she thought it was more proper to update Nate and I together.

It also could be that she doesn't feel that severed heads make for great pillow talk.

"What does that mean?" Nate asks, taking the words out of my mouth.

"It means he was not who he says he was. His identity was faked; there is no Sean Connor that could possibly fit his description. The only ones that might be close are alive, heads fully intact."

"Did you learn where he lived?"

"I know where he said he lived," Jessie says. "I got it from your amnesia group. It was an address in Clifton, but unfortunately, he never actually lived there. The residents of that address are an elderly woman and her daughter. They've owned the house for thirty-five years, and they never heard of Mr. Connor."

"What about the credit card receipt that said he was in the bar that night?" Nate asks.

Jessie shrugs. "I can't speak to that, because I don't know his real name, so I can't access his credit card accounts. But based on what I'm seeing, I think you can safely assume that everything he said to you was a load of horseshit."

Jessie has a delicate way of phrasing things.

"We need to run his DNA," I say. "And get a sketch out to the media, to see if anyone comes forward and identifies him."

"What I can't figure out is why he came to you in the first place," Nate says.

"He obviously wanted to draw me into investigating Carlisle, though I don't know why. Of course, there is still a remote chance he was telling some version of the truth."

"How do you figure that?" Jessie asks.

"Well, he could have legitimately thought he might have been responsible for Carlisle, and wanted me to find out. But then he could have left himself an out by faking his identity; that way if I learned that he was the perpetrator, he could have vanished without me knowing who he really was."

"You believe that crap?" Nate asks.

"No."

We don't have much to do at this point, so I leave Nate to wait for more information, while I go to the coffee shop where I had breakfast with Connor, or whoever he was. I'm in luck in that the waitress who had taken care of us is there.

"Excuse me, I had breakfast here the other day . . ." is how I start, but she interrupts.

"Full stack of blueberry pancakes, sugar-free syrup, and coffee. You cleaned your plate."

"How did you remember that?" I ask.

She shrugs. "It's a gift."

This woman might well be out of central casting for the perfect witness. "I was here with a guy . . ."

She nods. "Just coffee, black."

"Right. Did you recognize him? He said he's been here before."

She shakes her head. "Nope. Never laid eyes on him. First time here."

"He recommended the pancakes," I say.

"Then someone told him they were good, because he's never been in this place. I've been here twelve years, so unless it was before that . . ."

"No, I'm sure it wasn't. Can I talk to the owner?"

"That's what you're doing," she says.

"You're the owner?"

"For the same twelve years. Don't look so surprised."

I've run out of questions to ask her. "Your pancakes are really good."

"Thanks. Waffles are even better. If the guy was a regular he would have known that."

This conversation has erased all doubt for me; there is nothing that Sean Connor told me that was true. I would bet that he was not even an amnesia victim. When you lie about pancakes, you'll lie about anything.

But if he wasn't an amnesia victim, then he was only at the group meeting because I was.

I was the target, but I don't know who was targeting me. And more importantly, I don't know why.

Nate and I aren't glued to each other
when we're on a case.

UNLESS IT'S SOMETHING IMPORTANT, OR A SITUATION THAT
could be dangerous, we go our separate ways. It maximizes what we
can get done; for example, if we are just interviewing a witness,
there is no need for us both to be there.

Nate says that we started working this way on the Liriano case,
but I have no idea who Liriano is, or what his case was, and it doesn't
seem important enough to ask.

Captain Bradley has assigned an unusually large contingent of
officers to work under us, so for now Nate is going to stay back at
the office and run the operation. I'm going to conduct the interviews in the field.

My first stop is the building in Englewood where I've been attending the amnesia group meetings. I think it used to be an American Legion hall, but it has been taken over by a group of shrinks
who use it to run support groups of various types. There is no name
on the outside of the building, probably to provide privacy and
anonymity to those who enter.

There are five rooms, four of which are set up to hold group
meetings. In the lobby is a schedule of the day's activities, and I

check it when I arrive. Only room number three is currently occupied, with an overeaters' support group. I would mention that to Nate, but he'd probably kill me for doing so.

The fifth room is for the administration office, so that's where I head. A woman named Carla Betts is there. She is not part of the psychology staff, but she appears to do everything else. She certainly always seems to be here.

She's never without a smile on her face, and this time is no exception. "Hi, Doug, didn't expect you in today. I don't think your group is meeting." The other thing about Carla is that she recognizes everyone and calls them by their first name. It serves to make the place seem more comfortable and unthreatening.

"It's not. I'm actually here on business."

"Oh?"

"Do you remember someone named Sean Connor? He attended some of the amnesia group sessions that I was in."

"Of course I remember Sean. Nice man. Your office called to ask his address. What's this about?"

The sketch of Sean is not ready to be shown in the media, so Carla would likely have no way of knowing what has happened. "I'm sorry to have to tell you this, but he's been murdered."

"Oh, no." She looks like I've hit her with a two-by-four.

"I'm afraid so."

"Wait a minute . . . that poor man in the park? Oh, my God. . . ."

I nod my confirmation, but caution her not to say anything until his identity is publicly released. Of course, there would be no harm in Sean Connor's name getting out, since that was a fake identity in the first place. "I need to ask you a few questions about him."

She just keeps shaking her head in sadness, then realizes what I said and finally responds, "Of course. I'm sorry."

"Did you handle the intake when he first came here?"

She nods. "Yes."

"Did he show you identification?"

"No, we don't require that."

"How did he present himself? What did he say?"

She thinks for a few moments. "It was fairly typical. He gave me his name and address, and filled out the form. I have it here, because I referred to it when your office called."

She takes it out of the drawer and hands it to me. "As you know, these aren't very detailed."

"What did he tell you about his reason for attending?"

"That he had been in an accident and had retrograde amnesia, and that he needed help dealing with it. I don't ask too many questions; it's not my area. And we're not really concerned about someone fabricating a story; there would be little reason for someone to come in under false pretenses."

"How did he pay?"

"With cash; I'm positive of that. It's unusual that someone would do that, which is why I remember it. He paid in advance for six sessions."

"How many did he attend?" Everyone has to sign in when they attend a session.

"Let's see . . ." She taps some keys on her computer and then says, "Three. Starting ten days ago."

"How many sessions have there been in that time?" I ask.

"Probably seven or eight. I could check."

"I think I've been in three also. Can you tell me if I was in all of the sessions that he attended?"

"I can cross-check it, sure," she says, and does so. "He was in every session you were in, and no others."

The odds of him just happening to show up at the same three sessions as me are pretty steep, but it doesn't surprise me. He was only there because I was.

"Carla, his name was not really Sean Connor, and I doubt very much that he was an amnesia victim at all. Is there anything you can remember that he said or did that might help me figure out who he really was?"

"I'm sorry, Doug, but I can't think of anything. He was just a guy who said he needed help. That's what we're here for."

"We've got a DNA hit," Nate says when I call in.

"WHO IS IT?" I ASK.

"I don't know; all I know is we got a hit. In fact, the message was that we got two hits, whatever the hell that means. They're sending me the information now. By the time you get back here we'll have it."

I head back to the precinct, but I think I know what "two hits" means. It's likely that the DNA was on two different lists, independent of each other. Most likely that means it was in both a criminal database and a military one.

Nate has already received the information by the time I get back. "His name wasn't Sean Connor, it was Connor Shawn, if you can believe that. Real smart guy; if he didn't do it that way, he would probably have had to write his new name on his arm so he could remember it."

"Who was he?"

"The two hits were military and criminal," Nate says, confirming my expectation. "He was in the Marine Corps, left with a dishonorable discharge after being court-martialed on multiple assault charges. Been living in Las Vegas ever since."

"What about the criminal hit?"

"Four arrests for various offenses, none of them very nice. One conviction for domestic assault. But here's the kicker: the latest information we have is that he works for Salvatore Tartaro."

"Who's Salvatore Tartaro?"

Nate shakes his head either in disgust or frustration, maybe both. "You think your memory deal is annoying to you? You should see it from here; it's like somebody dropped you from another planet."

"Just tell me who the guy is."

"He's head of a crime family in Vegas, and he used to do a lot of business with Nicholas Bennett. You know who that is?"

I know very well who Nicholas Bennett is. He was the leading crime figure in New Jersey. You could accurately say we had been enemies; he killed a teenage boy that I cared deeply about, and he was also responsible for me being shot. He was, in my humble, unbiased opinion, a piece of shit.

But I am responsible for him being dead, which effectively ended our rivalry.

"Which brings us to Joey Silva?" I ask. Joey Silva is the hood who took over Bennett's operation. Bennett was a smooth operator, a guy who fancied himself a respected citizen of charm and manners who could reliably be found at elite charity dinners. Silva, on the other hand, wouldn't know a salad fork from a forklift.

Nate nods. "He's the leader in the clubhouse. If Shawn was still working for Tartaro, then he wouldn't be here unless Silva was in the loop on it. And if Silva is involved, then we are dealing with something much bigger, and much different, than we thought."

"But if Silva is behind it, and Tartaro sent Shawn here, then why the hell is his head sitting in the morgue? Somebody killed him, and did it in a way to send a message. Shawn didn't disappear; his death was engineered in a way to be as noticeable as possible."

"Maybe we have a war going on."

"Maybe," I say. "But that's not what we should be looking at. That's not the key factor."

"What is?"

"Rita Carlisle. The only role Shawn had in this whole operation, as far as we can tell, was to bring us into an investigation of Carlisle. He was lying about the scrapbook bullshit, but what he set out to do was clear. He wanted us to look into Carlisle. And he accomplished his goal, because that's exactly what we're going to do."

"Captain Bradley is not going to like it," Nate says.

"He'll just have to deal with it. Let's go."

"Where?"

"To his office. He asked to be updated, so we'll update him."

We go to Bradley's outer office, and as soon as his assistant tells him we're here, he calls us right in. "I hope you've got something for me, because I'm tired of telling the chief it's too early. He's called three times already, and the last time he mentioned something about me sitting around with my thumb in my ass."

"We've got an ID on the head."

"Talk to me."

So we do; we tell him everything that we know so far. He doesn't say a word, just listens as we tell him about Shawn, and Tartaro, and Silva.

When we're done he asks, "So how do you read it?"

"Everything they've done has been in full daylight," I say. "They practically . . . hell, they literally . . . begged us to come in. And the trigger is Carlisle. It has to be."

I expect an argument but don't get one. Instead Bradley nods and says, "I know." Then, "Shit."

"It doesn't mean that Nicholson didn't do it," I say. "It just means that they want us looking at Carlisle. There could be other reasons that we don't know about."

Nate says, "So they bring Shawn in from Vegas to bullshit you about his amnesia and his scrapbook. Then when he does his job, they kill him, and make sure you know that they did it. And they had to know we'd get a DNA hit, which means you'd know the whole amnesia story was faked."

I nod. "That seems to be where we are."

"What do you need from me?" Bradley asks.

"You can contact the Feds. They may know things about Tartaro and Silva that we don't."

"But then they might want to come in on this. Once the door is open a crack . . ."

I shake my head. "You can finesse it and not let on why you're asking. If need be, just tell them it has to do with an ongoing investigation of Silva. They would have no idea it's related to Carlisle. Besides, nothing I see in the files mentions that the Feds were even involved in Carlisle."

He nods his agreement. "Okay. What else?"

"Full permission to follow this wherever it goes, including Carlisle." I'm asking because I want him to think he's making the call, since we'll need his support down the road. But I'm going to do it anyway, and he probably knows that.

He nods. "You got it." Then, "With one condition. At least for now you don't go public with the fact that this might be about Carlisle."

That seems reasonable enough, especially with the "for now" attached, so we agree to it.

Bradley has one more inspiring message for us before we leave. "Don't screw this up."

"You've got to be kidding."

I'M TALKING TO LIEUTENANT ZACK ROBERTS OF THE LAS VEGAS Police Department, Organized Crime Division, and I've just told him that Connor Shawn has turned up decapitated in New Jersey. Roberts is expressing his surprise at the news.

"I didn't even know he was there," he continues.

"Well, I can't speak for the rest of his body; for all I know it's sitting in one of your casinos sucking down vodka gimlets. But his head is definitely here."

"What was he doing there?"

"I was sort of hoping that I would be asking the questions, and you'd be supplying valuable insight."

"Good luck with that."

"Let's try it anyway. What can you tell me about him?"

"Well, for one thing, he wouldn't have been there on vacation. He wasn't taking in a show or visiting the Statue of Liberty. There was no casual side to Shawn."

"How long has he worked for Tartaro?"

"Well, that's interesting, because he seems to have left Tartaro a couple of months ago. We have that on pretty good authority."

"So is it possible that Tartaro ordered the hit? Maybe revenge for Shawn bailing out on him?"

"With Tartaro you never know, but I doubt it. Why do it there? Here Tartaro has the home field advantage, and there are multiple ways to arrange untimely deaths right here in Las Vegas. We invented many of them."

"What about the style? The decapitation and leaving the head where it could be found?"

"That's the other reason I doubt it; it's definitely not Tartaro's style. He makes people disappear, and he never invites media attention. The only way it would make any sense would be if Shawn was disloyal, and Tartaro wanted to send a message to his own people about the downside to disloyalty. But there are even problems with that."

"And they are?"

"First of all, we'd probably know if there was an issue between them, if Shawn had turned on him. But more important, if Tartaro wanted to send a message to his people in Las Vegas, he wouldn't leave the head in New Jersey."

"What about Tartaro's relationship with Silva?" I ask.

"I haven't seen any, but it could exist without me knowing it. Tartaro doesn't branch out much; he's always been pretty happy to stick close to home."

"He did a lot of business with Bennett," I say, only because Nate told it to me. "They were pretty close."

"That was the exception," Roberts says. "And I'm not sure 'close' is the word I'd use. They didn't have pajama parties; they occasionally found business reasons to cooperate. The funny thing is that from what I understand, Silva is more Tartaro's style."

By that I assume he means more prone to violence and driven by temper rather than a coolheaded, albeit deadly, businessman.

"If Shawn was back working for Tartaro, would he have been sent into Silva's territory without Silva knowing about it?"

"I don't see it," he says. "There's no upside to Tartaro making powerful enemies, no matter where they are."

"So far you haven't done much for me," I say.

He laughs. "So come out here. We can go talk to Tartaro, and I'll get you comped at the Excalibur."

"No thanks."

"I can tell you this," he says. "If Shawn was back working for Tartaro, and if he was sent to New York, it was for something important. Because Shawn was a top guy, not someone you wasted. And if Tartaro sent him, he did it quietly."

"What do you mean?" I ask.

"Let's just say we have a surveillance presence in Tartaro's life. We have people in his organization, though not at the center of it. And we have an electronic operation as well; if Tartaro sneezes, four guys in unmarked vans say 'Gesundheit.'"

I debate whether to tell Roberts about my connection to Shawn, and his amnesia deception. I ultimately opt not to; he's made it clear that he had no idea that Shawn was even here, or what his assignment from Tartaro might have been. My goal is to get information, not provide it.

I also don't mention Carlisle for the same reason. It wasn't a case that made national news, so I doubt he would even have heard of it. And there seems no reason to believe he'd have insight into Connor's relationship to it. Also, I'm trying to honor Bradley's goal of keeping Carlisle as much out of the spotlight as possible.

"Does Shawn have a family?" I ask. "Anybody you might want to notify? Maybe somebody who would know what he was doing here?"

"He had a wife, but she left him and moved somewhere in the Midwest. I'll check and see if he has a mother, or if he just grew out of the dirt. I'll let you know if I learn anything."

I thank Roberts and end the call. He hasn't helped us a lot, but if he's right about the things he's said, then he has made a few things clear.

The one thing I know for sure is that Shawn's mission was in some way related to the Carlisle case; the entire fake amnesia–scrapbook conversation proved that. So whether or not Shawn was here to do Tartaro's bidding, Carlisle must have implications that spread to Vegas. We had never had any idea of that before.

Of course, it's always possible that Silva prevailed upon Tartaro to send someone to approach me, sort of a rent-a-thug agreement. Silva might have been afraid that if he used someone local, his cover could be blown. But Roberts didn't seem to think that Tartaro and Silva had the relationship that Tartaro and Bennett had, so that would make lending Shawn to Silva less likely.

Nate comes in and asks, "What did you find out?"

"That we could get comped for a room at the Excalibur."

"Well, now we're getting somewhere. Would they throw in Cirque du Soleil?"

"What is Cirque du Soleil?"

He shakes his head in frustration. "It's sort of a circus, but it's in some kind of soleil."

"That clears it right up. So they have that out in Vegas?"

"Are you kidding? There's a hundred of them. You throw a dart, you hit a Cirque du Soleil. And you should see the women in those shows. They bend in directions you wouldn't believe. It's like they're elastic."

"Thanks for sharing that, Nate. Now let me ask you this. Why would a three-year-old kidnapping of a woman who was a mid-level executive at a local hospital be important to a pair of mob bosses twenty-five hundred miles apart?"

Nate shakes his head. "Beats the shit out of me."

Salvatore Tartaro found out about Shawn's death the way the public did, through the media.

NOT DIRECTLY, SINCE TARTARO NEVER WATCHED THE NEWS OR read a newspaper himself. He had people to do that, and to inform him whenever there was something that directly affected him or his business. His disconnect from the non-Tartaro part of the world was total and remarkable; Tartaro had recently heard the term "ISIS" for the first time, and asked what it meant.

In the case of Shawn's murder, Tartaro's true right hand, Dominic Romano, came to him with the news. "Shawn is dead; got his head chopped off," he said simply. Dominic was a needed calming influence on his boss, and his manner of speech reflected it. His announcement of Shawn's fate was given with the same matter-of-fact tone he might have used to comment on the weather.

Tartaro tried never to show surprise; he felt it detracted from the impression that he was always in total command of every situation. But he was alone with Dominic, and he trusted him as much as he trusted anyone. So he let his face betray his shock at hearing this news.

"Where?"

"New Jersey. They put a sketch out in the media. I could tell it was him, but I confirmed it with some people we know there. It's definitely Shawn; the state cops now have the ID."

"What the hell was he doing there?"

"That I don't know."

"Was it Silva?"

"I don't know that, either. Feels like his style, but I don't know of any problems we have with him. Things have been working pretty well, and I can't believe he would pick this time to screw with us. He has as much invested in our business as we do."

Tartaro nodded. "Things are going better than I thought. After Bennett I figured we'd have some difficulty. Does Silva know Shawn wasn't working with us anymore?"

Dominic shrugged. "Not from me. Maybe the asshole thought we sent Shawn to somehow horn in on his territory."

"Then he should have come to us direct. We're partners; that's not how partners behave. I'll cut the bastard's heart out."

"We don't know it was him," Dominic said, concerned that his boss was going to get ahead of himself and make a mistake. When Tartaro made mistakes, they were almost always of the violent variety.

"So who else could it be?"

"I don't know."

"And you're sure we haven't had any business problems with Silva?" Tartaro asked.

"No. Going better than ever. Volume last year doubled the year before. And there's one more thing."

"What's that?"

"The state cop on the case is the one who killed Bennett."

Tartaro laughed. "The guy who can't remember where the hell he's been the last ten years? That's funny."

"Bennett didn't think it was so funny. We've got a lot to lose here."

"So find out what is going on. Make a meeting if you have to."

"Silva won't come here," Dominic said. "Will you go there?"

Tartaro shook his head. "No way. But you will."

Connor Shawn's death has effectively and completely reopened the investigation into Carlisle.

UNTIL HIS HEAD SHOWED UP IN EASTSIDE PARK, NOT ONLY WAS I expending very little effort on it, but I was approaching it the same way it was done last time. My assumption was that Nicholson had done it, based on motive, evidence, and opportunity. But I had never considered that it might have much larger implications. Rita Carlisle had not seemed like someone who could possibly have had mobsters interested in her.

So much for that approach.

We have people digging into Shawn's history, but short of finding out that he was Rita Carlisle's cousin, it seems as if we've been looking at it the wrong way. Shawn came here and fabricated an elaborate ruse to get me to look into the kidnapping, and he didn't do that without a very important reason.

This is not proof positive that Nicholson is innocent. It's conceivable that he had a reason to commit the murder beyond the apparent lovers spat that was the basis of the prosecution. For all we know, Nicholson could have had organized crime connections himself, and some larger reason for wanting Rita dead. But if he did, no one ever found it, or even suspected it.

Bradley calls Nate and me into his office, and I assume he's looking for an update. If he's expecting fast progress on this, he's going to be one disappointed captain. Because the truth of the matter is that we are going to have to re-create the Carlisle investigation from scratch. In retrospect it seems not to have gone so well the first time, and now it's three years older and colder.

But Bradley isn't looking for information; he's called us in to provide some. "I spoke with Special Agent Wiggins of the FBI about Shawn."

"Anything interesting?" Nate asks.

Bradley nods. "In a way. The most interesting part was how our conversation came about. I didn't call them; Wiggins called me before I had a chance to."

"He knew it was Shawn?"

"He did."

I'm surprised by this, because Shawn's identity has not been made public. "How did he know that?" I ask.

"That's exactly the question I asked him, and he wouldn't answer. So I pressed him again, and he said there was an investigation going on and that Shawn was one of the people under surveillance. I asked why, and he said that he wasn't at liberty to say."

"Let me guess," Nate says, "he wants us to lay off."

Bradley smiles. "Not in so many words; he can't expect us to not investigate a murder. But he wants to be apprised of any developments."

"Did you mention Carlisle?" I ask.

"I did; I said we thought it was related. He asked why I thought that, and I said I was not at liberty to say. He wasn't thrilled with that answer."

"Tough shit," Nate says.

"You're going to get pressure from above on this; the Feds are going to go to the chief," I say.

Bradley nods. "I'll handle it. But it will be easier to handle if we solve the damn thing sooner rather than later."

"Did you learn anything else?"

"I asked him if he had any idea why Tartaro might have sent Shawn here, and he said Shawn doesn't work for Tartaro, that Tartaro has nothing to do with this. He was so adamant I thought he was going to tell me that Tartaro doesn't actually exist."

"Bottom line, they're going to be more of a pain in the ass than a help?" I ask.

Bradley nods. "I would say that's a safe bet. In the meantime, we're putting surveillance on Silva." Then, "You guys getting any-where?"

I update him on my conversation with Roberts, the Vegas cop. It actually fits with Bradley's discussion with the Feds, at least as far as Shawn no longer working for Tartaro. "But he must be working for somebody," I say. "He didn't wake up one morning and decide to fake amnesia. And I don't think he was into scrap-books."

We don't have anything else to tell him, and nothing ends a meeting quicker than lack of any progress to talk about. Nate and I head off to our own office to plan our next steps.

"You think we should go to Vegas?" he asks.

"Is this about the elastic women again, or did someone tell you about the buffets?"

"Wiseass."

The idea of going to Vegas and questioning Tartaro is one that I've been kicking around, but it's way premature. What we need to do now is focus on Carlisle. Shawn's lying to get me to look into Carlisle is by definition a reason to do so.

Bradley has wanted us to downplay it, to not make public the fact that we are reopening that case. Of course the problem with that is when we talk to witnesses, those witnesses are going to know we are not just rekindling old memories.

Those witnesses are going to be upset and curious, and they're going to talk to people.

But first they're going to talk to us.

> "How many people have I shot, Nate?"

IT'S A QUESTION I'VE WANTED TO ASK FOR A LONG TIME, BUT haven't had the nerve. Nate and Jessie talk of me as having been such a hothead that I'm afraid I used to have gunfights in front of city hall three high noons a week. If I've actually shot or killed someone, I sort of feel I owe it to the victims to know their names.

Since we're on the way to the coroner's office, it feels like an appropriate time to ask.

"Total?" Nate asks, making it sound like there's a list long enough to require a printout.

"I'm not talking about since the accident. I know about Bennett and that operation. I'm talking about before."

"How many do you remember?"

"One. A drug dealer named Richie Zimmerman. He came at me with a knife, and I shot him in the arm. Were there any others?"

"Let's put it this way. The guys at the station used to call you Wyatt Earp."

"Come on."

"Okay, there were two, at least that I know of. Three if you're including Zimmerman. One was a guy who kidnapped a kid, and the other was a hostage situation after a bank robbery. You passed the internal investigations with flying colors; both were justified."

"The guys I shot . . . are they living?"

"They were until you shot them. Then they weren't. Could have been a coincidence."

Hearing about my life secondhand is always weird, but this time it's even weirder than usual. "Were you there when I did it?"

"Of course. We're partners."

"Did you shoot anyone?" I ask.

"No way. You're the psycho nutjob, not me."

I think about this for a minute, but all I can think of to say is, "Shit."

"Hey, they were scumbags," Nate says, momentarily appearing to feel bad that he upset me. "And in both cases you saved innocent lives. Even Bradley said you did the right thing."

I nod. "Okay. Thanks."

"No problem, Wyatt."

Anthony Ruggiero is the Passaic County coroner, and because the head was found in Paterson, he was the lucky recipient of it. He's waiting for us when we arrive, and ushers us right into his office. He's new on the job, which means he hasn't been around long enough for me to forget him.

On the way back to his office, we can see through clear windows into the refrigerated room where the bodies are kept, and the table on which the autopsies are performed. Everything is perfectly clean and polished; there is no way those bodies are going to get an infection and die.

"This place gives me the creeps," Nate says, and it's a feeling I share.

We've already seen Ruggiero's report on Shawn, and it's skimpier and less specific than most, for obvious reasons. Nate thought we should talk to him, to see if he had other impressions not in the report, and I agreed that was a good idea.

Once we sit down, I'm glad that Ruggiero gets right to it, without any small talk. Even asking "what's new?" to a coroner can open up unpleasant conversational pathways.

"This was an unusual one," he says, smiling. "And I've been doing it for a while."

"Glad we could expand your horizons," I say.

He nods. "Pretty much every day it's 'been there, done that,' but not this time."

Autopsying the head really seems to have enriched his life. "So your report says that you can't be specific as to cause of death," I prompt.

"Right. No way to tell without the rest of the body. But you want an opinion?"

"Of course."

"Best guess is he was already dead when the head was cut off; at the very least he was completely immobile."

"Why do you say that?" Nate asks.

"The cut was neat, almost surgical; I couldn't have done a better job myself. If he was moving around, scared or resisting, that couldn't have happened. And the knife was very sharp; this guy didn't use a chainsaw, that's for sure."

I nod. "And the time of death? Can you be more specific than in the report?"

He shakes his head. "Very hard to tell; I wouldn't even want to venture a guess. No way to measure rigor, and no way to know if the head was preserved, maybe in plastic. But it was only in place for no more than two hours."

"How do you know that?"

"It was raining a little more than two hours before the jogger found it, but it obviously wasn't rained on. So I'm basing it on that; no medical reason."

We ask a few more questions, but Ruggiero has no more insight to provide. As we're leaving he says, "Good luck; you need to get this guy off the street."

"Why do you say it like that?" I ask.

"A guy who can slice a head off like that, living or dead, unless he's in my job . . ." He pauses and shakes his head. "There was no emotion; this is a bad guy. You think you could do what he did?"

Nate and I answer together. "No."

Hector Davila has more seniority than
anyone in the department.

THE JOKE IS THAT HE HAS MORE SENIORITY THAN EVERYONE PUT
together, but it's not a great joke, and definitely not one that anyone
actually says to Hector's face. Hector does not have a great sense of
humor about his age, and yet he still seems young enough to kick
anyone's ass.

Nate tells me that Hector is fifty-six, and has been in the department for thirty-four years, the last twenty-eight as a detective. Obviously, he could have retired with a full pension a while ago, and just as
obviously he likes what he's doing enough to want to keep doing it. I
have my doubts that I'll follow Hector's career path.

Hector was the lead detective on the Carlisle case; I worked
under him. The reason I was the arresting officer, again as Nate tells
it, was strictly a matter of being in the right place at the right time.
It was Hector's case all the way. Of course, I may be relying too
much on Nate to tell me things that went on in the past; he doesn't
really seem like the historian type.

The only way that Hector might be sensitive to the reopening
of the Carlisle investigation is if he happens to be like every other
cop in America, me included. In his mind, like everybody else's for

the last three years, the case has been solved, and the guilty party is in prison.

To question that is to invite Hector's wrath, and Hector gets very few wrath invitations. He's a scary guy. That's why Nate and I flipped a coin to see who gets to talk to Hector.

I lost.

"I hear you're reopening Carlisle," he says, before I am even settled in his office.

"Looks that way," I say, wishing that I had left his office door open behind me. I might need to make a quick getaway.

"Good."

Obviously, I'm surprised. "Why is that good?"

"Why wouldn't it be good?" he asks.

"I don't know; I figured you might not be happy about the possibility that you . . . we . . . got it wrong the first time."

"If I got it wrong, I'll be pissed," he says, emphasizing the "I." This is not a guy who shirks responsibility. "But that's still better than it staying wrong. There's a guy sitting in jail for it."

"I think that's a great attitude."

"I live to please you. Now what do you want?"

"Nicholson told me that Rita Carlisle told him she couldn't see him anymore, and that's what the argument was about. He thought she might be having an affair."

"So?"

"So he said she seemed stressed about something, maybe even afraid."

"I know. I was there for this, remember? Oh, that's right . . . your mind is a blank." He doesn't say that in a nasty, sneering way; it's more a statement of fact.

I nod. "This unfortunately falls into my dark period."

"We knew all that; Nicholson's lawyer made it very clear. And we followed up on it." He frowns at the memory. "But not maybe as hard as we should have."

"What do you mean?" I ask.

"Nicholson was perfect for it. He was there, he was pissed at her, and he went after her. There were traces of her blood in his car."

Nicholson claimed that she had torn a nail while in his car a few weeks earlier, and that was the source of the blood. Quite obviously we didn't believe him, and the jury didn't, either.

Hector continues. "So we treated everything he said as bullshit, and didn't try to confirm it as hard as we might have. And if that was a mistake, it's my mistake. Because from the beginning something didn't feel right."

"What do you mean?"

"Well, for one thing, Nicholson was too easy for it; it was all laid out there for us. For another, he never had any history of violence. For a guy like that to kidnap and kill a woman because she broke up with him, or whatever the reason, didn't ring completely true."

He pauses for a moment, remembering. "But most of all, what happened after she left the bar didn't make sense to me. At least not in my gut."

I'm very surprised by his attitude; I expected him to be much more defensive about his actions, and more certain that he got it right.

"Tell me about that," I say. "Please."

"She was pissed at him, or at least that's how she was acting. She ran out of the bar. He chased after her and grabbed her when they got outside, but she pulled away. At that moment, she wanted no part of the guy. We have that on video."

"Right."

"But there were people on that street; a few people came forward and said they saw live what we saw on the video. Yet no one saw anything after that; no one actually saw her go with him, or get into his car."

"So?" I ask.

"So her behavior that we could see was such that she wouldn't have just gone along; there would have been some kind of struggle, some kind of argument. Somebody would have seen something, or heard it. But she just disappeared. She wouldn't have walked away; her home was twenty miles from there. She would have called a friend, or a cab, and waited to get picked up."

I see what he's saying, but I can't say I find it terribly compelling. "Maybe he talked her into getting into the car."

"Maybe. There's one more thing," he says. "There's no audio on the videotape; it's silent. But when he grabs her, she says something to him. Look at it; I think you'll be able to read her lips."

"What do you think she's saying?" I ask.

"I'm pretty sure she's saying 'I can't.' Not 'leave me alone,' or 'I don't want to,' or 'get your hands off of me.' She's saying, 'I can't.'"

"And you think someone was stopping her?"

He nods. "I think it's possible. And I also think it's possible that the person who was stopping her was waiting for her. And that's the car she got into."

Joey Silva did not believe in an open-door policy.

WHEN HE TOOK OVER THE OPERATION FROM THE RECENTLY deceased Nicholas Bennett, there were close to eighty people in his full or partial employ. He had since expanded it by almost thirty; a sign of the aggressiveness with which he attacked the "business."

But with all of that, only two of those employees were allowed direct contact with him. In fact, no one else had permission to talk to him unless spoken to first. And those two were also strictly aligned in a "chain of command."

Number two under Silva was Tony Silva, Joey's younger brother by two years. His loyalty was unquestioned, and he was the only person allowed to openly disagree with something Joey had done or was doing. Of course, that open disagreement had to be done in private, when the two of them were alone.

The truth was that Tony got the better of the deal when their mother was handing out brains, and on some level Joey knew that and utilized it to his advantage.

Joey, on the other hand, got the major share of toughness and ruthlessness, which explained his number one position on the "family" tree. But Tony was a strong and respected number two; no one doubted that to go against Tony was to go against Joey.

And no one went against Joey.

Number three in the organization was Ralph DeSimone, though no one called him Ralph. He was universally referred to as Philly, since Philadelphia was where he was born. Nicknamers in the Silva operation were not particularly creative, which might explain why Joey was called "Joey," and Tony was referred to as "Tony."

So "Philly" DeSimone was allowed access to Joey Silva, though it was well understood by him that Tony was his primary contact. He never expressed any problem with that, probably because the number three position in the Silva family was a powerful and lucrative one.

When it came time to take a meeting with Dominic Romano, it was therefore no surprise that the New Jersey delegation consisted of Joey and Tony Silva, plus Philly DeSimone. Romano, Salvatore Tartaro's number two, only brought from Vegas two of his "soldiers," strictly for protection.

Knowing that modern technology left no indoor location 100 percent safe from surveillance, the decision was made to meet outdoors, but in a private setting.

The location they settled on was the Castletop Petting Zoo in Pompton Lakes. It covered three acres and had an assortment of ponies, donkeys, goats, and cows that for some reason attracted enough families each weekend to allow it to keep operating. The star attraction was a large bull that did nothing but stand there and look large and bullish.

Philly knew a guy who knew a guy whose brother-in-law owned the zoo, and a modest financial accommodation was made to arrange a takeover of the place at ten in the morning, when it was closed anyway.

Joey sent an advance party to the zoo that morning to make sure there was adequate security, and installed men at the gate and the perimeter. Joey loved money and power and women and food, but his number one priority was personal protection.

Joey's men ushered Dominic and his two bodyguards in when they arrived and brought them to where Joey, Tony, and Philly were waiting on benches in front of the pony ride booth. The expression on Dominic's face as he looked around was the same as if he had just tasted some expired milk; the Castletop Petting Zoo was a long way from Vegas.

Hands were shaken, and brief regards were offered. Dominic and Joey had met before, shortly after Bennett's death, when their business arrangement was being cemented.

Once the pleasantry phase was concluded, Joey said, "Let's take a walk." His second comment was, "Watch out for the goat shit."

So they started walking, Joey and Dominic together, and Tony and Philly a couple of steps behind, straining to hear what was being said. Soldiers on both sides walked in front of and behind the group. No one was inclined to stop and pet any animals.

"Mr. Tartaro is very unhappy about what happened to Shawn," Dominic said, referring to Salvatore Tartaro by his last name, as he always did. "He insists that I find out how it went down."

"So what are you coming to me for?" Joey said. "I had nothing to do with it. I didn't even know he was here."

"A guy like that comes into your territory and you aren't aware of it? That surprises me."

"What do you think, I have a booth set up at the airport? Where people have to sign in? This is a big place; I don't care who's here and who's not here. If they bother me, or my business, then I get involved."

"If one of your people came to Vegas, we would know about it, and he'd be protected."

"I would tell you he was coming," Joey said. "Which is what you should have done. If you asked for him to be protected, he'd be walking in goat shit with us right now."

"He didn't work for us anymore."

"Then why does Tartaro give a shit about him?"

It was a good question, and one that Dominic didn't want to answer, since an accurate response would have been to say that this was really about Tartaro not trusting Joey, and thinking that Joey might be trying to screw him. The truth was that Tartaro didn't care if Shawn was alive or dead; he only cared about Joey's involvement.

So Dominic ignored it and said, "We have done very profitable business together. And we're going to do even more in the future."

"Damn right, so let's not screw it up," Joey said, and then went to his version of conciliatory. "You tell Tartaro that I value his friendship, and his partnership. I had nothing to do with Shawn getting hit; I mean, what's with this 'cutting off the head' shit? That's crazy." He turns around and asks Tony, "What's the name of those nuts that cut off heads again?"

"ISIS," said Tony.

Joey nodded. "Right. ISIS."

"Mr. Tartaro still wants to know who hit Shawn," Dominic said.

Joey nodded again. "So do I, and I've got people on the street trying to find out right now. Just tell Tartaro I had nothing to do with it. But I also want to know what the hell Shawn was doing here. Maybe you can find that out, huh?"

"Maybe," Dominic said, with no enthusiasm or sincerity whatsoever.

Joey smiled. "Good. You do that."

"This is very unexpected," Daniel Lewinsky says.

I DON'T RESPOND TO THAT FOR A FEW REASONS. FIRST, AND
most important, I really couldn't care less about what he was expecting. But also, I have taken something of an instant dislike to him;
he's a guy that is clearly impressed with himself, and less so with me.

But the other reason I don't respond is because I don't want
him to think we're having a conversation. I'm here to ask questions,
and his only function right now is to answer them.

Lewinsky is the general manager of Bergen Hospital, which I
believe is the largest in New Jersey. It's a sprawling complex, and one
that fashions itself as the equal of any hospital in New York. I have
my doubts about that, although I did get excellent care here after
I was shot.

I'm here first because I want to learn what I can about Rita
Carlisle, and I'm putting off interviewing her mother, who seems to
be her only close relative. I'm delaying the reopening of her wounds
for as long as possible, though I expect I'm going to have to do it
sooner or later.

When I don't respond to Lewinsky's comment about how he

didn't expect my visit, he continues, "And I must say there's a bit of déjà vu in play here as well."

"How is that?" I ask.

"You know, you questioning me like this about Ms. Carlisle. It's reminiscent of three years ago. It's quite disconcerting, actually. Brings back memories of that awful time."

I could tell him some things about bringing back memories, and that if *USA Today* published a list of the top déjà vu practitioners nationally, I'd be at the top, but I don't.

"Would you mind telling me why this issue has come up again?" he asks. "Have Ms. Carlisle's whereabouts become known?"

Lewinsky is the leader in the clubhouse for the position of "guy I'd least like to sit in a bar and watch a football game with." Even the way he talks gets on my nerves. For example, in the mouth of a normal person, "Have Ms. Carlisle's whereabouts become known?" would come out, "Did you find Rita?"

I don't know if I felt differently about him three years ago, but if I liked him back then, I have clearly changed even more than I've been told. "This is a normal follow-up, Mr. Lewinsky."

"You mean because she's still missing?"

"We'll get through this much faster if I ask the questions."

"Very well," he says, in a tone that indicates he thinks it's far from very well.

"What was Ms. Carlisle's job here?"

"That hasn't changed in the past three years; she was in administration."

"That would be a good answer if I asked what department she was in. I asked what her job was."

"She was responsible for contacts outside of the hospital. With other hospitals, government agencies, hospice services, plus of course pharmaceutical companies . . ."

"Why do you say, 'of course'?"

"Well, that was probably what she spent the most time on."

"What was she doing in that regard?"

"Purchasing drugs to meet the needs of the hospital. Negotiating prices as well."

That's particularly interesting to me, because drugs would certainly be something that would interest both Tartaro and Silva. "Did she have a staff under her?"

"Yes, she did. I believe three people full-time, with occasional additional, temporary help. Her responsibilities were substantial."

"How long did she work here?"

"Really, Detective, you must still have all of this information," he says, his annoyance evident.

I nod. "I must. How long did she work here?"

"Almost four years."

Time to change topics. "Are you aware of any romantic relationships she might have had with any of her coworkers?"

"No, I certainly am not."

I ask him to give me a list of people in Rita's department back in the day, and he tells me that a number of them have left. When I press him, he agrees and asks his assistant to have someone named Mitchell Galvis come in.

Galvis gets here so fast that I think he must have had his ear pressed to the door. Lewinsky introduces us, and we shake hands. I've got the feeling that Galvis is staring intently at my face, as if trying to remember where he saw me. I get that a lot, now that I'm semi-famous.

"Mitchell, Detective Brock will need a list of people that Rita Carlisle worked with, as well as contact information for those that are no longer with the hospital."

Galvis nods. "I'll get right on it. How can I reach you, Detective?"

I give him my card, and he assures me that I'll be hearing from him soon. I then tell Lewinsky to send out a memo saying that everyone in the hospital that I might contact should speak to me.

He agrees to do so, sporting a facial expression that identifies that agreement as very reluctant.

It's while I'm on my way home that I realize I have an early morning session with Pamela tomorrow. It's a few seconds later that I realize I'm not going to keep it. I call her office and get a machine, so I tell her that I'm sorry, but work is going to keep me from seeing her in the foreseeable future.

I don't mention that "the foreseeable future" is going to last for the rest of my natural life. And the same is true of the amnesia group.

I'm through talking.

Now if I can just get someone to tell Jessie.

Jessie updated Nate on the department's surveillance of Silva, and he has news when I return.

"TARTARO'S TOP GUY IS IN TOWN, AND HE MET WITH SILVA THIS morning. His name is Dominic Romano."

"We have audio?" I ask.

"No. They met outdoors, at some zoo in Pompton Lakes, so we couldn't listen in. It's a new world; even the assholes are getting smarter."

"So we don't know what they were meeting about?"

"Not officially, but smart money is on it being about Shawn. Romano flew in, had the meeting, and went straight back to Vegas. I bet he wanted to hear firsthand how their boy wound up without a head on his shoulders."

"So now it definitely looks like the relationship that Tartaro had with Bennett has continued with Silva," I say. "But we don't know if Shawn had anything to do with that, or if he was here with his own agenda."

"But we know that whatever it was, it had to do with Rita Carlisle. And if Tartaro and Silva are involved, then they must be making money off of it."

"I think it's about drugs."

"How do you figure?" Nate asks.

"I just met with Rita's boss at the hospital, guy by the name of Lewinsky. Among Rita's responsibilities was buying the hospital drugs from the drug companies."

"Those hospitals use a lot of drugs," Nate says. "And Silva sells a lot of drugs. So let's talk this out. Suppose Rita was manipulating drug sales, maybe ordering more, concealing it, and funneling them to Silva."

"Bennett," I say. "At the time Rita went missing, Bennett was in charge."

He nods. "Right. But as the number two to Bennett, Silva would have been in on it. Either way, she could have been supplying the drugs."

I shake my head. "Doesn't make sense. If she was supplying them, why would they get rid of her?"

"Maybe she wanted out," he says.

"They wouldn't have let her out; they had too much on her. I think it's more likely that she found out it was going on, and that's why they got rid of her. They wanted the operation to continue, so she was a threat and had to go. Which would explain their current interest; they might still be getting drugs from the hospital. The conspiracy is probably ongoing."

He nods. "So we need to find out who's in her job now."

"I'm going to be getting that information soon. But if she wasn't involved, and simply found out about it, then it wouldn't matter who took her place. They were getting it with the help of someone else on the inside."

"Still doesn't explain two things," Nate says. "One . . . why did Shawn dig up all this ancient history? And two . . . why would Tartaro be involved? I don't see any reason why Silva would want or need a Vegas connection. He can handle his drug operation on his own, right here on his own turf. Silva isn't into sharesies."

Our intercom buzzes, and I pick it up. It's Sergeant Graves at the front desk, and he says, "You've got a call from a Mitchell Galvis. Says he's from Bergen Hospital."

That's the guy I met in Lewinsky's office, who was going to get me the personnel information. Right now, though, I want to talk to Nate about our next moves. "Tell him I'll call him back," I say.

"I already did. But he says it's really important."

"All right; put it through."

Once Mitchell is on the line, he reminds me who he is and says, "Detective, I will have that personnel information for you tomorrow."

This is what he thought was so important? "Good, call me when you do."

"I was hoping we could meet about it."

"Why?"

"There's something I need to talk to you about. It's a significant matter."

"Fine. Call me and you can bring it here, or I can stop by the hospital."

"It would be better if no one knew we were meeting. That would be crucial, actually."

This conversation just got a whole lot more interesting. "I see. Call me when you have the information, and we can arrange a meeting wherever you like."

He sounds relieved. "Excellent. Thank you for understanding. I'll contact you in the morning."

I hang up the phone and turn to Nate. "I've got a good feeling about this one."

Paramus Park exists in one of the densest shopping areas in the world.

SHOPPING MALLS IN THE PARAMUS/TEANECK AREA OF BERGEN
County are ubiquitous and have been in place for many years. Anyone who has driven on Route 4 or Route 17 on a Saturday knows what a mob scene it is. The collection of shopping havens attracts people from throughout North Jersey, and they even get many of the more mobile Manhattan residents as well.

If you can't get find something in Bergen County, it doesn't exist.

The Paramus Park mall is unique in a couple of ways. First of all, it is now the only fully enclosed mall in North Jersey; two others that had been enclosed have since opened up and let the air in. Second, it claims with some justification to have invented the concept of the food court. They trumpet that fact, though as inventions go, it ranks somewhere below the wheel and lightbulb.

The food court at the Paramus Park mall occupies the entire mezzanine level, so hungry patrons can take a quick escalator up from the main shopping floor. There are no public stairs leading up there, a fact that hasn't exactly led to a storm of protests. Patrons who are going to sample the kind of calorie-laden fast food that the court provides are not likely to insist on exercising their way up there.

There are eleven fast-food options on the mezzanine level, ranging from American to Mexican to Asian and back. Prices are higher than at the same chains at other, freestanding locations, but people are paying for the convenience and the multiple options. Parents out to efficiently use their time for bargain shopping can bring their children up there knowing that each will find something to their satisfaction, without ever having to leave the building.

Saturday is by far the busiest day of the week at Paramus Park for two reasons. Most people are off from work on the weekends, so they have time to spend shopping. But even more significant is the fact that Bergen County is the only county in the entire United States that is fully governed by so-called "Blue Laws."

Originally started in 1854, and amended somewhat in the intervening years, the laws state that almost nothing can be sold in Bergen County on Sundays. This is not just a ban on alcohol sales, as exists elsewhere . . . if you so much as want to buy a diaper in Bergen County on a Sunday, you're out of luck.

Efforts to repeal these laws have failed over the years; residents feel that the lack of shopping on Sunday gives them a better quality of life. Store owners often feel differently, especially Orthodox Jewish ones who keep their own stores closed according to their faith on Saturdays. Once Saturdays and Sundays are eliminated, there aren't many weekend days left.

Apparently the good people of Bergen County are literally the only people in America who have discovered the joy of shopless Sundays.

So Saturday is the huge day each week for all the Bergen County shopping malls. Peak time is between one and three o'clock, especially in the food court, where lines stretch out from the more popular venues. Most of the common tables are filled by patrons who have gotten their orders from the counters, and are settled in to eat before going back to resume their shopping.

It is, of course, a given that almost everyone walking around the mall is carrying at least one shopping bag to carry their purchases. Many people have multiple bags, as shoppers patronize more than one store on each trip, so as to efficiently use their time. It stands to reason that many of the food court tables being utilized will therefore have shopping bags lying next to them and under them, as people eat.

On this particular Saturday, a lone patron named Nick Saulter sat at one of the tables, munching on a slice of pizza. He did not have a shopping bag with him, because he was not there to buy anything.

Saulter was there to observe, and to plan, and to confirm that the food court at Paramus Park was in fact the perfect target.

Next time he came there, he would bring a shopping bag.

"He doesn't want to be seen with me,"
I say to Jessie.

SHE SMILES. "I KNOW EXACTLY WHAT HE MEANS. IT'S EMBAR-
rassing."

I return the smile. "Among the things I've obviously forgotten is how nasty you can be."

I'm in Jessie's office, and she's fitting me for a wire to wear to record my conversation with Mitchell Galvis. Based on how he sounded yesterday, as well as this morning when we set up the meeting, it seems like it's a conversation I might want to preserve.

"Take your shirt off," she says.

"Why does sex have to be your answer to everything?"

"You're right. I need to cut back on that."

I start taking off my shirt. "On the other hand, it's a decent answer for pretty much any question I can think of."

"What do you think this guy is going to say?" she asks, indicating that the banter portion of this meeting has concluded.

"I have no idea. Could be he's going to implicate someone, or maybe he thinks he's James Bond and the idea of clandestine meetings with law enforcement about kidnappings is exciting."

She's just about finished taping the wire to my chest. "Well, whatever it is, we'll all hear it."

"This could turn out to be the most boring secret recording of all time," I say.

The door opens and Nate pops his very large body into the room. "Galvis is on the phone. I switched it in here." On cue, the phone rings, and Nate points to it. "And there it is."

I pick up the phone, and again I'm talking to the apparently nervous Mitchell Galvis. "Can we meet this morning?" he asks. "I took off from work."

"Do you have the information?"

"What? Oh, yes, of course I do."

I have the strong feeling that the information I asked for is, at least in Galvis's mind, the least important part of this upcoming meeting. "Where would you like to meet?" I ask.

"I was hoping we could go for a ride. Maybe you could pick me up, and we could go someplace, or even talk in your car."

"OK. Where are you?"

"There's a place on Route 17, the Village Diner."

"I know it," I say.

"I'll be in the parking lot to the rear of the store. I'll be in my car, all the way in the back by the fence. It's a gray Fusion. When I see you, I'll get out and come in your car."

"Why so secretive?" I ask.

"I have my reasons, believe me. But you'll understand when we meet."

I tell Jessie and Nate about the call when I get off, and Nate says, "I'll go with you."

"No. I don't want to scare him off."

"I'll smile a lot and buy him a donut."

"No."

"Then I'll follow you," Nate says. "I don't like this secrecy shit;

you shouldn't be alone with him. Especially with you driving. He could be armed."

"I agree with Nate," Jessie says.

"No. This guy is not a threat."

"That's what you said about John Smith," Nate says.

"Who's John Smith?"

Nate shakes his head in disgust. "You forgot him, too? Guy was a wimpy librarian; we were investigating him for a possible drug buy. He pulled a gun on you, and I had to save your ass."

"You're making that up," I say.

Nate nods. "Yeah, but it could have been true."

Jessie laughs. "You couldn't come up with a better name than John Smith?"

Nate shrugs. "Hey, I was under a lot of pressure."

"I'm leaving, but I'm going to watch for you," I tell Nate. "If I see you come out that front door, I'm going to run you down. It'll total the car, but it will be worth it."

I arrive at the Village Diner about ten minutes early, and the parking lot is still fairly crowded with what must be a late-eating breakfast crowd. I drive around toward the back, and I see Galvis sitting in the driver's seat of his car. He sees me, as well, and gets out. He's carrying a small briefcase.

I pull up in front of his car, and he quickly opens the door and gets into the passenger seat.

He seems out of breath, but he's only walked about ten feet. "Thanks," he says. "I made sure I wasn't followed."

"That's a relief."

He is aware enough to know I'm being sarcastic. "You think I'm being too careful," he says. "But I'm not. These are dangerous people."

"Who is it we're talking about?"

"Let me start from the beginning," he says.

So he does.

"You have to keep my name out of this,"
Galvis says.

THAT IS THE SAME REQUEST THAT CONNOR SHAWN MADE WHEN he told me about his scrapbook. It was the last time I saw him with his head on his shoulders. Hopefully this will work out better for Galvis.

"I'll do what I can," I say. We've left the diner and pulled into an enormous parking lot in a mall called Paramus Park. We can sit in the car here and talk without anyone noticing us.

He shakes his head. "No, that's not good enough. You have to promise me you won't tell anyone about this conversation. Otherwise take me back to my car."

"OK. Just between us." Technically my promise has no meaning, since a recording of this meeting is being done, and therefore other people will learn about it without me having to tell them. Jessie and Nate are no doubt listening to us right now. But I'll try to stick to the spirit of the agreement in any event.

I can see him relax with relief, and he takes a folder out of the briefcase. "First of all, these are the people that Rita worked with. Some of them are still with the hospital, some not. I included whatever contact information we have for the people that left."

"What about people she dealt with at other places? Lewinsky said she was involved with dealing with outside companies, including drug manufacturers."

He nods. "Whatever I know about is in there."

"Great."

He takes a deep breath and launches into his story. "There is something else, something that until now I've kept to myself. I know that was wrong, but what's done is done."

I don't say anything; I think it's best in these situations to interrupt as little as possible. When someone wants to talk, let them talk. I may have learned that at the police academy, or since, but I just don't remember.

"There have been some . . . let's call them irregularities . . . in the way the hospital buys drugs."

He pauses, waiting for me to jump in, so I just ask what he means by "irregularities."

"Over time the amount we've been buying has increased, but the usage hasn't. And it's not being reflected in our inventory. I've seen the orders, and the payment authorizations, but when I look in the system, the numbers are different. It's happened too many times for it to be a mistake."

"What kind of drugs?" I ask.

"Mostly opioids. The kind that would have a serious street value."

"Who is in charge of this?"

"You made a promise, right? My name stays out."

"Right."

"It has to be Lewinsky . . . my boss. He's the only one in a position to cover this up. I don't know who he is working with inside the hospital. He'd need help, but nobody else could do it without him."

"How much money is involved?"

"I don't know; it depends when it started, and I don't know the answer to that. But it's got to be at least seven figures, and that's not taking into account the street value of the drugs. That would be through the roof; I can't even imagine how much. You'd probably know better than me."

"Is this ongoing?"

"I think so, but I can't be sure," he says. "But they don't know that anyone is on to them, so I can't see why they'd stop."

"Why are you coming forward now? And why to me?" I ask.

"Because of Rita, and the fact that you seem to have reopened her case. I know I should have thought of it earlier, but I never connected the possibility of Rita's disappearing to the situation at the hospital. It just seemed like her boyfriend was guilty, and that was that."

The words are coming easier to him as he's getting more into the revelations. "Was she in a position to have been working with Lewinsky to get these drugs illegally?"

"I guess so, but I knew Rita, and I don't believe it. She was a good, honest person. I was thinking maybe she discovered what was going on, and they silenced her. They could have killed her to prevent her from talking. Maybe that's crazy . . . I hope it is . . . but . . ."

"Who's 'they,' Mitchell?"

"What?"

"You said 'they' could have killed her. Who are 'they'?"

He looks around, as if trying to confirm that we're alone, even though we obviously are. "My name goes nowhere. Promise me again."

"We've been through this twice, Mitchell."

"I don't care. I'll deny everything, and I'll never testify. You need to make the promise again."

"I won't reveal your name. Now who are the people that could have killed Rita Carlisle?"

He takes a deep breath. "I overheard a phone conversation that Lewinsky was having; he didn't know I could hear it. He sounded like he was afraid of something, like he was doing damage control. I heard him say, 'It will be fine; I can handle it. Please tell him that.'"

"Do you know who he was referring to?"

Galvis nods, pauses for a moment, and then says, "Lewinsky said, 'Tell Mr. Silva not to worry.'"

"For now, let's keep this within this room."

THE ROOM I'M TALKING ABOUT IS JESSIE'S OFFICE. SHE AND NATE heard my conversation with Galvis through the wire as it was happening, and were as stunned by it as I was. I've come straight back to talk to them about it.

"If we don't tell the captain, he'll have our asses," Nate says. Then, to Jessie, "I'm talking about Doug's and my asses, of course."

"Thanks, Nate; that's a relief," she says. "Why within this room?" Jessie asks me. "Because of your promise to Galvis? Because, technically, if one of us tells the captain, or if we just play him the tape, you're in the clear."

"That bothers me some, but that's not really it. I just think we should wait until we have it nailed down more."

"We've got testimony about a felony conspiracy at the hospital, we have a potential perp for Carlisle, we've got a motive, and we've got Silva connected. All wrapped up in one taped conversation. What more do we need?"

I nod. "We do have all that, but in the eyes of a prosecutor, we have nothing. We have no proof of the drug thefts at the hospital; in fact, Galvis said Lewinsky has covered those tracks. We have no proof that Rita Carlisle was either part of the conspiracy or knew about it. We don't even know for sure it was going on back then. And we have no way to tie Silva in, at least not in a manner that would be admissible. All we have is one witness, who, by the way, has sworn he'll deny all of it and never testify."

"He's on tape," Jessie says.

"It's not enough. No prosecutor in his right mind would take this anywhere near a courtroom."

"We could probably get a warrant to examine the hospital books based on Galvis's statements," Nate says.

"Without using his name?" Jessie asks.

I nod. "Probably. I would just have to swear that he's a reliable guy who is absolutely in a position to know what he's talking about. But it likely wouldn't get us anywhere, since Galvis has already said that the books have been cooked to look normal. And if we made that move, we'd tip off where we're heading with this."

"We might have to do that anyway," Nate says.

"Not a good move. We want to do more than nail a hospital administrator for drug crimes and fraud. We want to get Silva on kidnapping and murder. And we need to convince a prosecutor to get near doing that."

"Absolutely," Nate says. "But nobody's talking about going to a prosecutor right now. This is about telling the captain."

"I know," I say. "I just think we should wait until we have a little more."

"You're worried he'll sabotage it? That he won't want to blow up the Nicholson conviction?"

"I don't think so, but it's possible. Maybe even subconsciously. Let's just give this some air, okay? Just a couple of days. There's also another angle we're not considering."

"What's that?" Jessie asks.

Nate answers the question for her. "Shawn."

I nod. "Exactly. Let's assume everything Galvis said was accurate, and let's further assume that Rita was killed because of the drug thefts. Maybe she was part of it and wanted to stop, or even confess. Or more likely she found out about it and they killed her to shut her up. You with me?"

Nate nods, and picks up the scenario. "And we can assume that Shawn knew all that, so if he wanted us to reopen Carlisle, then he wanted Silva to get nailed for it."

"Right," I say. "For all we know he might have slipped us more evidence if he had lived. So Silva makes sense for having killed Rita, but the bigger question is, why was Shawn trying to bring Silva down?"

"Maybe he was doing it for Tartaro," Jessie says.

"Maybe, but why? What would Tartaro, sitting in Vegas, gain from Silva going down? And why go about it this way? If he wanted Silva out of the way so bad, why not hire somebody like Shawn to put a bullet in his head? Why would he rely on us? Unless I'm forgetting even more than I think I am, our record of going after people like Silva is not exactly filled with lightning-fast successes."

Nate seems to think about this for a few moments, and finally nods his agreement. "Okay, we sit on it, but not for long."

"Thank you. Now, we need to proceed like before, like we're investigating Shawn's murder, and Carlisle as well. But we do it looking through the prism of what we know, of what Galvis told me."

"Makes sense," Nate says.

"We go slow," I say. "We need to take it one step at a time."

Jessie says, "Wow."

"Do you believe this guy?" Nate asks her.

She just shakes her head, and I ask, "What the hell are you guys talking about?"

"You wanting to take it one step at a time, to go slow," Jessie says. "That will take some getting used to."

Nate adds, "In the old days, you would be strapping on your gun belt to go in shooting."

I'm not sure why, but I'm finding this really annoying. "So I've changed, okay? There's the old me, and now there's the new me, and all of us, especially me, have to deal with it. So can we stop going back down memory lane to the old days? Because for me there aren't a hell of a lot of them, and I don't need to be reminded of it."

Jessie and Nate exchange looks; it seems like they feel bad for upsetting me. Nate is the one who speaks. "Okay, Doug. And if it makes you feel better, I do want you to know that the old you and the new you have one thing in common: You're both a pain in the ass."

I can't help it; I start to laugh. "Well, all right then. Glad we cleared that up."

Tony Silva and Philly DeSimone would have occasional conversations about someone they considered dangerous.

THAT DANGEROUS PERSON WAS THE ONE ABOVE THEM ON THE organization personnel chart, Tony's brother, Joey. Joey could be erratic and make impulsive decisions; it was certainly understating the case to say that he was not a master strategist. And when he flew off the handle, the net result was that it could be dangerous for all of them.

Tony and Philly knew that, and had long ago come to openly share that view with each other. So they would meet to discuss how they could guide Joey in a more productive direction on various issues that came up.

They were not being disloyal in the process and were not trying to undercut Joey at all. Rather they were just working to come up with approaches that could benefit Joey and the organization, and then figuring out how to persuade Joey that their approach was best. They actually viewed such conversations as both an act of loyalty and self-preservation.

Inevitably, it fell to Tony to bring their ideas to Joey. He was the number two man in the organization, and while Joey did not doubt either man's loyalty, Tony had a special position as Joey's brother. Joey had a tendency to anger when his views and decisions were challenged, but Tony could get away with much more than anyone else, including Philly. It was a tactic he had developed and perfected over time.

Discussions like this between Tony and Philly were not a frequent occurrence. Despite the breadth of the Silva family's organization and business interests, it ran smoothly and usually without crises. Employees from Tony on down knew their jobs and executed them well, helped along by the fact that they rarely had to face new and unexpected challenges.

But just such an issue had arisen, at least as far as Tony and Philly were concerned. They were not particularly happy with the meeting at the zoo between Joey and Dominic Romano. They found it pretty much impossible to believe Dominic's statement that he and his boss, Tartaro, had no idea why Shawn was on the East Coast.

They didn't know what Shawn was doing there, who killed him, or why it was done, but they didn't buy Tartaro's supposed ignorance of it. It seemed to them that he was trying to pin it on Joey, while knowing better. Even worse, it also seemed like he might be setting Joey up for something down the road.

They felt Joey should have taken a more aggressive attitude, a rarity since they usually were trying to temper Joey's aggression. But Tartaro was Joey's partner, and they didn't think he was behaving the way a partner should.

The way the conversation with Dominic was left, in their view, was that Joey was unconvincing in his denial of involvement in Shawn's death, even though he in fact had nothing to do with it. This could prompt an excuse for revenge by Tartaro, something they needed to be prepared for.

Perhaps even more troublesome was the fact that, since the Silvas actually had no responsibility for hitting Shawn, it meant someone else was out there, cutting off the heads of made guys. It was possible but very unlikely that Tartaro had sent Shawn and then ordered him hit. The only possible reason for doing that would be to enable him to blame Silva, though that made little sense. Among other things, it could imperil their ongoing and increasingly profitable business partnership.

So at the very least this was an issue that needed to be discussed. The plan was for Philly to come over to Tony's house in North Haledon on this night, so that they could talk through the best way to broach this with Joey. Like all such meetings, Joey was not aware it was taking place, and so as to preserve that secret, Tony sent away the two men who served as guards on the property. If word ever got back to Joey, he might ask uncomfortable questions.

Tony welcomed Philly as he always did, with a bottle of red wine and a plate of cheeses. The two of them had grown comfortable with each other over time; they had literally been through wars together.

The meeting was held at Tony's instigation, so he started it. "I think Dominic was full of shit. He knows we didn't hit Shawn, but he was trying to pin it on us."

"I don't know how Joey didn't see it," Philly said.

"But here's what I don't get," said Tony. "Why would Tartaro send Shawn here, and then press the button on him? What the hell was he doing here in the first place?"

"What does Joey think?"

"Joey has no idea. But I don't think Tartaro would send his own guy here and then kill him. And we didn't give the order. So if we didn't, who did?"

Tony got up to get some more wine, turning away from Philly in the process.

"I did," Philly said.

It took a moment to register, but then Tony realized what he'd said and responded, "What does that mean?"

As he turned, he learned exactly what that meant, as Philly was holding a gun on him. "What the hell are you doing?"

"I brought Shawn here, and then I killed him. I'm the answer to all your questions. It's too bad you're not going to be around to see how it all works out, because you'd be impressed," Philly said. "Maybe I'll give you a look at the future on the way."

Tony looked to his right and realized that two other men had just entered the room. He didn't recognize them; he had never seen them before. One was pointing a gun at Tony, the other held some kind of satchel.

"It doesn't have to be this way, Philly. We can work out whatever the problem is. We're family."

"It's all going to work out fine, Brother Tony," Philly said. "Just fine. Now let's go."

The call is routed to Nate and me,
which by itself is surprising.

I QUESTION IT, AND AM TOLD THAT CAPTAIN BRADLEY HIMSELF
gave us the assignment. That is even stranger, since he wants us laser
focused on Shawn and Carlisle.

Once we're on the way and we get more details, the mystery is
cleared up. We're heading to a small shopping mall in Elmwood
Park, a town just east of Paterson that actually used to be named
East Paterson. A body has been discovered in the back sitting on
top of a closed Dumpster.

Well, not actually a body.

A severed head.

If you're figuring the odds, the chance of two unrelated severed
heads being found so close to each other in both time and distance
is pretty small. Bradley's assuming it's related to our case, and his
decision to send us therefore makes sense.

We arrive on the scene in the middle of a driving rainstorm,
and one look at the head shows that we don't need an odds maker to
tell us that Bradley made the right call. The head used to sit on the
body of none other than Tony Silva. The pelting rain makes it look
like Tony's head just got out of the shower.

"Holy shit," Nate says, a reaction that makes perfect sense.

This time the discovery was not made by a jogger, but by a short order cook arriving for work at a coffee shop in the mall. Despite that, there is another similarity too obvious not to notice.

This head was also meant to be found. Not only was it left in a place where it would easily be discovered, but the killers made sure to put it on top of the closed Dumpster.

They could have put it in a Dumpster, this one or another one, or they could have left it on the ground. But the former would have meant it might not be found, and the latter could have resulted in an animal carrying it off. They also could obviously have buried it in the woods, or under the end zone at Giants Stadium.

Sitting on the Dumpster as it was, it was put on display, and might as well have had neon lights shining on it.

"There's going to be a goddamn war," Nate says.

"Tartaro and Silva?"

He nods. "Tartaro's guy gets hit, and then Tony Silva gets it in the same way? You got another idea?"

"There could be a third party involved."

He shakes his head. "Who is nuts enough to piss off both Tartaro and Silva?"

"I have no idea."

"It's got to be between them; maybe some business deal gone bad. But this is personal, and Joey is going to go batshit. I'll bet you they're going to the mattresses now."

"Going to the mattresses?" I ask. "Who are you, Clemenza? Actually, you're built like him."

Nate and I hang around until the forensics people have had a chance to do most of their work, and the head is taken off to the coroner's. There's little to be found here, and certainly nothing that will lead us to the perpetrators.

We have officers canvass the local neighborhood, but by the

time we leave, nobody has seen anything or added to what we know. No houses have a view of this alley, and if we assume the head was left during the night under cover of darkness, then the businesses would have been closed as well.

We finally head back to the precinct, where Captain Bradley is waiting for us. "I've already heard from the Feds," he says. "They're opening a full-fledged investigation."

"It's our case," I say.

"That's not exactly how they look at it. They're assuming this is Tartaro versus Silva, which is Nevada versus New Jersey, which means they're crossing state lines. In fact, if you remember what a map looks like, many state lines."

"They won't give a shit about Carlisle," I say. "We need to make that right."

Bradley nods and proceeds to surprise me. "I agree. I said they were moving in; I didn't say we were backing off."

"Good," Nate says.

"We now have two murders to investigate, and that's what we're going to do. Doesn't matter if they're gangsters or Boy Scout troop leaders; we can't have people getting killed like this in our backyard. But I'm not interested in refereeing a cross-country gang war. If that's where this leads us, then fine, and we work with the Feds. But it's not our priority."

I nod. "Understood. But we're going to find out it's all related. And the answer is still Carlisle."

"How do you figure that?"

"Because Shawn's sole purpose in being here, at least that we know of, was to draw us into reopening Carlisle. Somebody didn't like that, so they killed him. The hit on Tony Silva was probably retaliation; but it all started with Shawn and Carlisle."

"You think that was retaliation?" Nate asks. "You ain't seen nothing yet. Joey Silva is going to go nuts."

I nod. "Yeah, but I don't give a damn about Shawn or Tony Silva. I care about Rita Carlisle; she somehow got herself in too deep with these assholes, and I don't think there's any doubt that she paid for it with her life. She's buried someplace where nobody is going to find her. And when I find out who put her there, then I'm the one who's going to go nuts."

It was left to Philly DeSimone to tell
Joey his brother was dead.

PRETTY MUCH EVERYONE IN THE ORGANIZATION ALREADY KNEW
it, because the media had the story. But Joey, not a consumer of
media, was still in the dark, and there was not exactly a throng of
people racing to enlighten him.

It was probably fitting that Philly should have been the one to
reveal Tony's murder, since Philly had been the murderer. But, of
course, Joey did not know that, which is why Philly continued to live.

Philly expected Joey to explode with anger at the news, since
Joey could explode with anger when informed that it was going to
rain. Anger was his default reaction to pretty much everything with
any negative connotations at all. And in Joey's line of work it could
be an effective governing technique, at least when tempered by
Tony's clear, calm thinking.

But if Joey's reaction to Philly's news was to be irate, he was hiding it well. He was quiet for a while after hearing the news, maybe
three minutes, but to Philly it seemed like three decades. Then, seemingly under control, he asked Philly to detail what he knew about it.

"Joey, you don't want to hear this," Philly said.

"Tell me or I will cut your heart out." He said it calmly and in control.

So Philly told him the details. Not the ones he knew, of course, since he knew them all. Rather he told him the facts that had been made public, including the graphic description of Tony's severed head sitting on top of the alley Dumpster.

"Come back in fifteen minutes," Joey said.

So Philly left, and Joey used the fifteen minutes not to plot his revenge, but to do something no one who knew him would have considered him capable of.

He mourned.

His brother had been killed. Tony was two years younger than he was, and he literally could not remember a day without Tony being present. He loved and trusted Tony in a way he loved and trusted no one else in the world. And he relied on him as well. On some level they both knew that Tony was smarter, and that Joey could get away with being erratic and impulsive because Tony was there to rein him in.

And now Tony was gone, and Joey was alone.

So he allowed himself those fifteen minutes to mourn before he called Philly back in. "Do whatever you have to do to find out who did this," Joey said.

"Come on, Joey, you know who did it."

"You think this was Tartaro?" Joey asked.

"You're damn right I do. Who else could it have been? Shawn gets hit, he blames us, and he takes out Tony. Who else could it have been?"

"Who killed Shawn?"

"I don't know," said Philly. "But it don't matter. Tartaro thinks that we did, so he took his revenge. That's all that matters."

"Do we know for sure that none of our people hit Shawn?"

"Absolutely."

"And Tartaro didn't hit him; Shawn was his own man."

"Maybe Shawn was disloyal."

Joey shook his head in frustration. Philly didn't understand what he was saying. Tony would have understood. It was distressing for Joey; he didn't want to assume the position as the logical thinker in the organization, since he knew it was not a job he was well suited for.

"Doesn't matter," Joey said. "If Tartaro put the hit out on Shawn, then he wouldn't have hit Tony for revenge. He would know we didn't do it."

"So what are you saying?" Philly asked. He was surprised and annoyed; he never expected clear thinking out of Joey, and certainly not after being told that his brother was dead.

"I'm saying that maybe there's somebody else out there doing the killing." Then, "Find out who it is, and bring him to me."

Talking to the family and friends of murder victims
is the worst part of my job.

I DON'T KNOW HOW MANY TIMES I'VE DONE IT OVER THE YEARS,
because, obviously, I don't remember some of those years. But I recall enough times to know I hate it.

Usually the conversations happen when the wound is fresh,
when the murder was recent and we're trying to find the killer.
We're looking for an instant reconstruction of the victim's recent
life, to find out who would possibly have wanted them dead. So often
the person I'm talking to is not thinking clearly, since they're
consumed by grief. I always feel like an intruder, but I have a job to
do, and down deep the people I'm talking to want me to succeed.

So because of the fact that years have elapsed since the crime,
this is a fairly unique situation. I've come to see Doris Carlisle,
Rita's mother. She works at an insurance agency in Hackensack,
and I could hear the tension catch in her throat when I called her
and told her I wanted to talk to her. She asked if we could meet at a
nearby diner during her lunch hour, so I'm here waiting for her.

A woman maybe sixty years old walks in and scans the room.
I don't recognize her, which is not exactly a news event, but her
eyes fixate on me and she comes over to my table. She sits down, not

even bothering to take off her coat, and says, "Is there a chance that Rita is alive?"

I'm not going to lie to her. "I don't have any knowledge of that one way or the other, but I don't believe that she is."

She nods; down deep she has known the truth all along. "Then please tell me what this is about."

"Some new information has come up about the case involving your daughter that requires follow-up. So I need to ask you some questions. I'm sorry about this, but it can't be helped."

"What kind of information?"

"I can't say at this point, but it could be important."

She thinks for a moment and then shakes her head. "No, I cannot go through this again. You have no idea what it's like."

Her reaction once again reminds me that this investigation is first and foremost about getting justice for Rita Carlisle. "You're right, I don't. It's unimaginable to me," I say. "But one thing I know for sure; you want to be positive that the right person is in jail for what was done. Because if he isn't, then the actual guilty party is out there free."

"Are you saying that he might not be guilty? How can that be? After all this time?"

Strangely, what I can say to her isn't that different from what I said to Nicholson. "All I'm saying, at this moment, is that I need to ask you some questions. And that when I know, you'll know."

She finally nods, giving in, and slips off her coat. "Ask your questions."

"In the last weeks before Rita disappeared, was there anything that she expressed fear about?"

She shakes her head. "Not to me. But she seemed distracted, maybe worried. She was not the type to burden other people with her problems, not even her mother. So she never came out and said anything, but I felt something might be wrong. I planned to ask her about it, but . . . I never got the chance."

"Was she having any problems at work?"

"I don't think so. She loved her job."

"She told someone that she 'didn't have a job anymore.' Any idea what she could have meant by that?" Nicholson had reported that Rita said that at the restaurant, after she said she was leaving town. Of course, since Nicholson is currently in prison for the crime, I can't just accept anything he says at face value.

"Who did she say that to?"

"I'm sorry, please, it will be much better if you just answer my questions. If she said that, that she didn't have a job anymore, do you have any idea what she might have meant?"

"No. I can't imagine her saying that."

"Mrs. Carlisle, I'm sorry to have to ask you this, but was Rita having an affair? Maybe with someone at work?"

She tenses slightly and doesn't answer for a few moments. There's no doubt that I've hit a nerve; the only question is whether it will provoke a response.

"They asked me that three years ago," she says, her voice getting lower. "In fact, *you* asked me that three years ago. I said no then."

"Was it the truth?"

"I didn't see what it could have had to do with what happened, and I didn't want to soil her memory. She was a good girl; she made a mistake."

"So she did have an affair?"

She nods. "Yes, but not with someone who could have had anything to do with what happened."

"I'm not saying he did, Mrs. Carlisle. I'm not saying that at all. I just need to know his name."

"He is a doctor; he worked at the hospital. I don't know if he still does or not."

"That doesn't matter," I say. "Please tell me his name."

"Cassel. Dr. Steven Cassel."

"I told you when you called that he was in surgery."

DR. STEVEN CASSEL'S RECEPTIONIST SEEMS ANNOYED THAT I didn't take her statement in our phone conversation as the last word in the matter. Instead, I've decided to come to his office; it's almost five o'clock, and I figure that at some point surgeries have to end, either positively or negatively.

"I remember that. You were very clear about it," I say.

"So why are you here?"

"Because I wanted to come by." I take a seat in the waiting area and pick up a brochure on thoracic surgery, which I take one glance at and immediately put back down. I then grab a three-month-old magazine and ask, "You got anything newer than this?"

She doesn't bother to answer and just sort of makes a huffing noise, which is fine. I assume if they had more recent magazines, they would have put them out. Either way, this woman is not about to go magazine hunting to find me something more current.

Doctors, and apparently their employees, are not used to having their directives disregarded. I'm told there was once a time when it was the same way with police officers, but that was before I lost my memory, and probably before I was born.

I'm guessing that Dr. Cassel is going to return after he's through with surgery. It's an educated guess; his bouncer would have probably told me if he wasn't coming back just as a way to get rid of me. Also, she's hanging around after hours, and I have to assume she's waiting for the boss.

I'm midway through my third outdated *Sports Illustrated* when a guy in what looks like a surgeon's outfit comes in the door. I'm figuring he's not a patient, since there's no doctor here to see.

He says, "Long day, Helen," and then notices I am sitting here, and says, "Oh."

Helen starts to do the introductions. "Doctor, this is Detective . . ."

"I know who it is, Helen," Cassel says. "Come in."

I follow him into his office. It's small and rather unimpressive, but I guess if you're going to spend the whole day in surgery, that doesn't matter. I take the seat he offers me, and he says, "I've been expecting you. When I heard that . . . never mind. What can I do for you, Detective?"

"You had an affair with Rita Carlisle."

"Is there a question in there?"

"Not so far," I say. "But jump in whenever you want."

"I'm a married man, Detective. I have two children. I am very protective of my family; I do not want them hurt in any way as a result of my mistakes."

"I have no interest in hurting your family. My interest is in accumulating relevant facts, and then trying to figure out what they mean."

He nods. "Very well. I'm not sure how relevant it is, but yes, I had a fairly brief relationship with Rita Carlisle. I regretted it then, and I regret it now. She deserved better."

"How brief?"

"Three months."

"Was it still going on when she died?" I ask.

"Not quite. It ended just two days before. She ended it."

"Why did she do that?"

"I'm not sure. She just said that she couldn't do it anymore. I assume she meant invading someone else's marriage. She was a very moral person, and was not comfortable with the role she was playing. Maybe she meant something else, but if so, she didn't verbalize it."

"Why didn't you come forward about this three years ago?" I ask.

"No one asked me. Had they done so, I would have told the truth as I'm telling it now."

"Did you have much interaction with her in doing your respective jobs?"

He shakes his head. "Some, but not much. I am one of the doctors on a board that deals with the administration about common interests and policies. So in that sense Rita and I had some contact. That's how we met."

"To your knowledge, was she happy in her job?"

He hesitates, and finally says, "I'm not sure I should go there. It would mean getting into hearsay and rumor, and I'm not really comfortable with that."

Since Cassel's comfort level is pretty far down on my list of concerns, I continue. "Doctor, these questions are going to be answered, one way or the other. You can answer them in a private setting, like this one in your office, with me, or in a more public forum in a place not of your own choosing, with a bunch of lawyers and a court stenographer. It's really your call, but you only have one bite of the apple."

"That's sounds like a threat," he says.

"Not to me. To me it sounds like a simple statement of fact."

"Okay. She was having trouble with the hospital general manager, Daniel Lewinsky. She was considering leaving her job."

"What kind of trouble?"

"I don't know, but I believe she disapproved strongly of something he was doing. I truly do not know what that was."

I tell Dr. Cassel that I may want to talk to him again, and he gets me to repeat that I have no interest in revealing his affair with Rita Carlisle. I've been promising so many people that I'll keep quiet that I probably should have Dr. Cassel operate to remove my larynx.

When I leave I call Nate to update him on my interviews with Helen Carlisle and Dr. Cassel.

"What kind of doctor is he?" Nate asks.

"A thoracic surgeon."

"What the hell is that?"

"You don't know?"

"Of course I know, I was just seeing if you did. He operates on thoracics."

"Exactly. I'll give you his card, in case you break your thoracic."

The Mirage is the one that started it all.

WHEN IT WAS BUILT IN 1989, IT WAS THE FIRST HUGE CASINO hotel/resort built in Vegas in fifteen years. But it was not the last; in fact, it set off a building spree that has still not stopped.

The Bellagio, the Venetian, the Mandalay Bay, the Wynn, and many, many more; one after another, they sprang up and came to dominate the Strip. They are remarkably large and ornate, with the finest restaurants, casinos larger than football fields, and show-rooms that can accommodate Broadway–style productions. Caesars Palace is the only hotel from the "old days" that has managed to compete with these newcomers.

As these enormous hotels were built, the smaller ones were gobbled up to make room. Most of the street-level casinos and gift shops on the Strip took the money and ran. They got outsized prices for spaces that housed businesses that would never have been able to compete with the "big boys" anyway.

One of the casinos that did not sell out was a small one near the Flamingo called "Lucky Linda's." Legend had it that Linda was an old-school casino operator who was too stubborn to sell and feisty enough to think she could make a go of it. Linda, the story goes, had started the place as a family business, and would never let go, no matter how big the offer.

Linda was revered as the last of a dying breed.

None of it was true. There were no big offers of a buyout; the place had the very unfortunate luck to be positioned in a location that no one really needed. There never even was a Linda; the original male owner just liked the name. The place had been sold a number of times over the years, sometimes to groups with multiple owners. It actually defied the odds that among all those owners, there had never been a Linda. Pretty much every other name was represented.

Except in conditions of inclement weather, every day movable glass walls were raised and the casino was actually open to the street. People passing by could just walk in, and there were gambling tables within five feet of the sidewalk.

Walking on the Vegas Strip is not easy. It takes a long time even to go from one hotel to another; they seem deceptively close but it takes forever to navigate the distance. Adding to the problem are pedestrian barriers that the town has installed for crowd and traffic control; the Strip is very definitely not conducive to long strolls and window shopping.

So Lucky Linda's, and a few others like it, have become rest stops for weary pedestrians. They walk in, take much-needed seats at slot machines and blackjack tables, and lose money for the privilege of doing so. The place doesn't get high rollers—you wouldn't even call their patrons "rollers" at all—but it pays the rent, one slot machine lever pull at a time.

The fancy casinos are among the most surveilled places in the world; there is not a square inch of them that is not being videotaped by multiple cameras twenty-four hours a day. You don't have to have seen any of the seemingly thousands of "Ocean" movies starting with *11* to know that the casinos are prime targets for thieves and gambling cheaters, and the video surveillance is designed to thwart that.

Places like Lucky Linda's have neither the money nor the inclination to duplicate the intensity of that security. There are cameras, and there are certainly security personnel, but the level is not on the same planet as their more well-heeled competitors. They have less to lose, and less to spend on protection.

Vegas has its share of rainstorms, and they can be sudden and intense. When that happens, the crowds on the sidewalks pour into places like Lucky Linda's for temporary refuge. The average crowd can more than double.

It would be relatively easy, during those times, for someone to sneak in and leave a device in a shopping bag, and then exit the casino undetected.

And if that device then exploded, the results could be catastrophic.

"Lewinsky said, 'Tell Mr. Silva not to worry.'"

JESSIE TURNS OFF THE TAPE OF MY INTERVIEW WITH GALVIS, which she, Nate, and I are playing for Captain Bradley.

"This is dynamite," Bradley says. "Nice work."

"It's unsubstantiated in a legal sense," I say. "But I think every word is true."

"It's a road map. If we get any corroboration at all, we can squeeze Lewinsky into implicating Silva."

I have some doubts about what Bradley is saying. Unless Lewinsky has been inhabiting another planet for most of his adult life, he would know what ratting out Silva would likely do to his life expectancy.

"Getting people to talk against Silva requires a lot of squeezing."

"I understand that."

"And I did promise Galvis anonymity," I say, as Nate winces. Apparently the diminished value of promises is something that I've forgotten along with everything else.

"Ask me if I give a shit about what you promised," Bradley says, confirming Nate's point of view. "This guy Galvis has admitted that he's known about stolen drugs going on the street and until now never said a word. He's one step above a pusher. The son of a bitch is lucky if we don't put him away for aiding and abetting."

I don't completely disagree with Bradley and Nate on this, but it doesn't matter, because my point of view is not going to carry the day anyway.

"We need to get search warrants to search the hospital records," Bradley says.

I shoot a glance at Nate; this is why I was opposed to bringing the Galvis information to Bradley.

"It's too soon, Captain," I say. "We'll tip them off."

"I understand that's a danger, but there's no way we're going to catch them in the act. There may not even be an act anymore; we have no way of knowing if this is ongoing."

"You heard Galvis say that Lewinsky has cooked the books to hide it all. The warrants won't turn up anything."

"Maybe, maybe not. But if he did, the only books he could cook are his own."

"What does that mean?" I ask.

"Jessie, this is where you come in. We'll prepare the warrant to go after both sides of the transactions."

"What do you mean?" she asks.

"We go to the suppliers, the drug companies. They know how much they shipped, and how much they got paid. If Galvis is right, then their figures won't match the hospital's. Which would give us the proof that the hospital is committing fraud. It will then be easy to make the jump to Lewinsky."

It's a good idea, so much so that I'm annoyed I didn't think of it, but I'm still worried that we're alerting Lewinsky and Silva that we're on to them too early in the process, but it's not like I have another, better idea. And Bradley's idea of getting the drug companies' books as a comparison could actually work.

Nate is going to prepare the warrants, with the help of our legal people. It's going to be tricky, because all we really have to go on is

Galvis, and we're not ready to name him yet. Since I'm the one who conducted the interview, my name will be on the warrant. I'll be vouching for Galvis's reliability as an upstanding citizen and someone in a position to know what he's talking about in this matter.

We've all heard the tape, so anyone in the department could be the person vouching for Galvis. Without saying so, Bradley is using me because of my recently earned reputation. I'm not sure why that bugs me, but it does. Not that there's anything I can do about it.

"We're going to have to go to the well with Galvis a few more times," Bradley says. "Jessie's going to need guidance about what to look for."

"He's not going to be happy about that," I say.

"That's too bad. If he resists, tell him you'll feed him to Silva."

"Two things are bothering me," I say. "One is Tartaro. What does he have to do with this, and why send Shawn to get us to reopen Carlisle? What does he have to gain if Silva goes down?"

"Excellent questions," Bradley says. "What's the other thing bothering you?"

"Nicholson. He's sitting in prison, and we've developed a theory about what went down that precludes his guilt."

"Not necessarily. He could still have killed Carlisle having nothing to do with this other stuff."

"That's bullshit," I say.

Bradley nods. "I know."

I leave Bradley's office and head back down to the prison to talk to Nicholson. I don't expect to get much in the way of information, but I feel like I need to make him aware that things are happening.

His first comment when he's brought in is, "I never thought I'd see you again."

"Sorry to disappoint you."

"You have any news?"

"Does the name Joey Silva mean anything to you?"

"The mobster?" he asks. "I've heard of him, but that's all."

"What about Salvatore Tartaro?"

He thinks for a moment. "No. Who is he?"

"He's the Joey Silva of Las Vegas. Do you have any idea why Rita might have had anything to do with these people, or people like them?"

"Absolutely none. And you could never get me to believe that she did."

"Okay," I say, not surprised by his answers.

"That's it?"

I nod. "That's it."

"I was hoping for more."

"All I can tell you now is that we're making progress."

"What does that mean?"

"I can't say right now. But for what it's worth, there's one other thing I can say. I no longer think you killed Rita Carlisle."

He takes a while to digest this, and finally says, "Good. Now prove it and get me the hell out of here."

Gail Marshall seems like a very nice lady.

SHE'S PROBABLY IN HER MID-SIXTIES, SHORT AND A BIT OVER-weight, pleasant looking and with an apparently perpetual half smile that never quite manages to break into a wide grin. I would bet my salary that she bakes and brings the fruits of her labors into the office to share with her coworkers.

Gail and those coworkers spend their days at Bergen Hospital. Gail works in administration; her title is Director. The reason I'm here to speak with her is because she moved into Rita Carlisle's job when Rita disappeared three years ago.

We're in her office, and I start by apologizing for taking up her time.

"Oh, don't worry. There's never enough time anyway, so this won't change anything."

"I understand you took over for Rita Carlisle three years ago?"

She nods, sadly but still maintaining that small smile. It's possible that it doesn't reflect happiness or pleasure; it might even have been surgically implanted into her face. "Yes, it's a promotion I wish I had never gotten."

It's interesting and pleasing that she does not ask me questions about my questions. Everyone else so far has wanted to understand what I'm doing, and whether the Rita Carlisle case is being re-opened. Not Gail; she is here to please and mind her own business.

"Did you work for Ms. Carlisle?"

She shakes her head. "No. I was here at the hospital, but in a different area. I was a nursing supervisor."

"Is that your background? Nursing?"

"Yes." She sighs. "Sometimes I miss it terribly."

"So why were you chosen for this new job?"

"I guess because I had been here so long, and I was so familiar with everything." She allows herself a small laugh. "And maybe people weren't thinking clearly."

"Did you know Ms. Carlisle?"

"Oh, yes. I've been here close to forty years, so people always come to me to understand how things are done. I didn't know Rita that well, but I considered her a friend. We had lunch quite a few times, and she was part of the group that always buys lottery tickets together. So far no luck."

"When you took over, was there anything about the job that surprised or troubled you? Anything you didn't expect?"

"There was plenty I didn't expect; it took me longer than I care to admit to get up to speed. But nothing troubling; it was mostly due to my unfamiliarity with all of it."

"Were you aware of any difficulties that Rita was having?"

"In her job?"

I shrug. "It's an open-ended question. Fill in whatever answer you can."

She thinks for a few moments, considering the question. "No. I mean, she wanted to make more money, and was unhappy with the way raises and promotions were given out, buy hey, join the club, you know?"

I'm getting nowhere fast with this; it's like asking Wally and the Beaver to talk about the dysfunctional aspects of the Cleaver family.

"Were you aware of her having any personal difficulties with anyone that she worked with?"

"I don't know of any, no. Rita was a very upbeat person. I mean, I know she wasn't crazy about the travel; she was a homebody like me."

"The job entails a considerable amount of travel?" I ask.

"Not so much; I mean, it's not what a jet-setter would go through, you know? But I like to be at home, and see my grandkids."

She points to a picture of the two kids on her desk; there are two more on the walls. I acknowledge their cuteness and ask what the traveling entails.

"Well, mostly conventions, conferences. Occasionally the hospital staff goes on what they call off-sites, but there's less of that these days. Money is pretty tight, apparently. I do it because it's part of the job, but I'm getting a bit old to run around the country."

"Must be tiring," I say.

"Yes." She leans in, as if sharing a secret. "Don't tell anyone, but my trip next week is the one I dread the most. It's so far. But it's our most important conference, so I have to go every year. I wish I didn't."

"Where are you going?"

"Las Vegas."

It's possible that the Rita Carlisle connection to Vegas has just been made.

COULD IT BE THAT EASY?

"Do you know if Rita also went to conferences in Las Vegas?" I ask, trying not to cringe as I wait for the answer.

"Oh, yes," Gail says. "Absolutely. Rita used to look forward to it. We talked about it a lot."

"What were those conversations like?"

She laughs. "I would tell her I had no interest in ever going there, and she'd say I was crazy. She said that even for people that didn't gamble, Vegas had the best hotels, and restaurants, and shows, and swimming pools. She said I'd love it if I'd give it a chance. Now I go, but believe me, I don't love it."

"Is the conference held the same time every year?"

She nods. "I think so. It had just been held a few weeks before I got this job, so it was almost a full year until I went. It made me sad to think about Rita."

"And it's always in Las Vegas?"

"That I know for sure, because Harriman Hospital in Vegas is the hospital that hosts it."

I ask Gail to check when the conference was three years ago, and she tells me a date that was indeed just three weeks before Rita's disappearance. I thank her, wish her a good trip, and tell her that my partner Nate recommends Cirque du Soleil. I don't mention anything about the elastic women.

Nate is in with Captain Bradley when I get back to the precinct, so I make that my first stop. "Where do we stand with the warrant?" I ask.

"Judge Kaplan just got back in town today. We'll have it in front of him by the end of the day," Bradley says. "He might not sign it until the morning, but it's looking good."

Judge Kaplan is considered the "easiest" judge to get to grant warrants, so whenever we have one that we're not positive will be approved, we "judge-shop" and get it to him. "Can you have someone call us to let us know? Nate and I will be in Vegas," I say.

"What are you talking about?"

"It's been confirmed that Rita Carlisle was in Vegas for a conference three weeks before she disappeared."

"So?"

"So there's been a Vegas connection all along with Tartaro that we haven't been able to figure out," I say. "Maybe something happened to her on that trip to trigger all of this."

"So you're going to walk around asking people if they remember seeing Rita Carlisle at a conference three years ago?"

"When we're not at the spa and blackjack tables."

"I call the window seat," Nate says. "Is it too late to order a special meal for the flight?"

"You're not both going," Bradley says, and then points to Nate. "More specifically, you're not going."

"Why not? And if you have to pick one of us, why would you choose Amnesia Boy?"

"First of all, I don't trust you; I don't think you'll ever leave the buffet. Second, it's not a two-person job; it's probably not even a one-person job. Third, Doug has done most of the interviews so far, and I want you here to follow through on this warrant. And fourth, and most important, I don't trust you; I don't think you'll ever leave the buffet."

I turn to Nate. "I don't want to start any trouble, but I don't think he fully trusts you. It might have to do with the buffet."

"This is bullshit. You'd better not go to Cirque du Soleil."

"I promise."

The truth is that I share Bradley's view that it's probably a waste of time, but it feels like a box we have to check. Even though Rita Carlisle's trip to Vegas could well have been a coincidence, especially since she went every year, there's always the possibility that it was a catalyst for what was to follow.

I leave Bradley's office and stop at what passes for our travel department, which is manned by Sergeant Willy Sano. Willy lost part of his right foot two years ago; he was giving out a ticket on a highway, and an oncoming car swerved at him. Most of him got out of the way, but his right foot didn't quite make it.

So Willy has been on desk duty ever since, and among his responsibilities is travel. We don't do much of it, so it's not exactly a time-consuming job for him.

"Where do you want to stay?" he asks.

"You tell me. You're the travel agent."

"I'm a cop, wiseass. How about if I just find a place listed under 'shitholes'?"

I'm forced to spend a few minutes kissing Willy's ass before he gets me into the nicest hotel on the department-approved list. It's the Paris, and Willy tells me they named it that because it looks like Paris.

Makes sense.

Next stop is Jessie's office to tell her what's going on, and her first reaction is, "Nate must be pissed."

I nod. "Yes, he must."

"Will you stay at my place tonight so I can give you your goodbye present?"

"The word that comes to mind is 'absolutely.' "

My next pre-trip move is to call Lieutenant Zack Roberts of Vegas PD, who I had spoken to for background information on Shawn and Tartaro. "I'm coming out there tomorrow," I say.

"Uh-oh. I lied about getting you comped at the Excalibur."

"That's okay. I'm at the Paris."

"You Jersey cops must be hot shit."

He offers me any help I need, and I say, "I'm going to want to talk to possible witnesses. Can you spare someone to give me cover?" As a Jersey cop I have no jurisdiction out there, and people might not see the need to talk with me. If I have a Vegas cop along, that would change.

"Witnesses to what?"

"Events," I say.

"You sure you want to be that specific?"

"Sorry. Maybe I'll be able to tell you more as I get out there and this unfolds."

"I'll see if anyone is free," he says. "But we're pretty busy. I'm booked solid."

"One of the people I'd like to talk to is Salvatore Tartaro."

"Then it's you and me, buddy."

"I thought you're booked solid."

"For Tartaro, I'll juggle my schedule. I like to talk to him; he's a hell of a conversationalist."

I tell Roberts that I'll call him when I arrive. Having him with me will make things infinitely easier. For now I head back to my office to do some research and make some more phone calls; I need to get the lay of the land and figure out who I want to talk to out there.

I'm sure I'll spend most of the flight tomorrow thinking about the parts of this case that bother and confuse me. In fact, the flight won't be long enough for that; that's how long the list is.

Moving up toward the top of that list is something I haven't spent much time pondering. That is the fact that the victims were decapitated, whether pre- or postmortem. Until now I've thought that it was done to send a message, first from Silva to Tartaro with Shawn's death, and then a return volley from Tartaro with the Tony Silva hit.

But now that I've thought more about it, that explanation doesn't hold up. I would imagine that both Silva and Tartaro have committed or ordered their share of murders in their long and glorious careers. Yet if they've ever separated the head from the body of one of their victims, I am not aware of it.

The "message" part is where the idea gets even shakier. They might do something like that for shock effect, and to scare the planned recipient of that message. But Silva and Tartaro are the last people on earth who would be shocked or frightened by violence, and they would both know that about each other.

Why send a message if you know the only person it won't impact is the one you're sending it to?

The news of Tony Silva's death hit
Salvatore Tartaro hard.

NOT NEARLY AS HARD AS IT HIT JOEY SILVA, AND OBVIOUSLY NOT as hard as it hit Tony himself. But Tartaro was affected for altogether different reasons, all having to do with his own self-interest.

He had met Tony on two occasions but really didn't know him, and certainly didn't care about him one way or the other. But Tartaro was smart enough to know that the hit on Tony, coming on the heels of the hit on Shawn, would look to Silva as if Tartaro was exacting revenge.

Which, of course, he wasn't.

There were two other problems with the situation, and they were connected to each other. Hovering over everything was the business relationship that Tartaro had with Silva, which had become increasingly lucrative over time, and which was going strong.

Rather than diminishing when Bennett died, as Tartaro suspected it might, Joey Silva had actually expanded the business relationship. So this issue with Tony could threaten that.

The other factor was that Tartaro, like everyone else, considered Tony to be the smarter of the two Silvas, though that might have been faint praise. But it was obvious that Tony was a calming influence on his brother, suppressing Joey's more volatile impulses. It was unlikely that anyone had enough credibility in Joey's eyes, or had enough of Joey's trust, to move into that role.

So Tartaro did what he always did in situations like this; he talked it out with Dominic Romano. He respected and trusted Dominic, who was to Tartaro almost what Tony Silva had been to brother Joey.

"Silva is going to think we hit Tony," Tartaro said. "Revenge for Shawn. That's what I would think if I were him."

"Even if he does, there's nothing he can do. And he wouldn't want to try anything now anyway. He's a businessman, and we've got more business coming up."

"I don't want to be looking over my shoulder all the time," Tartaro said. "Maybe I should talk to him directly."

"Won't do any good," Dominic said. "He wouldn't believe you anyway, and it would show weakness. Joey eats weakness with a spoon."

"We shouldn't have gone in with him in the first place," Tartaro said. "We could have done this on our own."

"It was good business, and it still is. And you didn't go in with him, you went in with Bennett."

Tartaro nodded. "But Bennett wasn't out of his goddamn mind; he understood how normal human beings behave. I didn't trust Bennett, but I could still talk to him, reason with him."

Dominic shook his head and said, "I understand that, but we're doing better business with Silva than we ever did with Bennett. He's not as cautious."

Tartaro thought about it for a few moments, and then said, "Set up a call."

"With Silva?"

"No, with JFK. Who the hell do you think?"

So Dominic started the process of arranging a call from Tartaro to Joey Silva. It was not a simple "pick up the phone" situation; no one involved had any doubt that every call they made on their normal telephones was listened to by some law enforcement agency somewhere.

But it was finally arranged on secure, throwaway phones, and Tartaro made the call. Tartaro set the dial to SPEAKERPHONE so Dominic could hear what was being said. In New Jersey, Silva did the same, so Philly could listen in.

Once the fake pleasantries were exchanged, Tartaro said, "Joey, I'm real sorry about Tony."

"Yeah, me, too."

"Terrible thing. I've got a brother, so I know what it's like." Tartaro didn't mention that his own brother was a philosophy professor at Cal State Fullerton, and that he hadn't spoken to him in six years.

"Yeah?" Joey asked. "You know what it's like? Did they find your brother's head sitting on a garbage Dumpster in an alley?"

"Okay, Joey, I just want to make one thing clear. I had nothing to do with Tony. I liked the guy, and you're my partner. I thought because of Shawn you might have other ideas, so I wanted to talk to you, direct, so that we understand each other."

The truth is that Joey did not think Tartaro was behind it, but he didn't want to give him that, at least not at this point. "I'll find out who it was."

"Good. And you let me know how I can help. My people are your people."

"I don't need no help. But the guy who did it, he's going to need plenty of help."

"I hear you, Joey. Just don't let this get in the way of business. Not now. You know what I mean."

"Yeah. I know what you mean."

The call ends, and Tartaro turned to Dominic. "What do you think?"

Dominic shook his head. "The son of a bitch thinks we hit Tony."

In New Jersey, Philly said to Joey, "The son of a bitch hit Tony."

This is the first plane I've been on in ten years.

NOT LITERALLY; I HAVE PHOTOGRAPHS OF JESSIE AND ME IN THE
Caribbean a few years ago, and I don't think we drove there. But I
don't remember any of the flights I might have taken, which I have
come to realize is the same as not taking them.

The experience is a lot different than I remember from long
ago. Everything is more crowded; the check-in areas, security, and
the plane itself. The crowds are all anyone talks about.

Every announcement they make relates to it. There are too
many passengers, so they'll give you a voucher not to fly. And there
are too many bags, so there won't be room for the carry-ons. And
clear the boarding area; there are too many people to all get on at
once, so your group number means everything.

It's not until I board that I find out there are no meals on the
flight, just these snack boxes to buy. And there used to be telephones
on the wall, but they're gone, too. And I don't see any movie screens,
but they tell me I can watch stuff on my iPad. Which would
be good, if I knew how to work an iPad, and if I had an iPad.

But they do have wireless, which is pretty amazing. And it
comes in handy, because when we're over Ohio I come up with one

of those ideas that I should have thought of earlier. Rather than wait to land, I can send an email to Nate and Jessie on my phone. What a world.

If Galvis's revelations are enough to get us a search warrant to look into the hospital and drug companies' records, then they should also be enough to examine Lewinsky personally. After all, Galvis claimed the frauds and thefts were being done under Lewinsky's direction.

I'd love to get a look at Lewinsky's emails, both personal and business. It's entirely possible that they could contain some information that, when matched up with other things we come up with, could be incriminating.

I would think that Lewinsky would be careful; anyone with a brain knows that emails are permanent and can come back to haunt the senders. But maybe even something cryptic or coded, seen from the correct perspective, can be helpful.

In any event, there is no downside to it. With a court order, the providers would be obligated to turn everything over, including current and future emails. They would also be under a directive to keep it secret, so that Lewinsky would not know he was being watched. I add that in addition to past and future emails, we want to be able to wiretap Lewinsky's phones.

Jessie gets back to me almost immediately. She says that Nate is out, but that she will convey my message. She also has some good news; Judge Kaplan signed off on the warrant. I have no doubt he'll also okay the surveillance on Lewinsky, since it's based on the same information.

The cab line at the airport is twenty minutes long, and then the ten-minute ride to the hotel costs sixteen bucks. The hotel looks exactly like Paris, except for the fact that it's filled with slot machines and looks nothing like Paris.

Of course, I've never been to Paris, or Vegas for that matter, or maybe I have and don't remember. For all I know I spent two years here dealing blackjack. But one thing completely surprises me: the casino is not filled with sounds of coin jackpots pouring out of the slot machines. I investigate it, because I am a professional investigator, and it turns out they don't use coins anymore. They use slips of paper.

I get to my room; if I brought in enough cots, it would be large enough to sleep a Marine battalion. There is a message on the phone from Lieutenant Roberts, telling me to check in with him when I arrive. Since I've arrived, I do that and tell him I'll meet him in front of the hotel, after I've grabbed a bite to eat.

An hour later I go outside and Roberts is waiting for me in an unmarked car. "Welcome to Vegas," he says. "You been here before?"

"I don't think so."

"Seems like the kind of thing you'd remember."

"Yes, it does."

Then he nods and says, "Oh, right. I checked you out. You're the amnesia hero guy."

"That's me."

"Okay, where to?"

"Harriman Hospital. I appreciate the ride," I say. "But I don't really need you here for this."

"Once you mentioned the name Tartaro you guaranteed yourself a sidekick for the duration."

Harriman Hospital is the closest hospital to the Strip, but it takes fifteen minutes to get there. The traffic is ridiculous; cops are not going to make a living giving out speeding tickets here. Harriman is the hospital that hosts the Hospital Administrators of America convention, which is held every year at the enormous convention center.

Betty Hedges is the hospital executive in charge of the annual convention. I've done some research on it, and it draws over eight thousand people, spread out over fourteen hotels. It is no small operation, and must require a huge amount of planning and preparation.

But you wouldn't know all that from Betty. She seems calm and in control, welcoming Roberts and me with a smile, an offer of something to drink, and a directive to call her Betty. "We'll try not to take up too much of your time," I say. "You must be busy with the convention happening next week."

"That's okay; we prepare fifty-two weeks a year, just so we don't have to go crazy at the last minute. I assume you wouldn't have come all this way if it weren't important."

"Did you look up the information I asked you about on the phone?"

She nods. "I did. That poor woman, Ms. Carlisle, was here four years in a row. The last time was three years ago."

"Did she have a special role of any kind, Betty? Anything that stood out to you?"

"Well, I'm afraid I wouldn't know; I've just been here for less than two years myself. I can't say I'd remember an individual anyway, there are just so many people. But she participated in two panel discussions, and she attended many of the other sessions. People sign in when they do so."

"Is there any way to tell who she interacted with? I assume there are dinners; is it possible to know who she sat with?"

"No, I'm afraid not. It's not formal at all; people sit wherever they want."

"Do people from this hospital attend?" I ask. "I don't mean people like yourself who are running the thing. I mean employees, maybe who have the same type job as Ms. Carlisle."

"Certainly. I can see who attended from Harriman."

"Great. And if you could tell me who her counterpart was."

"It'll just take me a few minutes," she says.

It winds up taking her twenty minutes, but when she comes back she has a list. "There were four hospital employees there as conventioneers. I have the names and current contact information, at least in cases where we have it. I'm not really sure exactly what Ms.

Carlisle's responsibilities were in her job, but I believe that the first person on the list, Janine Seraphin, would be the closest."

"Does she still work here?"

"No. Doesn't appear so."

"When did she leave?"

Betty looks at her records and says, "I can't be sure; certainly personnel could give you the date. But I can say that the convention three years ago was the last one she attended."

I look at the records. "Where does she work now? That doesn't seem to be listed here."

"That's all we have. I assume it's her home address."

We thank her and leave. Roberts hadn't said a word during the entire interview other than hello. And all he says when we get in the car is, "Nice lady."

We head for the home address that was on file for Janine Seraphin, which is a garden apartment complex in Henderson. The name on the apartment buzzer is Lansing, and no one responds when we press it. So we find the building manager, who tells us that Janine Seraphin moved out a few years ago.

"Her mother came, paid her rent, and got her stuff."

He has no idea where she lives now, or who her mother is. When we get back in the car, I ask if Roberts can use the resources at his disposal to find Seraphin's mother.

"I'm sure I could, but I'm not getting the feeling there's a free flow of information going on here. It all seems to be going in one direction."

"I'll tell you what. You find the mother, and while you're buying me breakfast, I'll tell you whatever you want to know."

The courier met Philly DeSimone at a highway
rest stop on the New Jersey Turnpike.

PHILLY AND TWO OF HIS PEOPLE WERE ALREADY THERE WHEN
the rented white van pulled up and the courier got out. He simply
asked, "And your name is . . . ?

"Philly DeSimone."

"Please join me in the van, Mr. DeSimone."

Philly took a briefcase out of his car and carried it as he and the
courier got in the van, which was empty except for a sleeping bag
and pillow, a large iron safe, and what looked like a freezer. Philly
instantly and correctly assumed that the man lived in here. "Doesn't
look too comfortable," Philly said.

"But the pay is good," the man said, without humor. "Which
brings us to the first part of the transaction."

Philly handed the courier the briefcase he had been carrying,
and the man put it in the safe without opening it. Philly wasn't surprised; considering the people that the man represented, he was
right in not worrying that he would be shortchanged. Not even Joey
Silva would be crazy enough to make enemies out of those people.

The man then opened the freezer, which turned out to function not as a freezer at all, but as a storage unit. He took out a bag, and Philly could see that there was another bag in there as well.

The courier told Philly to lift the bag, "to understand the weight." Philly did so, and was surprised that it was not more than six or seven pounds.

"Pretty light," Philly said. "You sure it's strong enough?"

"It will be more than adequate for the purposes described."

He gave the bag back, and the courier opened it and took out the device, placing it on the cot. He then demonstrated that he was far more than a courier, as he expertly gave Philly a tutorial on the workings of it.

"What is it, exactly?"

"It's called C-4. Did you ever see those videos where they take down those big buildings, or stadiums? This is the material of choice."

Philly had seen those videos, so he had no doubt that the courier was right. It would be more than adequate for the purposes described.

The whole thing made Philly uncomfortable, but he would have been more uncomfortable with anyone else handling it.

When the demonstration was finished, and Philly was confident in the remote manner of detonation, they left the van. "You make the drop in Vegas yet?" he asked.

"Next."

"How do you get it there? Wait a minute . . . you're driving all the way there?"

"You have a better way?" the courier asked.

Of course that made perfect sense; it would be way too risky to try and bring it on an airplane. "No," Philly said. "Drive carefully."

"Those buffets are for suckers," Roberts says.

"WHAT DO THEY CHARGE, TWENTY-FIVE BUCKS? MOST PEOPLE don't eat ten dollars' worth. They give you these small plates, and then you have to reach under the glass to get the food. People don't want to deal with it. So they overpay and then tell everyone at home how great the buffets are."

Roberts and I are having breakfast in a coffee shop about ten blocks from the Strip. It's decent food, although eggs are eggs. I have to admit that I wish we were getting ripped off at one of the buffets, especially since it's on the department's tab, but I don't mention it.

Instead I tell him about the case, starting with Rita Carlisle and working my way up to now.

"So you think it's about drugs?" he asks.

"Don't see any other possibilities."

"I don't get the Tartaro–Silva connection," he says. "Why would they need each other? A Vegas–New Jersey underground drug rail-road? If either of them needed to hook up with other organizations, they both could have found business partners a lot closer."

"I don't know, but I'm sure they have a damn good reason.

Because they're definitely doing some business together, Shawn's presence proves it."

"That's for sure. Take a look at this."

He hands me a sheet of paper, which looks like a long list of phone numbers. "What is it?"

"Shawn's cell phone records. He got three calls from a phone registered to Joey Silva in the two weeks before he died."

"You subpoenaed this?" I ask.

"You think we've just been sitting on our ass? Shawn was a citizen of the great and peaceful state of Nevada, but he made the fatal mistake of traveling to the violent hellhole that is New Jersey. We're trying to find out what happened to the poor man."

"I would have thought Silva would be more careful. He knows phone records can be checked."

"Maybe he didn't care who knew about it," Roberts says. "But we don't have a transcript of the calls. Silva called on a cold phone, and we weren't covering Shawn's phone."

"So you've been sitting on your ass."

He nods. "Guilty as charged. You want to talk to Tartaro this morning? I combed my hair and everything."

"Why are you so anxious?" I ask.

"Any day I can hassle him is a good day."

"Well, your hair looks great, but I want to track down Janine Seraphin first. You have any luck with that?"

"I would have to say that the answer to that is yes and no."

"Start with the yes."

"The yes is that we know where she is. The no is because she's in a cemetery. She died in a car crash."

"Let me guess. Just under three years ago."

"You New Jersey cops are really smart. It was investigated at the time and ruled an accident."

"Maybe a reinvestigation is in order. What about the mother?"

"We found her; the woman's name is Denise Keller."

"So Seraphin was Janine's married name?"

Roberts shrugged. "That's one of the mysteries that the mother can help us with. I spoke to her; she's waiting for us."

We drive out to Denise Keller's house, passing along much of the Strip on the way. The hotels are amazing; they're like cities. I briefly think that maybe I should bring Jessie out here, and then reject the thought seconds later. Jessie's idea of a great vacation is an outdoor camping and hiking trip. I don't think a hike from Caesars Palace to the Venetian would do the trick.

Denise Keller lives in a rather depressed area of Vegas; not a slum but another world from the neon glamour of the Strip. I imagine it's where the casinos draw their thousands of cocktail waitresses, dealers, and housekeeping crew members from.

She comes out onto the porch in front of her home when we pull up. She looks anxious about our arrival, as if she thinks we might be bringing her bad news. Unfortunately for Denise, the bad news that a parent never wants to hear came three years ago. Nothing anyone will ever say to her again could match that.

As we enter the house, I whisper to Roberts, "You take this one."

Denise offers us coffee and these small cookies that she's baked, and we take some. I'm still hungry, which I'm sure I wouldn't be if Roberts hadn't talked me into missing the buffet.

"This is about Janine, isn't it?" she asks. It's a slightly strange question for her to ask, since there was never a police involvement in the death. The crash was ruled an accident.

"In a roundabout way," Roberts says. "It's more about a situation at the hospital, where she worked. We're talking to many people that worked there during those years."

"What kind of situation?"

"I'm afraid we can't say at this point, in case it doesn't come to anything. We don't want to hurt the hospital's reputation."

"I understand, but I don't know how much I can help. You know that Janine has passed away, don't you?" Denise says.

Roberts and I both nod sympathetically, and he says, "Yes, I'm very sorry. It was a car accident?"

"Yes. She hit a tree; it broke her neck." I can see the words catching in her throat as she says it; it is something a parent should never have to say.

"Was Janine having any trouble at work? Did she mention that there was anything unusual going on?"

"Well, obviously."

I'm about to jump in with the question, but Roberts beats me to it. "Why do you say obviously?"

"Because Janine quit her job. About three weeks before she died."

"Why did she quit?"

"She didn't tell me, but I think she was having trouble with some of her coworkers. It upset her a great deal. She went away for a while to a cabin she had, and when she came back, she had the accident. So we never really got to sit down and talk about it, or anything else."

"Where was this cabin?"

"Up north, near Carson City. It was her husband's, and she got it in the divorce."

"When did they get divorced?" Roberts asks.

"Oh, at least seven years ago. Walter, that was her husband, went back east to live, where he's from. Somewhere in New England."

"Were you surprised when she left her job?"

"Very. She always talked about how much she liked it there. But she was one of only a few women in that department; who knows . . . maybe some men made some advances on her. You know how that is these days."

"Yes."

I finally ask one question. "Did Janine ever mention someone named Rita Carlisle?"

She thinks for a while. "Not that I remember."

Denise has nothing more to tell us, so we leave.

Once we're in the car, I say, "So Rita Carlisle goes missing and Janine Seraphin dies, a short time after they attend the same convention. Small world."

"Yeah, real small. We see Tartaro tomorrow?"

"I'm not sure we have much to accomplish by that," I say.

He smiles. "That's okay. It will be nice to catch up."

It's only been two days, but I'm missing Jessie.

IT'S THE FIRST TIME WE'VE SPENT TIME APART SINCE WE'VE been a couple. At least that's true to the best of my recollection, but my recollections really aren't anywhere near the "best."

I order coffee from room service and call her, and it's nice to hear her voice. "Have we ever been apart?" I ask. "I mean since we've been together?"

"You went on that white-water rafting trip in Maine," she says. "And then there was the time that I went to Bermuda with my girlfriends."

"Right. I mean except for those times."

"You don't remember them? Well, just so you'll know, you loved white-water rafting. We said we were going to go together."

"Sounds like fun." I don't know why I always get embarrassed by my inability to remember events. I obviously know intellectually that it was the result of a physical injury and it's not my fault, but I can't seem to wrap my defective head around that fact.

"I've got some good news on the investigation," she said. "The judge approved everything, and we're moving ahead. I'm even going to have the first look at Lewinsky's emails tomorrow."

"Great."

"In addition to his private line in his office, there are two cell phone numbers in his name, his and his wife's. Because he's listed for each of them, I've included them both. Of course, it would be nice to know exactly what I'm looking for."

"Well, first choice would be an email to Joey Silva saying 'now that we've kidnapped Rita Carlisle, we can keep stealing drugs.'"

She laughs. "Got it. Anything else?"

"Anything related to the drug situation at the hospital would be ideal," I say. "And certainly anything related to Carlisle or Silva. But it's a long shot."

"I'll do my best. When are you coming home?"

"We're going to talk to Tartaro in a little while, so maybe I can get a late-afternoon flight."

"Will you come straight here? Bobo and I miss you."

"Try and stop me," I say.

I place a call to Nate, but he's not in, so I leave a message that I'll call him later. Then I go down to the buffet in the hotel, which is not remotely the rip-off that Roberts said it was. There is enough food there to feed the Russian Army, and not a single one of them would say *nyet* when presented with the chance to eat here.

As soon as I'm finished I head outside, and five minutes later Roberts pulls up. "Big day today," he says. "Just so you'll know, when we see Tartaro, it's okay with me if you shoot the son of a bitch."

We head for the Aria Hotel, and on the way I suggest that Roberts take a look at Harriman Hospital in terms of whether the same kind of drug thefts are taking place there that we think are going on at Bergen Hospital in New Jersey.

"Way ahead of you," he says, meaning that they're already on it. Roberts is a smart cop.

We get to the Aria and take the elevator to the top floor. According to Roberts, Tartaro has a home in Vegas but lives in the hotel almost exclusively. He has half a floor, and when we get off the elevator, we see one of Tartaro's men acting as a security guard/bouncer.

Roberts shows his badge to the guy and says, "You're doing a hell of a job." We then just walk by him, and he doesn't try to impede us.

"They know we're coming?" I ask.

He nods. "I called and spoke to Dominic Romano; he's Tartaro's number two. He wasn't happy about it, but he'd never say no."

"Why not?"

"He knows I'd find an excuse to bring Tartaro down to the precinct and ask the questions there. The hotel is more to his liking." Then, "This is not our first rodeo."

As we approach the door, it opens and a man lets us in to what looks like a den. I suspect it's just one room in a multi-room suite. "Hello, Dominic," Roberts says. "Where's your boss?"

"Right here." It's a man I assume to be Tartaro who has just entered from another room. Nobody really seems into doing introductions. "Lieutenant Roberts, always a pleasure to see you. This the Jersey cop?" Then, to me, "I was there about thirty years ago, did I forget to pay a parking ticket?"

I turn to Roberts. "You were right. He's hilarious."

"So what do you want, Jersey cop? I'm busy."

This guy immediately gets on my nerves, as does Dominic, who stands to the side with a practiced sneer on his face. I shoot a glance to the terrace outside the sliding doors, and momentarily picture myself throwing them both over the rail and down to the street. It's an impulse I probably should control.

"First let me tell you what I know. Then I'll tell you what I want." I sit down on the couch and make myself comfortable, even though I wasn't invited to do so. Roberts goes to a refrigerator and takes out two Diet Cokes and hands me one.

"Make yourself at home," Dominic says, insincerely.

"I know about Joey Silva ordering the hit on Shawn, I know

about the drug thefts from the hospitals, I know about the business you're doing with Silva, I know about Rita Carlisle, and I know about Janine Seraphin."

Tartaro turns to Dominic. "What the hell is the Jersey cop talking about?"

Dominic shrugs and fakes a derisive laugh. "Beats the shit out of me."

"I can't prove any of it yet, at least not enough to take to a jury, but I'm getting close. What I care about, and what I want from you, is Silva."

"Silva," Tartaro says, not as a question, but as a statement. "I don't believe I know a Silva."

"Google him," I say. "Then get me the proof I need, without implicating yourself. That's what I want. I want Silva, not you."

He points to Roberts. "What about you? What do you want?"

Roberts shrugs. "It's his show."

Tartaro says, "I give you Silva, and you leave me alone?"

I nod. "Right."

"Get the hell out of here."

"You won't get another chance," I say.

"You heard him, Jersey cop," is Dominic's response.

So we start to leave, and on the way out, Dominic comes up to me and says, "You're a bigger asshole than Roberts."

I feel an anger probably greater than any I've felt since I was shot. I grab Dominic by the shirt. Then I let my arms move to his sides, and I lift him up and half throw-half push him over a chair and onto the floor.

He jumps up and makes a motion to come toward me, but doesn't. Not doing so is the smart move for him to make, because the next thing I'm going to throw him over is the terrace railing.

When we get on the elevator, Roberts smiles and says, "We have self-control issues, have we?"

I nod. "So I'm told."

Nate is waiting for me at baggage claim.

"WELL, THIS IS PRETTY GOOD SERVICE."

"We aim to please," he says. "How was Vegas?"

"Wild. Two days of huge buffets and elastic women. They actually have the elastic women at the buffets, which saved a lot of time. I'm exhausted."

"Asshole."

"So what are you doing here?"

"We got a hit on Lewinsky's emails," he says.

"What kind of hit?"

He tells me that he'll show me in the car, and goes off to get it. I retrieve my bag and go outside, where he picks me up. I can definitely get used to this kind of treatment.

When I get in the car, he says, "Jessie and her people started going through the emails. They began by focusing on the period starting two months before Carlisle went missing."

"Personal or business?"

"Personal, for now. Anyway, about three weeks before Carlisle disappeared, Lewinsky sent an email with just two words... William Simmons. That's it, just the name."

"Who did he send it to?"

Nate shrugs. "We don't know. The recipient was listed with a fake name, and the account was closed the next day. So no way to know who it was."

"And who is William Simmons?"

He takes a manila envelope that was on the dashboard under the windshield and hands it to me. "I'll drive; you read."

So I read, and on the first page I learn that my question should have been, "Who *was* William Simmons?" because he is dead. And he died in Bergen Hospital nine hours before Lewinsky, the head of that hospital, sent the email consisting only of his name.

Simmons died of a fractured skull, inflicted by an assailant who has never been found. He was homeless and spending the night in an alley behind a Hackensack restaurant when he was attacked. It was considered a random killing; Simmons was thought to have just been in the wrong place at the wrong time.

There are some pages that construct as best as possible the life of William Simmons, and they read as an American tragedy.

For years William Simmons was a productive model citizen. He grew up in Fair Lawn, raised by a single mother who died when he was fourteen. He went to live with family members in Ohio, but came back to New Jersey to attend Rutgers. He graduated with a degree in business administration, and ultimately wound up having his own insurance agency.

Simmons married and had two daughters. Life was apparently good, and Simmons seemed to be leading it the right way. He gave to charity, was active in his church, listed himself as an organ donor, and even took on a close but unsuccessful run at city councilman. Friends and neighbors described him as someone who was always there for them, ready with a smile or anything else they needed.

It was six years ago that Simmons' wife and one of his daughters were killed in an automobile accident driving on Route 80.

Simmons and his other daughter were also in the car, and suffered injuries that were not life-threatening.

A drunk driver's car went over the center median and crashed into them head-on; they never had a chance. Simmons had vision problems, so his wife was driving, and he was a passenger. He and the surviving daughter were in the backseat.

As so often can happen in situations like this, Simmons's life went into an almost immediate descent, spiraling out of control. He lost his business and his home, and wound up on the streets. Those same friends and neighbors that had praised him completely lost track of his whereabouts, and apparently didn't care enough to do anything about it.

Then came that night in the alley that ended it all. The cause of death was a crushed skull; someone literally stomped his head into the pavement and left him there to die.

Because Simmons was not thought to have any possessions of value, robbery was eliminated as a motive. It was thought to be a random thrill-killing, and the killer left no forensic trace. The most unusual thing about it was that it was apparently the killer that called 911 and alerted authorities to the crime.

First responders were there within minutes, but the assailant was gone, and there was no saving William Simmons. He died at Bergen Hospital within minutes of his arrival; there was nothing doctors could do.

The official time of death was three minutes past midnight, just nine hours before Daniel Lewinsky sent an email consisting only of his name.

I've just finished reading the materials when we pull up to Jessie's house. "Come on in," I say. "Let's kick this around."

Jessie opens the door as we approach, and her greeting is a warm one, including a significant amount of hugging and kissing. It's far preferable to the welcome I got from Nate at baggage claim.

"Am I the only one getting nauseous?" Nate asks.

"I think you are," I say.

We go inside and sit around the kitchen table as Jessie makes coffee. She puts down some cookies as well, and Nate eyes them. "What's in those?" he asks.

Jessie shrugs. "I don't know; cookie stuff."

"Fattening? Because some cookies contain, like, no calories. Some people are on all-cookie diets."

Jessie smiles. "Every time I want to lose some weight, I eat a few hundred of them."

I don't take any cookies, but I give Bobo a few dog biscuits; I want to get on his good side.

Nate puts five cookies onto his plate. Then, with his mouth full, he asks, "What do you think about William Simmons?"

"The head of the hospital sends an email mentioning a person who died at that hospital the night before. There could certainly be a benign explanation for that."

"He sent it to someone who was concealing their identity, and who closed the account after getting the email. Maybe Lewinsky wasn't supposed to have communicated that way, so they blew it up."

"How does it fit into our overall theory?"

Jessie says, "It doesn't yet. We're going to do a full dive into Simmons' life. At this point there's no drug connection; but that's not to say there isn't any."

"What about the toxicology report?"

"No drugs in his system. His uncle in Ohio said he'd never used them, that he hated them."

I nod. "Also get the hospital records. For all we know they'll show that Simmons was given heavy drugs for weeks, even though he died that night. It could be a way to explain how all the drugs they took in were accounted for."

"Good idea."

"If you guys are right that this is significant, then we need to make a connection. Simmons at one point had an insurance agency;

did he ever sell life insurance to any of the players? Or to a lot of other people that might have died at this hospital?"

"He was out of that business for years," Nate says.

"But insurance policies live on. I doubt we'll find anything; maybe there's nothing to find."

We talk for a while longer, and then Nate says, "So what's on television? I'm not tired at all."

Jessie and I look at each other, and she says, "The television is out, Nate."

"Then what do you have to eat?"

"The refrigerator is out, Nate."

"Anybody up for three-man poker?"

"You're out, Nate," I say.

He shakes his head and stands up to go. "Did I mention that you guys make me nauseous?"

Everything was the same as it had been in New Jersey.

DOMINIC ROMANO MET THE SAME COURIER THAT PHILLY HAD met. He was driving the same van, and they met behind an abandoned warehouse. He was also delivering the exact same kind of package.

Dominic was considerably more comfortable receiving the material than Philly had been. He had joined the Army coming out of high school, and served in a combat role in Iraq. So he had handled explosives; he learned how to handle and respect them.

He also was familiar with C-4 plastic explosives, and knew without asking what the courier had to tell Philly . . . that this amount was more than sufficient to handle the job it was being called upon to do.

But Dominic took nothing for granted, and once he made the required payment, he listened carefully as the courier explained the workings of the device. Once that was completed, he asked a few pertinent questions to make sure he was thoroughly confident and comfortable.

The courier noticed the difference between Dominic and

Philly when it came to their competence regarding this specific situation. He knew that the Vegas side of the operation had a substantially greater chance of success.

But he didn't say anything, and the truth was he and his people didn't much care. Once the packages were delivered, they were somebody else's property and someone else's problem.

Dominic made sure the package was locked away, concealed and secure, then he went back to the hotel, where Tartaro was waiting for him. They had not had a chance to talk much since the cops had been there, and he found Tartaro to be surprisingly agitated.

"I think we should pull the plug on this thing," Tartaro said.

"Why?"

"Because we're being watched too carefully. The cops are all over us, and the Feds can't be far behind."

"You heard them," Dominic said. "They don't know anything."

"Right now they don't. But they know something is happening."

"I don't think they do. And it wouldn't matter anyway. They won't be able to tie us to it. We've got every base covered."

Tartaro got angry. "How about if you stop arguing with every goddamn thing I say? Okay, Dominic? I'm not saying we cancel the sixteenth; I'm saying we wait until the pressure is off. You understand?"

Dominic had spent enough time with Tartaro to know when it was time to back off. "I understand."

"Call Silva's people and tell them. Make sure they hold off as well, and don't let them give you any shit. When we do it, we do it at the same time."

"I'll take care of it right away," Dominic said.

He left Tartaro, ostensibly to make the phone call to Silva. But he had no plans to make that call, even though he would tell Tartaro that he had.

Tartaro was in the dark about it, but Lucky Linda's Casino was going to experience a moment of very bad luck, and nothing would delay it.

It was not the first time that Dominic disobeyed Tartaro, and it certainly would not be the last.

I'm spending the day at Bergen Hospital.

MY FIRST MEETING IS WITH DR. STEVEN CASSEL, THE SURGEON who admitted to me that he had an affair with Rita Carlisle, which ended shortly before her death.

Not wanting to tangle with his protective assistant again, I've called ahead and learned that he is not doing surgeries today, but rather just doing office visits and rounds of his patients that are in the hospital.

He suggested that we meet in the hospital cafeteria for coffee, which was fine with me. I asked that he get the hospital records for William Simmons on the night he died, and he agreed to do so. Since Dr. Cassel is worried that I'll reveal his affair to the public, and therefore to his unsuspecting wife, it's fair to say that I have some leverage on the good doctor.

We're meeting at 10:00 A.M., so the good news is we're able to get a table near the back, away from any other patrons who might overhear our conversation. The bad news is that the array and quality of food in this cafeteria is never going to be confused with the buffet at the Paris.

Once we're settled in, I ask if he had a chance to go over the

William Simmons records, and he points to a small folder he has in front of him. I assume that means the records are inside. "I have," he said. "They're not very complicated."

"Were you on duty the night he was brought in?" I ask.

"I have no idea; it was a long time ago. But I very much doubt it. In any event, I had nothing to do with his treatment. The records obviously list the doctors involved; they were emergency room personnel. Dr. Ziskind, a neurosurgeon on staff here, was called in, but there was no opportunity for him to successfully intervene."

"What do the records show?"

"He was near death from a fractured skull when he was brought in; actually the skull was mostly crushed. The pressure on the brain was enormous, and it had sustained catastrophic damage; there was no possibility of survival. Based on what I see here, I'm surprised he made it to the hospital alive."

"Is there anything you see in there that would have gotten the attention of top management?" I ask.

"Hospital management? Well, the man died, so certainly that isn't a desired outcome. That's obviously taken seriously, and there are procedures in place."

"I understand, but is there anything unusual about hospital protocols as they were followed in this case, anything strange or surprising in the way the hospital handled this?"

He shakes his head. "Nothing that I see."

"Were drugs administered?"

"Yes, of course. Antibiotics, a drug to reduce swelling and pressure in the brain, but the treatment seems to have been discontinued quickly, since he was only here for a matter of minutes before he died."

Dr. Cassel's answers don't surprise me; I haven't been able to see what the death of William Simmons could possibly have to do with what we believe has been going on at the hospital.

The only connection we had was Lewinsky's cryptic email, but for all we know, he could have been replying to someone asking the name of the murder victim. It's just not possible to infer guilt from it, much as I would like to.

Dr. Cassel goes off to do his rounds, but before I leave I decide to stop in and talk to Mitchell Galvis, second in command at the hospital to Lewinsky. Once we told Captain Bradley about Galvis pointing us to the drug issue, and Lewinsky's culpability, he directed us to keep pressing him.

This seems like as good a time as any.

I'm sure that Galvis would want to talk to me again at some clandestine, out of the way location, but I'm not going to indulge that. I've been talking to a lot of people at the hospital, and Lewinsky had somewhat reluctantly instructed people to cooperate. So I would have every reason to talk to Galvis without arousing suspicion.

When his assistant tells him that I'm here to see him, I'm ushered right in. "You said you'd leave me out of this" is his way of greeting me. He seems to be in a perpetual panic, and since Silva is involved, it's not a reaction that surprises me.

"No, I said I'd keep your name out of it. You placed yourself in the middle."

"I never should have spoken to you. Lewinsky has been acting funny toward me ever since. Is there any way he can know?"

"Not from me," I say, which is true.

He doesn't seem appeased. "What do you want?"

"I need proof that drugs are being stolen."

He shakes his head. "I told you, Lewinsky has covered it up. The books won't show anything."

"Then how did you know about it?"

"Because I work here; I see a lot and people tell me things. And I saw it as it was happening."

"Is it still happening?"

"Of course," he says. "Why wouldn't it be?"

"Then get me the proof before Lewinsky can change the books. Mitchell, right now you're my only witness to bring down Lewinsky, and then Silva. If I have physical evidence, I don't need you. If I don't, then your testimony becomes crucial."

"I won't testify."

"Mitchell, don't push me. Do the right thing, and so will I."

My meaning is clear, and Galvis is no dope. "Okay," he says. "I'll do what I can."

The message is waiting for us when we get in.

BRADLEY WANTS TO SEE US; I ASSUME IT'S FOR THE PURPOSE of downloading him on our current progress, or lack of it. I haven't even told him about what happened on my trip to Vegas, and I'm sure he'll want details. I should have taken a cell phone picture of the buffet.

I tell Jessie to come in with us, since she's involved with a number of important aspects of the investigation. But when we get to his office, we discover that Bradley is not alone. There are two men with him, and just based on my first impression of their manner and dress, they are Federal agents.

Bradley does the introductions. "Lieutenant Doug Brock, Lieutenant Nate Alvarez, Lieutenant Jessie Allen, this is Special Agent Alex Wiggins and Special Agent Randall Kiper. They are with the FBI."

"I thought you said there would just be the two of them," Wiggins says. I get the hunch that he's the leader of the pair; maybe he's the more "special" of the two special agents.

"Jessie is a part of the team," Nate says. "Easily as important as we are." I'm glad he said it; I wish I had.

Wiggins just nods. It's an acceptance of reality, not an acknowledgment of having been rebuked. "Very well." Then he turns to Kiper and says, "Show them."

Agent Kiper takes his cell phone out of his pocket, presses a couple of buttons, and then points it at the wall. It projects an incredibly clear photograph that takes up most of that wall.

"That is very cool," I say, a comment which draws a response from absolutely no one.

The photo is of a crowd of people, but it's obvious that the man in the center was the target of the photographer. The camera is above him, and he's not looking at it, but rather straight ahead. It appears to be a crowded airport, or train station . . . something like that.

"Do any of you recognize him?" Wiggins asks.

Jessie says, "No," while Nate and I shake our heads.

"Ever seen him before?" Wiggins asks.

Another "no" from Jessie, and this time one from Nate as well. I say, "I don't think so."

"You might have?" Wiggins asks.

"Don't go there," Nate says, and Bradley quickly tells him that I've recently experienced some memory loss. Wiggins nods as if he already knew that.

I want to move this along. "Who is he?"

"He has at least forty names that we know of, and while we think we know his birth name, it is unimportant. He hasn't used it for many years. For the past two weeks, while he was in this country, he went by the name Isaiah Butler."

"Why are you asking us about him?"

"Ten days ago, he entered the country and rented a van at Newark Airport. Yesterday he died in that van in an accident on Route 15 near Baker, California."

"Do we know it was an accident?" Bradley asks. My guess is that he already has been briefed and knows where this is going.

Wiggins nods. "We have high confidence that it was. There

were high winds, and a car swerved into his. A father and son in one of the other cars was killed, and the driver of a third car suffered a broken leg. The accident is not suspicious, at least not at this point."

"Why do you care about him?" I ask.

"He's part of a group that supplies arms, explosives, and advice to bad actors; if you want to kill people in large numbers, and you have a lot of money to spend, these are the people you turn to for your equipment and expertise."

"What does this have to do with us?"

"Through the GPS on the van, we were able to track its movements since he rented it. It made stops in New Jersey and Vegas that we believe were drop-offs."

"Drop-offs of what?" Nate asks.

"Without knowing exactly, we know it is something we would be very interested in finding."

"They are aware of our investigation, and think that Butler, or whatever his name is, might be involved," Bradley says.

"You think the drop-offs were to Silva and Tartaro?" Nate asks.

Wiggins answers with a question to me. "What were you doing in Vegas?"

"How did you know I was there?"

"We know a lot of things. What were you doing there?"

I'm about to tell him to kiss my ass when a slight nod from Captain Bradley indicates that I should answer the question. "Talking to witnesses."

"Tartaro is a witness?" Wiggins asks.

The question tells me that they've been monitoring what I've been doing; either that or they're monitoring Tartaro and I got swept up in it. "He's a suspect in a drug investigation."

"So what did you learn out there?"

"That the buffets are worth every penny."

Wiggins doesn't seem amused; either he didn't appreciate the joke or he has a different view of the buffets. He tells Bradley that he and the Bureau need to be kept informed of any progress in our investigation, and Bradley agrees, which annoys me.

The meeting breaks up, leaving Bradley, Nate, Jessie, and me alone. Jessie asks the obvious question. "Why would Silva and Tartaro need explosives to peddle drugs?"

"I could have twenty people on this and not get through it," Jessie says.

"IT'S LIKE PROOFREADING THE LIBRARY OF CONGRESS."

Jessie is sitting at her computer in her house; when everything you do is online, it's pretty easy to bring your work home with you. Nate and I don't have that luxury, unless we decide to hold a criminals dinner party.

"Talk to Uncle Dougie," I say.

"Uncle Dougie is going to find himself sleeping on the couchie with Bobo if he keeps talking like that."

"Sorry. Tell me what's going on."

"Okay. The hospital records and the drug company records have been coming in, and by 'coming in,' I mean we are being flooded with them. Do you have any idea how many drugs a hospital this size uses? Do you know what their damn aspirin bill is?"

"No."

"Good. You don't want to know. But it's huge, and Tylenol is even more."

"Those aren't the drugs we're interested in."

She stares a dagger at me; this is not going well. "I know, but what I don't know is what the hell we *are* looking for. You know all the opioids, all the names of drugs that would have street value? And then their generic names?"

"No."

"Then how the hell should I?" she asks.

"Maybe we need to get you some consulting help, like a doctor, or better yet, a pharmacist."

"Doug, this is impossible."

"Don't focus on the drugs," I say. "Focus on the money."

She shakes her head. "No, that's what I've been doing, but it doesn't work. Let's say the hospital bought a million dollars' worth of drugs from a company, and believe me I'm using a low amount just to make it easier."

"Okay."

"So the books show that they paid the company a million dollars, and the company's books show that they received a million dollars. Looks good, right?"

"In that case, yes," I say.

"But it's not, or at least we don't know one way or the other. Because we don't know what happened to the drugs. Let's say the hospital actually dispensed three-quarters of what they received to patients. That leaves a quarter million dollars of drugs at wholesale price that were never dispensed. You know how much street value that would have? A fortune."

"Okay, I see what you're saying. So focus on the dispensing side."

"How? If it says Sylvia Swathouse got twenty OxyContin for pain, how can I know if she did? For all I know she's allergic to the stuff, or she had pneumonia and no need for pain meds, or there was no Sylvia Swathouse in the first place.

"And if I knew how to get through all of this, there still might be nothing to find. Galvis said that Lewinsky covered his tracks, remember? The dispensing would be the easiest thing for him to fake, because it's all internal."

I have no answer for any of this, so instead I just ask another question. "And how would Rita Carlisle know about it?"

"What do you mean?"

"I mean, she was in hospital administration. How would she know if the medicine was actually prescribed? That wasn't her area at all."

She nods. "True. Maybe she was told about it by someone else. Or maybe she overheard something she shouldn't have. Or maybe she was the ringleader. Who the hell knows? We need Galvis to catch him in the act."

"Won't happen," I say. "Galvis is scared to death, and sorry he came to me in the first place."

"He should be scared, because based on what that FBI agent said, Silva might be about to kill a lot of people, maybe blow up the hospital."

The FBI briefing, if that's what it was, is something I've been trying to ignore. I simply cannot make the connection to the Carlisle case. Maybe Silva and Tartaro are planning some terrorist plot, but it seems very unlikely and out of character. These guys are interested in money and power; they are not ideologues. What would they have to gain by killing a bunch of people, or taking down a building, or both?

Whatever that is about, I'm operating under the assumption that it is separate and apart from our Carlisle drug investigation. It is not stretching logic to think that organized crime figures can do two illegal things at the same time. They can steal and chew gum.

The only similarity and possible connection is that it involves both Tartaro and Silva, possibly working in tandem. But even that is not a surprise; if they have a good and profitable working relationship, it can be varied.

"Let the FBI handle that side of it," I say. "We've got enough on our plate."

Jessie nods. "More than enough."

Galvis is ready to meet with me again.

AND AGAIN HE DOESN'T WANT IT TO BE AT THE HOSPITAL, HE wants me to pick him up behind the Village Diner, like last time. Since last time worked out pretty well, I agree.

"When?" I ask.

"Fifteen minutes?"

I go along with it, even though it will not give me time to get fitted with a wire. This conversation will therefore not be recorded, and will rely on my memory, which is fairly ironic. I can just imagine a defense attorney having a field day with that.

Once Galvis is in the car, I ask if he got what I wanted, which was current evidence that Lewinsky was involved in the drug theft and fraud.

"In a manner of speaking," he says, which doesn't thrill me.

"Let's hear it."

He holds up a folder and says, "In here are the medical records of one Travis Mauer, a fifty-two-year-old with two herniated disks. The records show that he was in the hospital for a solid week on pain meds and epidurals. He went home with a healthy supply of those meds as well."

"So?"

"So Travis Mauer doesn't exist. He was never a patient at the hospital, and certainly never received any medication. Believe me, Travis is not alone; I would think the list of nonexistent patients is a long one."

"Why did you say that you have what I asked for, 'in a manner of speaking,'" I ask.

"Because I don't have proof tying Lewinsky to it. I can prove that Travis Mauer was not a patient and that his medical records are a fake, but I can't prove that Lewinsky did it."

"Is there anyone else that could have?"

"I don't see how; not without it being detected."

"I understand. Get me more."

He just about moans his distress. "Come on, I did what you asked."

"And I appreciate that. Now do it again."

"I don't work for you," he says. He's a little feistier this time.

"No, you work for a crook, and you need to help me put him away."

He thinks about it for a few moments. "I'm getting tired of this."

"Join the club," I say. "Does the name William Simmons mean anything to you?" I've gotten the medical assessment of Simmons' case from Cassel; I want to find out if Galvis can learn whether or not Lewinsky had anything to do with it.

"I don't think it does. Who is he?"

"A murder victim who died at your hospital a while back. Look him up, see if there's anything unusual in his records."

"Unusual how?"

"I don't know; I'm hoping you'll tell me. Maybe he didn't exist, either."

"Okay. I'll find out what I can." He hesitates for a moment, then adds, "There's one other thing."

"What is it?"

"I think something is going to happen on the sixteenth."

The sixteenth is only one week away. "What is going to happen?"

"I don't know; I heard Lewinsky mention it on a phone call." He explains, "My office is right next to his; if I put my ear to the wall, I can hear everything he's saying."

I don't tell him what I'm thinking, that the sixteenth could be the date that the terrorist action the FBI is expecting could happen. I still don't see what Lewinsky and the drug conspiracy could have to do with it, but I think there's a lot that I'm not seeing.

I take Galvis back to his car and then head to the office. I give Jessie the medical records of the nonexistent Travis Mauer with his nonexistent herniated discs, so that she can examine them. Maybe it can point her in the right direction as she works her way through the subpoenaed documents we have.

Nate comes in for a strategy session. We both have the feeling that we're just running in place; we might be getting a little closer to nailing Lewinsky, but it isn't moving at the pace we'd like, and taking the next step of getting Silva seems way off in the distance.

"We need to move this along," I say, and Nate nods in agreement. "Otherwise this is going to turn into a pissing contest between two sets of accountants looking at two sets of books."

"So we pressure Lewinsky."

"Yes, we do."

We find Bradley and tell him what we're going to do, and Bradley agrees. I think he's getting increased pressure from the chief to make progress, which is why he grabs onto the idea without having to be convinced.

Sitting in Bradley's office with him and Nate, I call Lewinsky. "Mr. Lewinsky, we need to have another talk."

"This is getting tiring, Lieutenant. People here are complaining about the intrusion."

"Well, this won't feel quite so intrusive, because the talk we're going to have will be down here, at the precinct."

He laughs a short laugh. "You can't be serious. I'm a busy man; I have neither the time nor the inclination to go to your office."

"I'm sorry . . . did I give you the impression this was voluntary?"

There is a silence of at least ten seconds, which seems a lot longer. Then, "Detective, are you attempting to arrest me?"

"We never 'attempt' to arrest, Mr. Lewinsky. They don't teach that at the police academy. We just 'arrest.' Which is something we are not doing now. But I strongly advise you that it is in your interest to come down here and cooperate."

Another pause. "Very well. I will be bringing my attorney."

"I'll make sure we have enough chairs."

We set a time for this afternoon and hang up. Bradley has one piece of advice for us.

"Rattle his cage."

Lewinsky arrives at 3:00 P.M. with his attorney,
Ronald Ranes.

IT'S NOT THE FIRST TIME I'VE BEEN SURPRISED THAT SOMEONE
who has never been charged with a crime has such apparent easy access to a criminal attorney; do people like him have them listed in their Rolodexes under *J* for "Just in Case"?

But Ranes is a top guy, very well respected, smart and tough. The two of them join Nate and me in an interview room with a one-way mirror so Bradley can observe. Nate and I have agreed that I will ask all the questions, and his role will be to look large and ominous. It's a look he can manage easily.

Once we're settled in, I inform them that the interview is being recorded and that they are free to end the session at any time. Ranes acknowledges that and says for the record that his client is here of his own free will and resents being dragged down here, that he is an upstanding citizen and deserves better treatment.

Our goal here is limited. With or without Ranes being present, there is no way that Lewinsky is going to say anything to incriminate himself. He's far too smart for that; the table we're sitting at would be too smart for that.

What we want to do is shake him up, to get him to take some

action that we can pounce on. We have surveillance in place on his phone and emails, so if he does or says the wrong thing because we have worried him, then we've got him.

I identify Lewinsky and his position at the hospital for the record, and then ask, "Mr. Lewinsky, are you aware of any fraudulent activities regarding the purchase and/or dispensation of drugs at Bergen Hospital?"

He pretends to be surprised at the question, and says, "I don't know what you're talking about."

"Please answer the questions that I ask you. Are you aware of any such activities?"

"I am not."

"Have you ever, in any manner, adjusted the hospital records showing the purchases of drugs, or the dispensation of them?"

"I have not."

I ask the question in different forms a few more times, and each time he denies them, showing exasperation at the repetition.

"Do you personally know Joey Silva?"

"Joey Silva?"

"Yes, that's correct."

He looks at Ranes, who nods. Then Lewinsky says, "I've heard the name."

"Have you ever met him?"

He shakes his head. "Not to my knowledge."

"Ever spoken to him?"

"Not to my knowledge."

I then ask him the exact same questions regarding Tony Silva and Philly DeSimone, and his denials are the same. Finally he says, "These are gangsters."

"Thanks for sharing that," I say. "Have you ever heard the name Travis Mauer?" Mauer is the fictitious patient that supposedly received treatment and drugs at Bergen Hospital.

"No, I don't believe so."

"What about the name William Simmons?"

That seems to provoke a slight reaction in him, but I can't be sure. "William Simmons?"

I nod. "That's correct. William Simmons."

"It sounds familiar, but I can't place it."

"Let me try and refresh your memory; he was a murder victim who died at Bergen Hospital."

"Perhaps I heard his name in that context, but I don't remember."

I tell him that we have no further questions, and ask him if he would be willing to take a polygraph. He says absolutely not, and expresses his resentment at being treated like a criminal.

I smile and thank him for his cooperation. He responds with, "I hope that this will conclude this matter, whatever it is you're doing."

I smile again. "We live in hope."

The meeting breaks up; whatever Ranes got paid for coming here today, he didn't break a sweat to earn it.

It's hard to know what effect, if any, the conversation had on Lewinsky. He was calm and under control; he certainly didn't break down and blubber out a confession.

Now the ball is in his court to see if he reveals himself in a phone or email correspondence, and in Jessie's court to monitor it.

Philly DeSimone knew all about Lewinsky's police interview within two hours of its conclusion.

LEWINSKY WAS SCARED, AND HE TALKED ABOUT IT TO SOMEONE he trusted and was comfortable with. And that person talked to Philly, who in turn talked to Joey Silva.

"We've got a small problem," Philly said. He was not used to having conversations like this with Joey; that used to be Tony's job. But he knew enough to know that he had to tread carefully.

"I don't like problems," Joey said.

"I know, Joey, but this one can be handled. The cops brought Lewinsky in for questioning."

"What about?"

"Drugs. They think he is stealing drugs from the hospital and giving them to us."

Joey laughs. "What did Lewinsky say?"

"He denied it, of course. But he's worried. And he thinks we should delay our plans for the sixteenth."

"We have the targets picked out?"

"We do," Philly said.

Joey shakes his head. "Then no chance; we move forward. If we give in to that little twerp, we'll never get him back under control."

"You need to call him and straighten him out."

"You do it."

Philly shakes his head. "Joey, it's got to come from you. You're the one he's afraid of, and he knows you're the boss. It's a two-minute conversation."

Joey sighed; this was something Tony could have handled. "All right, let's get the asshole on the phone."

So Philly prepped Joey very carefully for what he should say, and then he did as he was told. He got Lewinsky on the phone.

"Lewinsky talked to Joey Silva,"
Nate says, hanging up the phone.

IT IS BARELY THREE HOURS SINCE HE AND RANES LEFT OUR
office, which is even faster than I could have imagined. Now Jessie
has called and says she's got the audio of the call, ready for us to hear.

Nate and I head for her office immediately, and she says,
"Here's a surprise; Lewinsky didn't initiate the call. Silva did."

She presses the button, and the first voice we hear is someone
answering the phone with, "Hello?"

The caller says, "You know who this is?"

There's a delay, and a very nervous-sounding Lewinsky says,
"Mr. Silva."

"I understand you had a conversation with the cops?"

"Yes." He seems surprised that Joey knows about that, as am I.
Could they be tailing him? He continues.

"So?" Joey is proving to be quite a conversationalist.

"The police questioned me."

"Local or Federal?"

"State. That guy Brock."

"And they asked you about drugs?" Joey asks.

"How did you know that?"

"I know a lot of things. What did you tell them?"

"That I didn't know what they were talking about," Lewinsky says. "But then they asked me a couple of names."

"Which names?"

"One of them I don't remember; I don't know who it is. The other one was William Simmons. He was a homeless guy who was murdered, and died in the hospital. We've talked about him before."

"I don't see no problems here. Just keep doing what you're doing."

"It's making me nervous," Lewinsky says.

"So be nervous. Just don't do or say anything stupid."

"I think we should delay our plans for the sixteenth; there's too much risk. Maybe push it back at least a couple of weeks."

"It goes as scheduled," Joey says. "You worry about your end."

"I think we should cancel it. Tony told me that . . ."

"Tony ain't here no more."

"I know. I'm sorry. I just don't think we should be doing this anymore."

Joey laughs. "Are you a religious guy, Lewinsky?"

"In a way."

"Do you know the line about giveth and taketh away?"

The calls clicks off with the sound of Joey continuing to laugh at his joke, whatever the hell it means.

We contact Bradley, who tells us to come in immediately. We say that it's best he come to Jessie's office, and he's here almost before we can hang up the phone. Bradley was making this a priority before, but after the meeting with the Feds, it's inched up a few notches.

"Lewinsky received this call a few hours after he left here," she says. Bradley listens intently, making eye contact with me when Lewinsky uses Joey's name in the call.

When it's finished, Bradley asks Jessie to play it again. After that, he says. "Get me a transcript ASAP."

"You need to get this to Wiggins," I say. "The Feds need to know this."

"Tell me something I don't know," says Bradley.

"There's plenty we don't know."

"Well, figure it out. And then hang that son of a bitch."

The intercepted phone conversation gives us a lot.

EVEN AN "INVESTIGATION HALF-EMPTY" GUY LIKE ME KNOWS that it advanced the ball considerably, just not quite enough.

First of all, it established beyond any doubt the connection between Lewinsky and Joey Silva. Lewinsky and Joey are doing business together, and doing business with Joey cannot have a benign explanation.

It also confirms our view that this is about drugs, which is what Mitchell Galvis has been telling us all along. Joey knew instantly that we must have talked to Lewinsky about drugs; it was the first question he asked.

The other important topic was William Simmons. We knew that Lewinsky had mentioned him in that cryptic email, but we thought it could possibly be legitimate hospital business. It's not; Lewinsky's talking about him to Joey places the dead man in the center of this investigation. Simmons died in the hospital, but it wasn't from cancer; he was murdered. Murder is a key part of Joey Silva's job description.

What the conversation didn't give us is proof of Lewinsky's guilt, at least legally. We know what it means, and we know that he's dirty, but it's not a smoking gun. Just based on this, we can't get it past a prosecutor. And if we can't do that, then we can't squeeze Lewinsky enough to give up Silva.

The other part of this, the scary part, is that we now have a deadline for another shoe to drop. Galvis had told me that he overheard that something was going to happen on the sixteenth, and now we have it repeated and confirmed.

That news, coupled with the terrorist implications that the FBI talked about, could be ominous. Or just as likely, it could be a day that they're going to take a whole bunch of drugs out of that hospital. Or it could be something entirely different. We've got a week to find out.

I'm still inclined to discount the terrorist side of this, no matter what the FBI said. How would Joey Silva benefit from a literally explosive terrorist action, and how could it possibly help his drug business, or any other part of his business? I also think that Joey telling Lewinsky to take care of his end of things argues against terrorism. What could Lewinsky's end of a plot like that be?

None of us understand Joey's comment about "giveth and taketh away," but I sure as hell didn't like the way he said it and then laughed about it.

For the time being, we need to focus on William Simmons. I've read the details of the investigation into his murder, but it presents only a surface picture of his life.

The cold truth is that he was a homeless guy who fell through society's cracks and who was believed to have been the victim of a random killing. I know the cops who handled the case, and they were professional and careful, but they didn't exactly marshal the full force of the department on it. They checked the boxes, but I'm sure they just moved on when their caseload got full.

Nobody cared about William Simmons in life, and nobody got too worked up over his death.

But William Simmons was not just another murder victim. There was something about him that is worrying the head of a hospital and an organized crime figure, even today. There is some connection between him and Rita Carlisle's kidnapping, and maybe between him and an impending disaster.

I think it's time to give William Simmons the attention he should have gotten in the first place.

Jessie uses her online magic to find Simmons's daughter, Patty, the one who survived along with him in the car crash that killed her mother and sister. She goes by her married name of Lynch, and lives in Leonia.

I call ahead, and she agrees to see us this afternoon. Nate and I go together, a reflection of the importance we're giving to learning what the hell William Simmons could possibly have to do with this case.

We arrive at a modest house with a carefully manicured lawn that can't be more than seventy square feet, surrounded by straight lines of neatly planted flowers. I have no idea what kind of flowers they are; roses are pretty much the only ones I can ever identify. If I wanted some enlightenment on the subject, and I don't, Nate is the last person that could provide it.

Patty Lynch lets us in; she's maybe twenty-five, and is wearing an apron and actually drying her hands on a kitchen towel. Two kids, maybe four and five years old, are playing with some toys in the den, with a cartoon on television.

"Come in the kitchen," she says. "I made some coffee." Then she turns to the kids and asks them to play nicely while Mommy is in the kitchen. They don't respond or seem to hear her, which is okay, because they're already playing nicely.

We sit down at the kitchen table as Patty pours coffee and delights Nate by putting out some donuts. "So you wanted to talk to me about Dad?" she asks, a little nervously. "After all this time?"

In these situations I usually do the talking, and Nate and I have agreed to the same this time. It's just as well, since Nate's mouth is about to be full of coffee-drenched donuts.

"Yes, we have a few questions. I'm sorry if this upsets you; that's not our intention. But the questions are important."

"It's okay; I'm just curious, that's all. It's been so long." Then, "Please ask your questions, maybe they'll answer some of my own."

We've decided to be straight with her, or at least as straight as we can be without revealing information we need to protect. "Your father's name has come up in another case we're working on, a case to which he has no apparent connection. So we're trying to make that connection, and to do so, we need to know your father a lot better."

"So you want me to tell you about him?" she asks.

"For now, yes. That's a good place to start."

"Okay. I look at it as though I had two fathers. There was the William Simmons before the accident, and the one after."

"You're talking about the automobile accident?"

"Yes. My mother and sister were killed, and my father and I lived. We were in the backseat, they were in the front, and the way the car was hit, that made the difference. It could just as easily have been the other way. I'm sure he would have preferred not to survive; you could easily argue that he actually died that day as well."

She's talking with intensity and emotion, and her voice cracks a couple of times. Nate has even put down his donut; for him that is a remarkable gesture of respect for her sacrifice.

"Before the accident, he enjoyed his life and his family. He owned an insurance agency—I don't know how much of this you already know—and was doing well. We had just bought a new house, although we never moved in.

"He loved my mother, and adored his kids. I know I'm painting a picture that sounds idyllic and unreal, and I'm sure he had problems that he was dealing with, certainly with his vision, but he never made us feel them. He made our world safe and happy."

"He had vision problems?"

"Terrible. He lost his eyesight over time, to the point where he was probably legally blind, though I doubt he got tested."

I ask her to continue, and she does.

"After the crash, it was never the same. It was like he couldn't function in the world, and didn't want to, but he didn't have the courage to put a gun to his head. So instead he killed himself slowly, and everyone who cared about him had a ringside seat. But there was a fence separating us from the ring, and he'd never let us come through it."

She takes a deep breath. "So I went to live with my grand-mother, and he disappeared. I tried to reach him, to find him, but I was never able to. And I probably didn't try hard enough, because I knew he did not want to be found."

"Did he leave a will?" I ask.

She shrugs. "Not that I know of. He had nothing anyway, so it really wouldn't have mattered."

"What happened to the insurance agency? The people that had policies through him?"

"I believe the companies themselves took them over, maybe re-positioned them with different agencies. He was not the insurer; he was the agent. He dealt with a lot of different insurance companies, and he wrote the policies through whichever one was best for a particular purpose."

"Can you think of anyone who might have wanted him dead? For whatever reason?"

"No. The only person who wanted my father dead was my father." Then, "Are you saying his death might not have been a ran-dom killing? That someone specifically targeted him?"

I nod. "It's a possibility."

She shakes her head in apparent amazement. "Wow. I can't be-lieve anyone would have done that, or what they would possibly have to gain. Certainly not money, and I can't imagine it being revenge. He never hurt anyone except himself."

What I don't tell her is that the cops doing the original investiga-tion believed that it was the murderer who called 911 and reported

Simmons' whereabouts. That was never consistent with a random "thrill" killing, but without anything else to go on, nothing ever came of it.

Of course, part of the answer is that making that call was not consistent with any kind of killing, be it random, thrill, or premeditated. Simmons was alive when the medical people showed up; a person intent on killing would not have called them in to possibly save the victim.

It could just have been a quirk of the killer; for example, maybe he waited around and got a kick out of watching the police and ambulances show up to see his handiwork. There's just no way to know.

I'm sure that Patty is telling us the truth to the extent that she knows it, but she's wrong about one thing, when she says that no one cared about her father.

Daniel Lewinsky and Joey Silva definitely cared about William Simmons. They still do.

The still-unanswered question is why.

Dominic Romano still hadn't told Salvatore Tartaro
that he'd disobeyed his instructions.

TARTARO HAD PANICKED—UNCHARACTERISTICALLY, ROMANO
thought—when the Vegas and Jersey cops came to see him. His response was to order Dominic to contact Silva and postpone the events set for the sixteenth. Dominic had not made the call, and in fact had never considered making it.

But this was the day that Tartaro was going to find out. Dominic came to see him in his suite at eleven o'clock in the morning and said, "Philly DeSimone is in town."

Tartaro was surprised by the news. "What's he doing here?"

"He wants to meet with us."

"What about?"

"I asked him that. He said 'business.' When I pressed him on it, he said he would only talk to you about it. He didn't want you to hear it from anyone else but him."

"Tell him to kiss my ass," Tartaro said.

"Salvatore, Silva must have sent him. He's our partner; you need to see him."

"They still think we hit Tony."

"He told me they don't. He says they know who did, and it's being taken care of."

Tartaro is surprised. "Yeah? Who hit him?"

"You can ask him that when we see him."

Tartaro thought about it for a few moments, but realized there was no way he could say no, not without blowing up the relationship with Silva. But he was still pissed off that Philly showed up unannounced, demanding a meeting. That was not an act of respect, and he would make that very clear to Philly.

"All right, let him come up."

Dominic shook his head and said, "Not here. Philly wants it to be in a public place."

"Public place? What kind of bullshit is that?"

Dominic shrugged. "Maybe he's not so sure we didn't hit Tony. Maybe he's just being careful in case we were looking to hit him as well. Can't blame him for being careful; you live longer that way."

"You pick a place? You better make sure we got it covered, wherever it is. Philly's crazy enough to come in shooting."

"It's all arranged. We're going to Spumoni's. Tommy's giving us the back room. I'm having our people pick Philly up; he doesn't know where we're going. And he's going to be alone."

"Okay. When?"

"Now."

"Who is going with us?"

"Ralph and Mike."

Tartaro nodded his satisfaction at that; having Ralph and Mike as protection was akin to employing a Marine battalion, but without being bothered by morals or the Geneva Convention.

Tartaro changed his clothes; he didn't venture out of the hotel much, but when he did, he liked to look good. Dominic waited for him in the den area, and when he was ready they went out the door.

Ralph and Mike were standing in the hall, and without saying a word they took their positions in front of and behind Tartaro and

Dominic. They were of course armed, and their weapons were within easy reaching distance.

They passed a housekeeping attendant pushing a cart filled with towels near the elevator. He saw them and then looked away; he knew exactly who Tartaro was, and eye contact with a mob killer was not what he was getting paid for.

They took the elevator, not to the lobby, but to the lower floor, where customers got their valet-parked cars. But Salvatore Tartaro was not about to stand there with a ticket, waiting for his car to be brought up. His car was waiting outside at a side entrance. Tartaro was not seen in public often, and he liked it that way.

Ralph drove the car, and Philly got in the passenger seat. Tartaro, as was his preference, sat in the back behind the driver, with Mike on the right side. The windows were tinted and could not be seen through from the outside.

They drove the fifteen minutes to Spumoni's, a small restaurant on the outskirts of town that was Tartaro's favorite. He rarely went to the actual restaurant anymore, but had food brought in from there often. The hotel food, in his view, was fine for tourists.

Salvatore Tartaro was not a tourist.

They approached the restaurant from the back, and parked in the small rear lot. They could see part of the front lot from where they were, and there were no cars to be seen.

"Where is everybody?" Tartaro asked.

"I don't know," said Dominic, looking at his watch. "It's early . . . Mike, go in and make sure everything is okay."

Without saying a word, Mike got out and went inside the restaurant through the back door. When he came back three minutes later, he was grinning. "What's so funny?" Dominic asked.

"Tommy closed the place for lunch when he heard we were coming. He said Mr. Tartaro wanted privacy, and that's what he was gonna get. We've got the whole damn restaurant; even Tommy just left."

Tartaro laughed; he was used to getting special treatment, but he never stopped liking it. Ralph got out of the car so that he and Mike were flanking Tartaro when he got out. They'd done it many times, and performed with Secret Service–like precision. No mob boss was going to get gunned down on their watch.

Dominic got out as well, and the four of them went into the restaurant through the back door. They went into the main area, and then into the private room that was off of it. They obviously had their choice of anywhere they wanted, but the smaller room had no window to the street, and was therefore safer and more private.

Once they were in the room, Tartaro said, "If nobody's here, how the hell are we going to eat?"

Dominic laughed. "I guess we're not."

"What time is Philly coming?"

"I guess he's not. He never flew out here. Didn't I mention that?"

"What the hell does that mean?" Tartaro asked.

"You're a smart guy, Salvatore," Dominic said. "You figure it out."

Even if Tartaro wasn't a smart guy, this wouldn't have been a tough one to figure out. Ralph, Mike, and Dominic had all taken out pistols, which they were pointing at him.

"What the . . . we can talk this out. Dominic, I've always taken care of you."

Dominic smiled. "Until now. Now I'm taking care of you."

"Why?"

Another smile. "I guess you can call it an old-fashioned power grab. But it's going to work perfectly. You're going to disappear, and then we're going to blow up a casino. And when they come looking for you, they'll assume you ran. They'll be searching for you forever; you'll be Hoffa, that DB Cooper guy, and that Earhart flying broad all rolled into one."

Tartaro turned to Ralph and Mike. "Whatever he's giving you, I'll do better."

"Bye-bye, Salvatore," Dominic said, just before pulling the trigger. "Sorry you couldn't get a last meal, but the restaurant is closed."

Roberts out in Vegas needs to be kept in the loop.

THERE IS NO DOUBT THAT THERE IS A VEGAS COMPONENT TO this; because of Shawn, we have known about this connection from day one. Roberts is smart, he knows what's going on, and he can be a valuable asset out there.

"I was just going to call you," he says, when he gets on the phone.

"Why?"

"You go first," he says, so I do just that. I update him on everything that has happened with Lewinsky, including the apparent importance of William Simmons. He, of course, knows nothing about Simmons, and therefore has no insight into the matter.

I also tell him about the references to something happening on the sixteenth, as well as the Feds coming to us about the death of the terrorist and possible supplier of explosives, who had made ominous stops in both Jersey and Vegas. He knows all about it, both because the car accident in which the supplier died was near Vegas, and because the Feds came to Vegas PD as well.

"They're scared that something is going to happen," Roberts says. "So am I. But it seems separate from our drug case, so I'm going to let them deal with that piece."

"Same here," I say. "How are you doing on checking into Harriman?" Roberts was investigating whether there were possible drug thefts going on there.

He tells me that they haven't found anything so far, nor have they made progress in reinvestigating the apparent accidental death of Janine Seraphin, Rita Carlisle's counterpart at Harriman.

It's disappointing, but not terribly surprising. He doesn't have probable cause to get a warrant to look at the drug records out there; we only had it because of Galvis's coming forward. And the Seraphin death is a cold case; if she was actually murdered, it was probably done by professionals and covered up well.

"We have some information that hospital records here show drugs dispensed in quantity to a patient who never existed," I say. "You could check that angle."

"Okay. Interesting idea."

"Your turn," I say. "What were you going to call me about?"

"Tartaro seems to be among the missing."

"What does that mean?"

"He left the hotel yesterday; we have two hotel workers who saw him head out with Dominic Romano and two soldiers. He never came back, either to the hotel or his home."

"Are you sure?"

"Who do you think you're dealing with?"

"Fair point," I say. "So where do you think he might have gone? And why?"

"On the 'where' question, I have no idea," he says. "On the 'why' question, I have absolutely no idea."

"Well, now we're getting somewhere. Has he ever gone off like this before?"

"I'm sure he has," he says. "But with all that's going on, lately we've been paying a bit more attention to Tartaro's travel habits."

"Maybe his severed head will turn up."

He laughs. "If it does, I'm going to stuff it and put it over my fireplace."

Roberts and I hang up, promising to keep each other informed of developments. Nate, who has been listening in on the conversation, says, "We need to squeeze Lewinsky."

"We tried that."

"I know, but he's having second thoughts. And now we have more facts to throw at him."

"The problem is he's more afraid of Silva than he is of us, and I can't say I blame him," I say. "What about talking to Ranes? Maybe get him to talk sense to his client?"

Nate shrugs. "It's worth a try. If nothing happens, we can always go to Lewinsky direct."

I can remember one time I dealt directly with Ranes on a case, and it went well; there may have been other times, but they're not part of my conscious recollections. He's a stand-up guy, for a defense attorney.

Ordinarily, a prosecutor would be contacting him, but since there was no prosecutor in our interview, it would take too long to get someone up to speed. It's not a violation of any rule or protocol for a cop to go to the attorney directly, so that's what I'm going to do.

I place a call to him, and I'm told he'll call me back, which he does ten minutes later. "I assume you're calling to apologize for harassing Mr. Lewinsky? I'll convey your regrets."

"You do that," I say. "And I have some other information you can convey to him."

"I'm having trouble understanding what your issue is with Mr. Lewinsky, Lieutenant; he's a well-respected executive who has never gotten a speeding ticket, and you spoke to him like he was Don Corleone, or Joey Silva, as the case may be."

"Good, now that we've got that out of the way, here's where we stand," I say. "I know things that you don't know, but your client does. And I'm about to tell you those things, so for now, please just listen."

"That's a little dramatic, Lieutenant."

"Yes it is. And I'll double down on that by telling you this may be the most important conversation you will ever have, with the exception of the next one you have with your client."

"I'm listening," he says.

"We have more information since I spoke to you last. I am not going to tell you how we got it, but it's real. Your client has been stealing drugs from the hospital by manipulating the books. He must have an accomplice internally to pull it off, but we don't know who that is yet. We will find out. We believe that Rita Carlisle somehow learned what was going on, and she was silenced."

"This is about Rita Carlisle?" he asks, and I can hear the surprise in his voice.

"And much, much more. Mr. Lewinsky has been participating in a conspiracy with Joey Silva to sell the drugs on the open market. There is a Vegas connection to it as well, which I won't go into now."

"Lieutenant . . ."

"Let me finish. There is a terrorism component to this investigation, an action is planned, perhaps more than one. The FBI is well aware of it, and they are very concerned. We do not know where, or exactly what is going to happen, but there is a concern that high-intensity explosives will be involved." I still don't believe that the terrorism investigation connects to ours, but I'm not about to tell Ranes that. I want Lewinsky scared that he's in over his head.

"You're not making sense, Lieutenant. Even if my client were involved in a drug trafficking conspiracy, which we categorically deny, what would such an operation gain by a mass killing?"

"That's a question we cannot answer yet, and I emphasize 'yet.' But I am telling you that all of this is something we know; this is not speculation."

"Yet you can't prove it."

"Correct, but we're getting close." I'm not telling him that we have his client on tape, because I don't want Lewinsky to be more careful in the future. "And I am not asking you to believe it or me. That doesn't matter at all. But here's the thing; your client knows that all of it is real. He knows that what I have told you is true, and he is scared. So I am simply asking you to tell all of this to him."

"For what purpose?"

"If any part of this happens the way I am saying, he will be taking the fall. He needs to think about that, because the alternative is that if he decides to make a deal, and helps us prevent this, you can do very well by him."

"I will convey your views to my client."

"Thank you. There is a lot riding on it."

It was the second full rehearsal.

IT COULDN'T BE CALLED A "DRESS" REHEARSAL, BECAUSE Nick Saulter did not wear what would be his disguise when he was doing it for real. On that day he would have facial hair and dark glasses, and knowing where the cameras were, he would never give them a head-on look.

But for now there was no danger of being discovered because he wasn't doing anything wrong. He was just out for a pleasant afternoon of shopping.

Nick bought a couple of shirts at the Gap, and a toy at a store called Cara's Village. He didn't pick the items at random, they qualified because they were the right size, and because the stores would gift wrap them. On the day when he had the package that he didn't buy in the stores, it would be a similar size, and it would also be wrapped.

So for the second time in as many weeks, he ascended the Paramus Park escalator to the food court, carrying the shopping bag. He went to the Burger King counter and ordered two hamburgers, fries, and a soda, carrying the tray and his shopping bag to a table near the center of the large seating area.

It was 1:00 P.M. and very crowded. He had no trouble getting a table, but even if he'd had, it wouldn't matter. This was fast food, and people who were there to shop didn't linger over their meals. The table turnover was rapid.

When he finished, he got up and left the shopping bag behind him. But he also left an uneaten hamburger, half of his drink, and a jacket that he draped over the back of his chair, so to anyone happening by they would think the table was still occupied, and perhaps the person was in the restroom.

One hour later the package, drink, and jacket were still there, untouched. This was the second time the exact same thing had happened, and in fact he knew it was far more than necessary. On the day in question, it would be all over within twenty minutes after he departed the food court.

Later that day, at Lucky Linda's Casino on the Vegas Strip, another man went through a similar rehearsal. He didn't bother doing any shopping; he brought a shopping bag with a wrapped "gift" in it with him.

He sat at a slot machine with the package on a ledge next to him. He played the machine for ten minutes, then got up and placed the package on the seat. He left a jacket on the back of the seat, so as to give the impression that he was coming back.

Forty-five minutes later, it was still there. So he stopped a casino official, and pointed out that the package had been left there, unattended, for a long while. The official looked at it, then took the jacket and the package to a security desk, which served as a lost and found.

The man behind the desk took it and placed it on a shelf behind him, not even looking at it in the process.

It was a completely satisfying result. The real package would very likely explode near the slot machine, where it would be left. But if not, it would explode behind the security desk. Either location would be fine for the purpose . . . maximum casualties.

I'm working late in the office, although I use
the word "working" loosely.

BASICALLY, I'M HANGING AROUND FOR TWO REASONS. ONE, I'M
hoping to get a call from Ron Ranes regarding the conversation he
was supposed to have with his client, Daniel Lewinsky. Second,
Jessie is working late hours digging into the hospital records, so
I'm waiting to take her home.

Nate is here also, for no particular reason that I can tell. One
thing is for sure; we're not accomplishing anything.

But whatever the reasons for my being here, it turns out to be
lucky, because the desk sergeant tells me that Daniel Lewinsky is on
the phone. I'm surprised, because I would have thought the call
would come from Ranes.

There's a recording system for incoming phone calls, which can
be activated with the press of a button. I press the button, because
I want a record of everything Lewinsky has to say.

"Hello, Daniel. What can I do for you?"

"I want to turn myself in," he says. "I want to make a deal. But
it's got to be now. I want to do it now."

"Smart move. I'll be waiting for you."

"No. He's going to kill me. I'm afraid to leave the house."

"Who's going to kill you?" I ask.

"Joey Silva. I'll tell you everything. All about the drugs, how we do it. And I know people that he's killed."

"Okay, stay where you are. We'll come get you. What's your address?"

He tells me, and I know the area. It's a very upscale neighborhood in Alpine.

"I'll have cops there in ten minutes," I say, and hang up.

Jessie just happens to be walking into my office as I'm ending the call, and she wants to come with Nate and me. First, we have the dispatcher get cars to the location; they'll be on the scene much faster than we will. The instructions are to stay there until we arrive.

Nate is the Dale Earnhardt of the department, so he drives. He makes it in fifteen minutes, ten faster than I could have done it. There are six cop cars in front of Lewinsky's house, and some neighbors standing outside. They must figure something significant is happening, and they are right.

As we walk toward the front door, Sergeant Luke Moore comes out, having seen us coming. "Where is Lewinsky?" I ask.

"Upstairs in his bedroom."

"Bring him down," Nate says.

Moore looks confused. "What do you mean . . . carry him? Forensics isn't even here yet."

Before I can ask the question, Moore sees the look on my face and says, "You know he's dead, right?"

Actually, no.

We go inside and find Lewinsky upstairs, dead from a bullet hole in the back of his head. There were no obvious signs of a struggle; Lewinsky didn't, or more likely couldn't, put up much of a fight.

About a half hour after our arrival, Ron Ranes shows up, and we send word to allow him into the house. He's already heard what happened, and is upset about it.

"He called us to say he was turning himself in," I say. "Ten minutes too late."

"He was? Why?"

"I assume it's because you told him what we talked about."

"I never spoke to him," Ranes says. "I left a message for him to call me, but he never did."

"I don't believe a word Lewinsky said on that call."

NATE, JESSIE, AND I HAVE STOPPED AT A DINER FOR A VERY LATE dinner after leaving Lewinsky's house. We hung around long enough to get the lay of the land and hear what forensics had to say, pending test results. It wasn't very encouraging; the murder was obviously done professionally.

"You don't? The guy said he was afraid for his life, and then he got killed. You don't think he was scared?"

"I do agree he was scared. But that was the only part I believe."

"Why?" Jessie asks.

"He was frightened out of his mind, right? Did you see the alarm system in that house? It was state-of-the-art. If he was that scared, it would have been activated if someone broke in, yet it never went off. There was also no sign of any forced entry, yet with his state of mind, he would have locked everything up tight and set the alarm. So he must have disarmed the alarm to let the killer in."

"Keep going," Nate says.

"The whole thing happened too fast. I checked; our people were there eight minutes after the call went out, which means ten minutes after Lewinsky got off the phone with us."

"Plenty of time to get in and shoot him."

"First of all, even if that were true, it's quite a coincidence that they happened to be there just as he called us. But besides that, how could it have gone down? Where was he in the house when he made the call to us?"

"I don't know," Nate says, and then adds, "probably the bedroom where we found him."

"Exactly. It's not on street level, so whoever he was worried about couldn't see him or shoot him through the window. That's where he would have been; it would be safer."

Jessie nods. "And the phone in that room was lying on the bed. The one downstairs was in the charger."

"Good catch. So he calls us from the bedroom, then he goes downstairs to let them in, and they take him back upstairs to the bedroom to shoot him? Why? And all in just a few minutes? Why not shoot him downstairs?"

"Maybe they somehow got through the alarm or he left something unlocked. So they come in, find him in the bedroom, and shoot him," Nate says.

"As unlikely as that is, he'd have heard them and closed his bedroom door. There's a lock on that door as well, but it wasn't broken into or jimmied in any way."

"So you think they were there while he called?" Jessie asks.

I nod. "I think they made him call, and told him what to say. It even sounded like he was reading it. Also, I spoke to Ranes at the house; he never spoke to Lewinsky and told him what we had on him."

Nate and Jessie think for a while, silently considering what I've been saying. Finally, Nate says, "You know, you're not as dumb as you used to be. Falling on your head might have paid off; or maybe not filling up your brain with memories opened up space for it to do other stuff."

"Thank you, Professor."

"So the killer was standing there, holding a gun and telling him what to say. Which probably means that everything he said was bullshit."

I nod. "Exactly."

"And the main thing he said was that Joey Silva was trying to kill him. If that's not true, why would they make him say it?"

"Because they want us to arrest Joey Silva for the murder."

"So what's our move?"

"We do not arrest Joey Silva for the murder."

A decision on whether to arrest Joey Silva is above my pay grade.

IT'S ABOVE NATE'S AND MY PAY GRADES COMBINED, EVEN IF YOU throw in Jessie's salary and the money I made for those ridiculous paid talks I gave before I got back on the force.

There are two people who would have to be convinced to make such an arrest; first Captain Bradley, and then the prosecutor. Both would have to sign on. If we can get Bradley to back off, then the prosecutor will never even get to participate in the decision. But Bradley is going to be very difficult to persuade; it's rarely in a police captain's interest to decline to arrest a mob boss when the evidence is there.

Nate and I are waiting in Bradley's office when he arrives at 8:00 A.M. Nate called him last night at home, updated him on recent events, and they arranged the meeting.

We start by playing the tape of the phone call from Lewinsky. As I listen to it again, I try and picture someone standing in the room, holding a gun on him as he talks. I still think I'm right about the circumstances, but I can't be 100 percent sure.

Once the tape is concluded, Bradley says, "We got Silva. This is enough to charge him."

We could let it go at that, and not tell Bradley what we think. He'll take it to the prosecutor, the decision will be made, and that will be that. No one could ever look back on this and say we did the wrong thing by making the arrest.

I don't know if I had a conscience in the past and have forgotten about it, but I have one now, and it's causing me to tell Bradley the truth.

"I think it's bogus," I say. "I think Lewinsky said what he said under duress."

Nate adds, "Major, serious duress."

"Why?" Bradley asks, and we tell him. We describe all the circumstances that make us believe that Lewinsky was saying exactly what he was told to say.

Bradley seems less than impressed. "You're advancing a theory, and this tape is a fact," he says, and he's right about that. "You're saying we let Joey Silva walk on a theory?"

I nod. "I'm saying we let Joey Silva walk, for the time being, based on our instincts and experience."

"Experience? You can't remember what you had for breakfast. You wouldn't know your experience if it walked into this room and bit you on the ass."

I decide not to punch him in the face for bringing that up; maybe I am maturing after all. "You put Joey away, and you're playing into their hands. We've been—I've been—playing into their hands since the day Shawn showed me the damn scrapbook."

He thinks for a few moments, not wanting to move quickly and do something stupid. "Okay. Tell me what you think is going on."

I nod. "Look, there are two possibilities here; Lewinsky was either telling the truth in that call, or he was being coerced into lying. I don't think he was telling the truth, but if he was, then we can arrest Silva whenever we want and hopefully put him away for years.

"Silva's not a flight risk; we always know where he is, and we can get him at our convenience.

"But let's say that Lewinsky was lying. Then two things can happen. One is that we figure out what the hell is going on and we get the real killer. The other is that we don't. But I think we have a better chance if we don't arrest Silva."

"Why?" Bradley asks.

"Because it shakes things up, and whoever is calling these shots gets thrown off their stride. They want to put Silva away, to get him out of the way, and they'll have to figure out another way to do it. Maybe we can watch and maybe intervene, but we can find out who benefits by him being put away, other than society.

"The way I figure it, it's one of two people. One is Salvatore Tartaro. First his guy Shawn's head wound up in the park, then Tony Silva's landed on a Dumpster. Now Silva gets set up to take the fall on this Lewinsky murder, and Tartaro goes underground, we don't know where."

"Maybe Tartaro is making sure he stays in a safe place until Silva is put away and peace breaks out. Or maybe Silva has already hit him; we won't know until we know. But Tartaro might stand to gain from Silva taking the fall."

"And the other possibility is Philly DeSimone?" Bradley asks.

"Exactly. It's no wonder they made you captain."

"Be careful," Bradley warns. "You may not remember what a prick I can be."

I nod. "Thanks for the reminder. But yes, Philly DeSimone. He's the number three man. Number two got his head chopped off, and now number one may go to prison. It's all working out pretty well for old Philly."

Nate asks, "With Lewinsky gone, the Silva family no longer has someone to get them the drugs. How does Philly gain by that?"

"Maybe he thinks it's done anyway. We're all over them, and we were all over Lewinsky."

"And the sixteenth?" Bradley asks.

"Unfortunately, that's where I run out of ideas. But I think we may have been making a mistake connecting whatever that is about with the drug dealing from the hospital supply. We connected the two because there is a Vegas connection to both, but maybe it's just an example of Tartaro and Silva working on two separate things."

"Okay," Bradley says. "You've convinced me. But I've got to share this with the chief."

"Will he overrule you?" Nate asks.

Bradley shakes his head. "He's better at complaining after the fact than making proactive decisions."

"What about Wiggins and the Feds?" I ask.

"I have to tell them about this, but Silva is our jurisdiction, not theirs."

"So we do nothing?" I ask.

Bradley stands up and nods. "So we do nothing."

I nod. "Good move."

The larger and more prominent the target,
the more careful everyone becomes.

WHEN SOMEONE LIKE JOEY SILVA GETS ARRESTED, ESPECIALLY
for murder, it's inevitably going to be a huge media story. So any
prosecutor who brings such a case is not going to do so unless he or
she is pretty damn certain they're going to win.

No young lawyer dreams of one day being just like Marcia
Clark or Christopher Darden.

Captain Bradley played the tape for his superior, and as Bradley predicted, the chief was not inclined to interfere with his decision not to make the arrest. Then Bradley brought Wiggins and the
FBI into the loop, and they also made no effort to get him to change
his mind.

What Bradley didn't know is that Wiggins did not try to convince Bradley because there was no reason to. He had already decided to nail Silva on drug and murder charges in Federal court, and
the tape would be a key piece of evidence. The Bureau would
claim jurisdiction by considering it a conspiracy that crossed state
lines . . . many state lines . . . all the way from Nevada to New Jersey.

Getting the Federal prosecutor to approve it would be an easy
maneuver, and Wiggins pulled it off with no problem. He never

mentioned the reservations that Bradley and his cops had; those were just theories and strategies, and in no way reflected the evidence.

Once the prosecutor approved Wiggins' request to arrest Joey Silva, then they moved into the planning stage. They knew it was highly unlikely that Silva would resist, but they would not take any chances. They decided to do it in public, specifically at Patrono's, an Italian restaurant Silva ate out at virtually every night. If he turned out not to be there that night, then they'd get him at home.

Wiggins sent an agent in plainclothes to the restaurant to sit at the bar and have a meal. He was a new guy, and certainly had never dealt with Joey, so they were certain he wouldn't be recognized. At seven o'clock, he texted Wiggins to say that Joey had shown up with his two bodyguards, and taken his regular corner table in the back.

Since Wiggins and other agents were waiting in cars within five blocks of the restaurant, it didn't take them long to get there. Wiggins and his partner pulled up first, leaving their car in front and going in. The two bodyguards were sitting near the door, and they stood up when they saw them. FBI agents as a rule are not hard to spot.

"Don't do anything stupid, boys," Wiggins said, and they walked toward Joey.

"Well, look who's here," Joey said. "Just in time to ruin my dinner."

"You're going to have to get it to go, Joey," Wiggins said.

"What the hell does that mean?"

"Here's the thing, Joey. You don't have the right to eat dinner, but you do have the right to remain silent. Anything you say can and will be used against you in . . ."

He interrupted. "What the hell are you doing? Are you arresting me?"

"Now you threw me off, Joey, just when I was on a roll," Wiggins said, and started again. "You have the right to remain silent . . ."

As Wiggins was reading, he saw that the bodyguards had taken steps toward him, but they backed off when the restaurant, as if by magic, filled with agents coming in from the front and back, ten of them. No one was going to take any chances with Joey Silva.

Wiggins finished reading Silva his rights, and another handcuffed him. As he was doing so, Joey asked, "What the hell are you charging me with?"

"Drug trafficking and the murder of Daniel Lewinsky," Wiggins said. "And that's just the opening serve."

"Daniel Lewinsky?" For a moment it seemed the name legitimately didn't register with him.

Then, when it finally did, he asked, "He's dead?"

I hear the news on the radio.

I'M ON THE WAY HOME, FOR ONE OF THE FEW NIGHTS IN RECENT weeks that I'm not staying at Jessie's. It was going to be a night of thinking about what our next move should be.

There aren't many details, just that the FBI executed an arrest warrant on Joey Silva at a restaurant while he was having dinner. The media is reporting that the arrest concerned drug charges and the murder of Daniel Lewinsky, an executive from Bergen Hospital.

I am sure that within minutes of Joey's arrival at the jail, he would have lawyered up. Joey Silva came out of the womb lawyered up. He wouldn't be answering questions, that's for sure, and I believe he will eventually be cleared, at least of the murder charge. But Joey will have a lot of time to remain silent. His arraignment will probably be tomorrow, and the judge will almost certainly deny bail, since one of the charges is murder.

All that the FBI will have accomplished is to do the bidding of whoever set Joey up, whoever really killed Daniel Lewinsky.

Within thirty seconds of the news coming on the radio, Nate calls me and asks, "Did you see what those assholes did?"

"Just now," I say. "We've got to go to Plan B."

"Let me know what that is. I didn't even know we had a Plan A."

As soon as I get off the phone, Bradley calls. He's pissed off, as he should be. "I should never have played Wiggins that tape," he says.

"You had to" is my reply, because he did. Information like that cannot be withheld.

"Yeah," he says, and hangs up.

While Joey is stewing in jail, we're going to have to be focusing our attention on everyone else. It's sort of like an inbounds play in basketball, when the defense covers everybody the person with the ball can throw it to, while leaving that person unguarded. He's standing out of bounds, so he can't hurt anybody. Sitting in prison, Joey is in the justice system version of out of bounds.

Having narrowed it down to Tartaro and Philly DeSimone as the possible beneficiaries of Joey's fall, that's who we're going to be paying attention to.

In Vegas, the job of watching Tartaro falls to Lieutenant Roberts, though his task is complicated by the fact that he has no idea where Tartaro is. He could be anywhere from the spa at the Palazzo to a makeshift grave out near Hoover Dam. I'm betting on the latter, since Tartaro didn't strike me as the hot stone massage type.

Back here, we are going to be all over Philly. We've gotten a warrant to surveil him electronically, and we'll have a tail on him wherever he goes.

So Nate and I need to get back to the nuts and bolts of the investigation, to keep digging until we manage to uncover something. It rarely gets us anywhere, but it certainly presents more opportunity for success than sitting on our asses and waiting for phone calls.

When I get home, I go through my notes and notice that I never heard back from Jessie on the cyber check she was supposed to do on Travis Mauer. Mauer is the guy, or non-guy as the case may be, that Mitchell Galvis used as an example of Lewinsky's drug thefts from the hospital.

Galvis gave me Mauer's hospital records, which showed that he had received a great many drugs in a fairly lengthy stay and post-op experience. The problem, according to Galvis, is that Mauer doesn't exist, and was never actually at the hospital.

If we're going to ultimately go to trial against Joey Silva or anyone else, we're going to need to lock all of this down. Galvis's word that Mauer doesn't exist will not be enough; we'll need to prove it to a prosecutor's and jury's satisfaction.

I call Jessie, and she says she's heavily into it and will have information for me tomorrow. She also says that she loves me, which means I get to end the day on a good note.

I don't sleep very well; I'm not sure if it's because of the case, or because Jessie isn't next to me. I've got a hunch that the reason might be missing Jessie, because I've been on the case for a while, yet haven't had sleeping problems at her house.

I get up in the morning and call Dr. Steven Cassel at his office. His assistant, the former SS officer known now as Helen, puts me right through. Since I know about Cassel's affair with Rita Carlisle, and since he knows that I know, he clearly has told Helen I'm to be given special courtesy.

She must hate that.

I tell Cassel that I am coming down to see him, and he doesn't put up any resistance. I bring copies of Mauer's records with me. Cassel is a major player at the hospital, so I can use him to get information and run interference.

"I expected to hear from you," Dr. Cassel says once I get into his office.

"Why?"

"With that horrible news about Daniel . . . Lewinsky . . . I assumed it must have had something to do with the work you're doing."

I don't say anything; I just start to open the envelope with Mauer's hospital records inside. He continues, "But they've caught the killer, right? That mob guy? I saw it on the news last night."

I ask, "Did I give you the impression that I was here to update you on the status of the investigation?"

He grins and says, "Sorry. It's simultaneously horrible and exciting. We deal with life and death around here every day, but not quite like this."

I nod and hand him the records. "Please take a look at these."

So he does so, page by page. He takes so long that I think he might be committing it to memory. Finally, he finishes and asks, "What about it?"

"You see anything unusual about those records?"

"Not on a first reading. Can you enlighten me on what I'm supposed to be looking for?"

"I'm told that Travis Mauer doesn't exist, that there is no such person. And obviously, if that's true, then those records are fakes."

He glances at a couple of pages again. "Then they would be elaborate fakes."

"I need you to confirm it for me."

"How?"

"Talk to the doctors and nurses that he's supposed to have seen. Find out from the kitchen if they served him meals. I don't know how this place works, but you do. You can figure it out."

He nods. "Okay. Can I be open about it? Can I say it's a police matter?"

"No. Make up a medical reason."

"I don't believe in lying, especially to people I care about," he says.

"You had an extramarital affair with a coworker, kept it secret from everyone including your wife, and you don't believe in lying to people you care about?"

"You're never going to let that go?" he asks.

"When all this is over, it will be wiped clean from my mind."

He considers this, and finally says, "Okay. I should be able to do it, but it may take a while. How much time do I have?"

"I need an answer by tomorrow."

He shakes his head. "You're a tough taskmaster, Lieutenant."

I nod. "It's part of my charm."

When I have some downtime on an investigation,
I make lists.

IN THIS CASE, THE DOWNTIME IS INVOLUNTARY; I JUST CAN'T think of anything else to do. So while I'm sitting here in my office, I might as well do the lists.

I do it in two columns. One column includes the things I know or think I know, and the other includes the things about which I don't have a clue.

The "things I know" list is unfortunately the shorter one, and I really don't pay much attention to it. It's the other list, the longer one of the things I'm in the dark about, that holds the answer to this case.

Most importantly, I don't know who has been committing these murders. Starting with Conner, then Tony Silva, and now Lewinsky, I feel like we're being led to believe that it's a mob war between Tartaro and Silva. But I just don't see why they would be fighting such a war, or what they'd have to gain from it.

I also don't know why Lewinsky would have been killed, since it likely ends the cash cow that the hospital drug flow represented. I don't think Silva did it, but whoever did was willing to cut off the drug supply. It's unlikely that Lewinsky was killed because he was turning himself in, because he had no reason to turn himself in. Ranes hadn't even talked to him yet, so Lewinsky should not have been afraid he'd be arrested.

What could the FBI's view that they had a possible terrorist case have to do with any of this?

Why would a homeless murder victim like William Simmons be something that Lewinsky and Silva would be concerned about three years later?

Where is Salvatore Tartaro?

Why did Shawn bring me into this investigation in the first place? What would anyone have to gain by our reopening the Carlisle investigation?

And maybe most important of all, what happened to Rita Carlisle, and why did it happen?

Reading this list and realizing how little I know at least leads me to one key decision; I'm going to stop making lists. It's too depressing.

Nate and Jessie come into the room, walking quickly as if something significant has happened. "We are in the presence of a genius," Nate says.

I shrug. "Thank you."

"I didn't mean you, asshole. I meant Jessie."

"I sensed that. What's going on?"

"You tell him," Nate says, and Jessie nods.

"I looked at the hospital records for Travis Mauer, the patient at Bergen that Galvis said was an example of Lewinsky's stealing the drugs. He said Mauer didn't exist, remember?"

I nod. "Yes, that's one of the things I remember." I've got to stop being so sensitive about memory comments; Jessie didn't mean anything by it.

"So he had an address, phone number, insurance information . . . all of that was faked. No such person."

"That's what Galvis said."

"Every patient has to list someone to be notified in the event of an emergency, and in the Mauer file it was a woman named Cynthia Crowder. There was an address for her in Garfield that was a fake as well. No one who is there has ever heard of Cynthia Crowder."

"So what's the big discovery?"

"The phone number for her had an area code for Des Moines, Iowa. It's a real number, but it's not listed to Cynthia Crowder; it's listed to Eileen Manningham. It struck me as strange that if Lewinsky was going to fake a New Jersey address he would use a Des Moines number, and a real one at that. I mean, where would that come from?"

I nod. "Definitely strange."

"Right," Jessie says. "So I called Ms. Manningham and asked her about it. She told me that Travis Mauer is her brother-in-law, and lives about a mile from her in Des Moines. And get this; he was visiting friends in New Jersey when he fell and hurt his back. He aggravated herniated disks."

"And they treated him at Bergen Hospital."

"You're not as dumb as you look," Nate says, jumping in to pick up the story. "So when Jessie told me about this, I called Mr. Mauer, with the medical records in front of me. Nice guy, had great things to say about the hospital, and he confirmed everything in the records. He even thinks the listing of drugs that they gave him is accurate."

"So the guy is real in every respect, except for his personal contact information?"

"Yes," Jessie says. "Apparently Lewinsky, or whoever, forgot to change that one phone number when he was changing the contact information."

Nate jumps in. "Which brings us to the question, why would Lewinsky fake records to steal drugs, if the patient actually got those drugs?"

"He didn't," I say.

"He didn't get the drugs?"

"No, he got the drugs. Lewinsky didn't fake the records."

"Somebody did, or at least they faked the contact information," Jessie points out.

I nod. "Right. But it couldn't have been Lewinsky. He had nothing to gain from doing so. The only reason to conceal Mauer as a patient would have been to pretend that he got all those drugs, when they really went to Silva. But there were no drugs to go to Silva, because they went to Mauer."

"So who changed the records?"

"My money's on Mitchell Galvis."

> While my money may be on Galvis,
> I'm not betting a lot on it.

IT IS CLEARLY SUSPICIOUS THAT GALVIS TOLD ME MAUER DIDN'T exist and was not a patient at Bergen, when in fact the opposite has been shown to be the case. But there are other conclusions to be considered before I jump to the one that makes him a bad guy.

Galvis said that Lewinsky faked Mauer's existence, and there remains the chance that he at least changed Mauer's identity in the hospital system. I don't know what he would have to gain from doing so, but there's plenty I don't know.

Maybe Galvis was wrong. Maybe there was some kind of administrative foul-up that confused Mauer's contact information with someone else, an innocent error that led Galvis to believe it was evidence of Lewinsky's drug maneuverings.

Then there is always the chance that Galvis faked the information himself, simply to provide me with the information I was asking for. He could have known that Lewinsky was dirty, and therefore might have felt that by making this up, he was serving the greater good. It would also have served the purpose of getting me off his back, something he seemed like he wanted to do.

To take a more negative view of Galvis, which is to say that he is the actual drug conspirator and was simply setting up Lewinsky to take the fall, presents some problems. When Lewinsky left our office after we brought him in for questioning, he spoke to Silva on the phone.

It's incriminating enough that Lewinsky spoke to Silva at all, but the fact is that they talked about the drugs. In my eyes that represents obvious proof that Lewinsky was dirty, so in pointing it out, Galvis was absolutely correct.

To make it even more negative, at least in terms of Galvis, it was Silva who placed the call. He already knew about Lewinsky's meeting with us, and even knew what had been discussed. Lewinsky must have told someone, and since we had his phones covered, it had to have been in person, at the hospital. Galvis is obviously the most likely, in fact the only, candidate for that confidence. And whoever Lewinsky told, that person must have called Silva and alerted him. I should have realized this earlier.

Could Galvis and Lewinsky have been coconspirators with Silva, and Galvis was trying to push Lewinsky out so he could take over by himself? That doesn't seem possible, because in alerting us to what Lewinsky was doing, Galvis was guaranteeing that the drug conspiracy would come to an end. Why would he go out of his way to take over an operation, if the act of taking it over rendered the operation defunct?

But the fact is, it is proving to be dangerous to be at the top of this investigation's totem poles. Joey Silva was at the top of his organization, and he's in jail. Tony Silva was second, and he's dead. Salvatore Tartaro was in charge, and he's gone. Lewinsky was the head of his area of the hospital, and he's currently residing on a slab.

Is it "revenge of the underlings," or just a coincidence? And does it matter at this point?

So my money is on Galvis, but I'm not giving odds on it.

There is one name that keeps bugging me:
William Simmons.

HERE'S A GUY WHO WAS HOMELESS, HAD NO MONEY, HAD ABAN-doned his friends and loved ones, and who had, himself, been abandoned by society. He was as close as a human being could be to being of no consequence to anyone, probably not even himself.

So why were Joey Silva and Daniel Lewinsky discussing his apparently random murder years later? What could they have possibly been concerned about?

I kick it around with Nate, and we come up with a plan of attack. He's going to dig into the possibility that Simmons might be representative of a larger group of victims. He'll check into whether other people that fit Simmons' profile were brought to Bergen Hospital; maybe we can make some sense of it that way.

One angle I haven't really looked at is Simmons' work life. He owned an insurance agency, which has some possible significance because insurance is all about money. Sometimes big money. The type of money that could interest Joey Silva.

Jessie finds out for me that the Simmons Insurance Agency still exists; it had been taken over by the insurance companies themselves, and eventually sold to a man named Ben Wilkinson.

I call Mr. Wilkinson, identify myself, and tell him I want to come talk to him. I guess the call is routed to him, because he says he's out in the field, which I assume means anywhere other than his office. He asks if it can wait until tomorrow, and I say no, so he agrees to see me at his office at two o'clock. I'm a tough guy to say no to.

My next call is to Agent Wiggins of the FBI, and I tell him I want to come down to see him as well. He'd find it easier to say no to me, but he doesn't. He says he can give me ten minutes, if I come right down.

So I've got a couple of meetings set for today, which has become my version of activity. I feel like I'm not getting anywhere, like I'm just trying to fill my day. This is how I'll be when I'm retired, maybe in Florida in a community with my fellow elderly people. Busy day today . . . shuffleboard in the morning, and then taking the tram to the market to buy fruit in the afternoon. And then some much-needed rest.

I think my old self may be returning, because rather than talking to people, I'd rather be punching and shooting them. I just wish I knew who to punch and shoot.

Wiggins is at the Bureau's Newark office, about a half-hour drive for me. I'm brought in to see him as soon as I arrive; his office isn't any nicer than mine. He stands when I come in and shakes my hand, and looks at his watch before he sits back down, a silent message that the ten minutes starts now, and I'm on the clock.

"I need some help," I say. "I need to know if you have any information on a man named William Simmons."

His face doesn't register any familiarity with the name. "Who might that be?"

So I tell him the story of William Simmons, or at least as much as I know about him. When I conclude, I say, "Silva and Lewinsky were talking about him, years after his death. They weren't reminiscing about an old high school buddy. It wasn't, 'Hey, do you remember who Billy Simmons took to the prom?' He was important to them."

"So what do you want from me?"

"To help me figure out why. To go through every database you have to see if anything pops up."

"Okay; I'll get it done. Is that it?" I'm sure he's wondering why I didn't just ask him this one over the phone, but I have another request.

"Almost. You can also tell me why you're so interested in what we're doing."

"What gave you that impression?" he asks.

"You've been hovering over this from day one. You called Bradley when Shawn got killed. You came to see us and told us about the courier. You've been in touch with Roberts in Vegas a bunch of times, trying to stay on top of what he's doing. You arrested Joey Silva when it should have been our call, and we didn't want to. Why are you so interested in a drug case? You're not wearing a DEA windbreaker."

He doesn't answer right away, and I suspect the decision he's making is between saying something truthful and throwing me out. Finally, he says, "I don't give a shit about your drug case, if that's even what it is."

"So what do you care about?"

"That courier I told you about; he wasn't just a normal courier. He didn't just do drop-offs, or make pickups. He was an expert in munitions; this guy could take a jar of peanut butter and some Krazy Glue and blow up Nebraska."

"But he's dead," I say.

"Yeah, but he was also the guy who would be sent to educate, to tell whoever was receiving the goods exactly how to employ them. And we know that he had a plane ticket; he was going to LAX. Which means he had already done what he set out to do."

He continues. "And there is one other thing; when he was taken out of that car wreck, he had a million five in cash."

"Shit," I say.

He nods. "Exactly. He didn't get paid that money for nothing. He brought the goods, and he showed them how to use them. And that's what they're going to do; they didn't pay a million five to use those devices as paperweights."

"Let me ask you this. Is there a technical way they go about it? How would something be detonated? Remotely?"

He nods. "Almost certainly. A simple call to a cell phone number on the device."

"Why did you arrest Joey Silva?"

"We wanted to pressure him and offer him a deal; all he had to do was tell us what was going to happen, and how we could stop it. We told him what would happen to him if he didn't go along."

"What happened?"

"We made him the offer, one so good that he couldn't possibly turn it down. Essentially he'd have immunity for every awful thing he's done in his life, and that covers a lot of ground. Just tell us about the explosives. And he turned it down."

"Why would he do that?"

"Because, and this is just my opinion, so I could be wrong . . . he didn't know what the hell we were talking about."

The SIMMONS INSURANCE AGENCY sign seems a strange homage to a forgotten murder victim.

IT MAKES IT SEEM AS IF WILLIAM SIMMONS, TOTALLY FORGOT-ten in life, lives on through this business. I doubt he would be impressed or touched.

The agency occupies a small office on Lemoine Avenue in Fort Lee, and currently has a SORRY, WE'RE OUT sign on the front door. I peer in, though, and I see a man sitting behind the desk. He sees me as well, then waves and gets up to open the door.

"Mr. Wilkinson?"

He nods. "Yes. Come on in."

"I'm Lieutenant Brock, I . . ."

He nods. "I know. I recognized you from television. Have a seat."

I sit down and accept his offer of a Diet Coke. "So you purchased this agency from William Simmons?"

He shakes his head. "No. A group of insurance companies had ownership after Mr. Simmons left. I have two other agencies down near Matawan, and wanted to expand into this area." He smiles. "Bergen County is where the money is."

"So you bought it from them?"

"I did. Two of those companies retain part ownership . . . fifteen percent each."

"Did you ever meet Mr. Simmons?"

Another shake of the head. "No. I'm embarrassed to say that I didn't even know what happened to him until about an hour ago. When you said you wanted to talk about him, I Googled his name. Terrible situation."

"But you didn't change the name of the business. Why?"

"Just for continuity's sake. His customers knew that name. Very often, when you sell someone a policy, especially life insurance, you don't hear from them for a very long time. I mean, until someone dies, there's no reason, right? So people knew that name, and if they ever needed to contact us, that would make it easier for them to find us."

"Would most of his clients have had a personal relationship with him?"

He shrugs. "Some, probably not most. But keep in mind, when I got the place, he had been out of it for a long while. The insurance companies were running it."

"So what I want to know is whether you have ever noticed any unusual activity on accounts that carried over from his day."

"Unusual activity?"

"Yes. Significant payouts, more of them than you'd expect, something like that. Anything ever happen that caused you to take notice, something out of the ordinary?"

He thinks for a moment. "No, I don't think so. I could run the numbers now, but if anything I think there's been less than my other offices. Insurance is a numbers business; if there was anything unusual it would stand out. But definitely nothing that has caused me to take notice."

I ask more questions, but I'm basically floundering in the dark and not getting anywhere. Wilkinson is far removed from William

Simmons, and though he inherited many of his clients, he's not noticed anything unusual about any of them.

I've accomplished absolutely nothing except filling up my day.

I check my voice mails, and there's a message from Nate telling me to come back to the office, that we "have something to talk about."

I would rather he said we have someone to shoot.

So I do as I'm told and head back to the office. Nate wastes no time, and starts by saying, "There were one thousand, one hundred and fourteen murders in New Jersey in the last three years."

"Have we solved any of them?"

"I have," he says. "You, not so much. But overall, forty-eight percent went unsolved. A total of five hundred thirty-four."

"Okay."

"Of the unsolved ones, eighty-one were in Bergen County."

"Seems high," I say, since Bergen is one of the more upscale counties in the state. There is very little gang violence, which can normally account for a high murder rate.

He nods. "It is. Bergen County has about ten percent of the population of the state, but fifteen percent of the unsolved murders."

The numbers he's quoting are surprising but not shocking. Hopefully, this is not just a statistics class, and he's going to get somewhere. "You approaching a point?" I ask.

"Stay with me. Bergen Hospital is one of six in the county, but half the victims in the unsolved murders were brought there. It's the largest hospital, but not by that much."

"I'm not following," I say, because I'm not.

"What if they were using these victims' presence at the hospital to fake drug orders? We get their records, and maybe we find out that they were using their identities as part of the fraud."

I shake my head. "We saw Simmons' records, and that didn't happen with him."

"But maybe he was the exception. Maybe something stood out about him, which made using him impossible. Maybe someone noticed something, which is why Lewinsky and Silva remembered him."

He pauses, and says, "Maybe Rita Carlisle noticed something."

Maybe she did.

In order to test Nate's theory, we'll need the hospital records of the victims.

THAT PRESENTS SOME PROBLEMS. WE COULD GET A SUBPOENA, but that would take a while, and would impact our ability to do it quietly. I can't go to Galvis, who has moved into Lewinsky's job at least on an interim basis, because he is very much under suspicion since Travis Mauer turned out to be real.

So it's back to the well that is Dr. Steven Cassel. He will resist and complain, but he'll do what I want, because he knows that I know about his affair with Rita Carlisle. I would feel guilty about taking advantage of him this way, if I were the "feel guilty" type. I'm not, and I doubt that I ever was.

He just about moans when I show up at his office, even though I had called and said I was on my way. "You're taking advantage of me, Lieutenant."

I nod. "I wasn't sure you noticed."

"Oh, I noticed. What is it now?"

I hand him the list of murder victims that were first brought to Bergen Hospital, more than forty people. Some were DOA, but many were not, although if Nate's theory is right, that shouldn't matter. It's their names and identities that were utilized.

He looks at the list briefly and asks, "What is this?"

I tell him what it is, and ask if the names are familiar to him.

"No, but that's not surprising. Most of this is handled in the emergency room; I'm only called in if specific surgery is called for. I may well have operated on a few of them, but I also may not ever have known their names, other than to see them on a chart."

"I need their hospital records."

He laughs at the ridiculousness of the request. "You do? All of them?"

"Yes. Humorous as it may seem to you."

"Come on, Lieutenant, this is crazy. I'm not in charge of records. Why don't you just ask Mitchell Galvis, and he'll tell the relevant departments to get them for you."

"I don't want to do that."

He reacts with surprise. "Are you telling me you don't trust Mitchell Galvis?"

"I'm not telling you anything. I'm asking you to do this. You've been here a long time; you must have friends in the records department, or whatever it's called. You can do it, and you can do it quietly."

"This will not be nearly as easy as you describe."

"Which is why they pay you the big bucks," I say.

"I never imagined that when I committed my indiscretion that someday I would be blackmailed by a state police officer."

"Yet here we are. Life works in mysterious ways."

He sighs. "I'll do what I can."

"And as quickly as you can," I say, starting to get up.

"When you came in I was hoping you were just going to ask me about Travis Mauer. I did not expect a new assignment."

I had forgotten that I had given him Mauer's records and asked him to find out if in fact Mauer was fictitious, and did not exist. Now that we have learned through Jessie that Mauer was real, I didn't think to follow up.

"What did you find out about Mauer?" I ask.

"I checked with the doctors and nurses that were listed on his records," he says. "And you were right."

"What does that mean?"

He shakes his head. "The guy was never here. No such patient."

Holy shit.

Dr. Steven Cassel lied to me.

THERE CAN'T BE ANY QUESTION ABOUT THAT. IT IS INCONCEIV-
able that he went to the doctors and nurses that treated Travis
Mauer for an extended period of time, only to have them tell him
that Mauer was never there. He was there, and they would know it.

Like everything else in this case, though, there are a number of
possible meanings to Cassel's lie. The most innocent version is that
he never checked with those people at all; that he got busy and just
went with what I had told him I believed in the first place.

The more likely interpretation is that Cassel is dirty, that he was
Lewinsky's coconspirator in the drug operation, that he was the
person Lewinsky told about his questioning by us, that he was the
person who alerted Joey Silva to it, and that he was involved with
getting Lewinsky killed.

All this time we thought it was Galvis, and it could be him as
well, though I would think it is unlikely that a conspiracy would
have that many pieces. There are law firms with less partners than
that. My guess is that Cassel told Galvis that Mauer was fake, and
Galvis just fed it back to me.

The other damning fact is that Rita Carlisle was having an

affair with Cassel, so it makes sense that she learned what was going on from him, perhaps by accident. Either way, she paid for it with her life.

At this point I can't trust either one of them, but if only one of them is guilty, I think it's Cassel.

I call Nate and Jessie and tell them what I've learned, and I direct them to get a warrant so that we can electronically surveil Cassel. At this point we have surveillance on half the citizens of New Jersey, but we don't really have a choice.

I also tell them to get an urgent subpoena for the records of the murder victims on the list I gave to Cassel. I didn't let on to him that I no longer trust him to get it for me, because I obviously didn't want him to think he's under suspicion.

But there is no longer an option to get the records quietly. If Nate is right, then a murder victim is an opening for drug records to be faked, and drugs to be stolen. And an explosion in a crowded place would be an ideal way to accumulate a lot of victims at once.

There is no time to waste. Today is the fourteenth.

We're two days away.

The warrant for the surveillance of Cassel
is gotten quickly.

MORE IMPORTANTLY, BRADLEY GETS A JUDGE'S ORDER TO EXPE-
dite the retrieval of the hospital records on an emergency basis, and
hospital administrative employees are served first thing in the
morning and ordered to immediately get those records.

I'm sure that Galvis, and probably Cassel, are aware, or about
to be aware, of what we've done. That's unfortunate, but at this
point there's nothing we can do about it. There is simply no way to
get the information without attracting attention.

Much to my surprise, I get a call from Mitchell Galvis shortly
after the subpoena is served. "What the hell is going on?" he asks.

"You want to rephrase the question?"

"A bunch of storm troopers came in here this morning, demanding my people drop everything and get records of hospital
patients, some of them two and three years old."

"So?"

"So why is this happening?"

"Because I want records of hospital patients, some of them two
and three years old. And I want your people to drop everything and
get them for me. Which part didn't you understand?"

"I thought we had a working relationship, Lieutenant. Rather than causing this kind of chaos here, you could have come to me."

"Yes, I could have, but I didn't."

"Well, I don't like it or appreciate it," he says.

If Galvis is one of the drug conspirators, then he is giving an Academy Award performance on this call. And I have to respect it; instead of curling up in a panic, he's taking the offensive.

"Let me ask you a question. You told me that Travis Mauer was never really a patient at your hospital, that he never really existed. Where did you get that information? Did you track it down yourself?"

He hesitates. "No. Someone told it to me."

"Who might that be?" I ask.

"I'm not sure I should share that with you." His tone has gone from aggressive to worried and unsure.

"Here's the thing, Mr. Galvis. If you don't share it with me, the next thing you're going to share is a jail cell." It's an empty threat, at least at this point, but I'm hoping it will intimidate him.

"Is the information not accurate?" he asks, possibly stalling for time.

"Who told it to you, Mr. Galvis?"

"It was told in confidence."

"This is the last time I'm going to ask. Who told it to you?"

"Our head of surgery. Dr. Steven Cassel."

All we can do now is wait for the records.

IF THEY CONFIRM NATE'S THEORY, THEN WE'LL ARREST A BUNCH of people, Cassel and Philly DeSimone at the top of the list. Many of the arrests won't stick, but we'll at least be able to keep them in jail tomorrow. And for what it's worth, tomorrow is the sixteenth.

We've sent a couple of officers over to the hospital to make sure proper attention is being paid to the collection of the records, and they confirm that it is. The age of some of them, and the sheer volume of hospital records in general, makes it a difficult and time-consuming task, even though they're electronic.

The subpoena provided for a 6:00 P.M. deadline, and the word comes in that they'll be able to meet it. Bradley orders a bunch of officers to stay around to help Jessie, Nate, and me go through it. He's pulling out all the stops, not all of them conventional. For example, he has a brother-in-law who's a doctor, and he brings him in as well, to help with the technical stuff.

They beat the six o'clock deadline by fifteen minutes, and it takes another half hour to print out copies for those of us who don't want to view them on the computer. Then we all dive into it, and about ninety minutes later we have the answer.

We were wrong.

There is absolutely no evidence that the victim's names were in any way used to serve as recipients for drugs that were never dispensed. On the contrary; they received very few.

There is a palpable feeling of depression in the room; we had high hopes for this one, and they were completely unjustified. It's possible that all the records were faked to conceal a fraud, at some point in the past, but I don't think any of us really believe it. In any event, we couldn't come close to proving it even if it were true.

Nate's response sums it up best. "Shit," he says.

The group breaks up and Jessie and I head to her house. I'm driving, but I have to admit that I'm pretty much lost in thought, and not paying the attention that I should be.

The flashing red lights on the car behind us make me somewhat more attentive. I pull over so that the cop can come and tell me exactly what it is I did wrong. Just what I'm in the mood for now.

The local cop comes up to the window and says, "Do you realize you went through a stop sign a couple of blocks back?"

"No, officer, I didn't see it," I say.

He looks carefully at me, trying to make out my face in the dim light. Finally, he says, "You're Doug Brock."

I nod. "I'm aware of that."

"I really admire what you did," he says, and I don't think he's talking about my missing the stop sign. "My name is Ted Rizzo."

"Nice to meet you, Ted. This is Jessie Allen."

Jessie and Ted exchange hellos. This is going on a bit longer than I am in the mood for.

Ted smiles. "I guess I'll let you off with a warning. Try and see the stop signs next time."

"Thanks, Ted, I will. Have a good night."

I wake up at three o'clock in the morning and can't seem to get back to sleep. Instead I play the entire day over again in my mind, including the fiasco with the hospital records, right up to my getting stopped for not seeing the stop sign.

And then I sit up in bed and yell, out loud even though Jessie is sleeping, "Holy shit!"

When you're a cop, your office is always open.

WE HAVE TO KEEP THE SAME HOURS AS THE WORLD AT LARGE, which is twenty-four/seven.

For some reason, my yelling "Holy shit!" in the middle of the night has woken Jessie, and by the time she can ask me what is wrong, I'm already up and getting dressed.

"I think I know what's going on," I say.

"Going on where?"

"With the case. At the hospital. I can't wait until morning to find out."

"What is it?"

"I don't want to say; not until I know for sure. I'm going down to the station."

"I'm going with you."

I'm dressed before Jessie, only because I have a head start. Bobo seems not to be impressed by the activity; I saw him open one enormous eye and then go back to sleep.

Before we leave I call Nate, who answers on the first ring. "What's wrong?"

I can tell that his mouth is full. "Middle of the night snack?" I ask.

"Just tell me what's wrong."

"Get your ass down to the station. I think I figured out what's going on."

I hang up, rather than wait for him to berate me and threaten me with death if I'm wasting his time. His curiosity will get him down there without me having to say anything else.

On the way I toss the possibilities around in my head, and it all makes sense. Horrible sense. Then I ask Jessie, "When was the last time you renewed your driver's license?"

"Last year. I remember, because I hate the picture."

"Did you take an eye test?"

"Of course."

We get to the station and I quickly take out the case files and look through them for what I need. Whether or not it's there, I know I'm right, but it would be nice to have confirmation.

I find it just as Nate is walking in. "This better be good," he says. "I don't know why you couldn't tell me on the damn phone."

"He hasn't told me, either," Jessie says. "And I was sleeping next to him."

I take the piece of paper out of the file and hand it to them. "Look at this," I say, and they do so together.

"So?" Jessie asks.

"Holy shit," Nate says, understanding where I'm going.

I nod. "You took the words right out of my mouth."

Jessie is frustrated. "Will someone please tell me what is going on?"

"As you can see, that is a copy of William Simmons' driver's license. He couldn't see five feet in front of his face. His medical records say that and his daughter said the same thing."

"So?"

"So according to the date on that license, it was issued three months before he died. He had no money, no home, certainly no car . . . so he went to get a driver's license? And they said fine, even though he couldn't see well enough to sign his name to the application?"

"I understand that is strange, maybe impossible, but . . ."

"Read the license, Jessie. Read everything on it."

So she does, slowly and carefully, to herself. Then she says, "Oh my God, he was an organ donor."

"Bingo. William Simmons was killed for his organs. They are harvesting human organs."

"Holy shit," Jessie says.

Jessie gets on the internet, which fortunately is also open twenty-four/ seven.

THE STATISTICS FOR ORGAN PRICES ON THE BLACK MARKET are stunning, as are the number of organs in the human body subject to transplant. There are stories about people dying and legally helping fifty people with their donated body parts.

In addition to heart, kidneys, lungs, and livers, the ones I thought obvious, we discover that things like eyes, tissue, stem cells, bone marrow, and much more are also valuable and in demand.

The black market is apparently worldwide, operating in the shadows and fueled by enormous amounts of money. It would seem, based on what she finds, that one person's intact organs could be worth well over a million dollars.

It's a world I knew very little about, and when this case is over, it will go on the short list of things I wish my amnesia would let me forget.

I have to assume that William Simmons' driver's license is a fake, though we have no opportunity to assess that right now. We don't even have the original, just a copy, and while it looks legitimate, I don't see how it can be.

Simmons would not have sought a license, and he would not

have been given one if he did. I assume that the licenses were forged after the fact to cover the hospital's actions.

At this point, we can't know the extent of the criminality. Was Simmons murdered simply to get his organs, or did the conspirators merely take advantage of a situation they did not create?

And if he was murdered for his organs, how many other similar victims were there? How many people were killed so that their body parts could be harvested?

I'm assuming there were also others, not necessarily murder victims, who had their organs taken, probably without the family's knowledge. Would every family member even know whether their deceased loved one meant to donate their organs? Would they think to question it?

And is this all doubled, meaning it is going on in Las Vegas as well? Are people at Harriman Hospital complicit, as they obviously are at Bergen?

Is that why this was a combination Tartaro/Silva operation? Is it because they're operating worldwide, and Tartaro was responsible for the western half of the country and Asia, while Silva covered the east and Europe?

Most importantly, and most horrifyingly, is the terrorist event possibly scheduled for today designed to accumulate victims so that their organs can be taken? Is it literally meant to be one last, huge killing?

These are all questions we need to answer, and answer as soon as possible. But one thing is very clear; we're going to need to act before we have all those answers.

Now.

"We need to get Bradley in here," I say.

Sometimes you just know when you're right.
You can feel it in your gut.

I KNOW WE'RE RIGHT ABOUT WHAT'S BEEN GOING ON AT THE hospital; it checks all the boxes. Nate and Jessie know it as well; even though this has been a case filled with maybes and what-ifs, they haven't pushed back on the theory at all.

I expect more resistance from Bradley, and I'm relieved when we don't get it. He doesn't even complain about having to come to the office at five o'clock in the morning, since he knows we wouldn't dare call him in if it wasn't tremendously important.

So he listens to a straight recitation of where we are and what we think. There's a lot to update him on; for example, we hadn't had a chance to tell him that Dr. Cassel lied about checking out Travis Mauer. But when I drop the bomb on him about the organ harvesting, he doesn't flinch.

"You guys nailed it," he says, when I'm done.

Nate asks, "So is Galvis bad, or just Cassel?"

"I don't know," I say. "But at this point it doesn't matter. We need to stop what might happen, and sort it out later. If I'm right, there is going to be an explosion today. Two in fact, one here and one in Vegas."

"But we don't have any idea where," Jessie points out.

"That's not entirely true. We have some idea. It's going to be where there are a lot of people, but more importantly, it will happen in a place where most of the victims will be taken to Bergen Hospital. We can figure out that radius."

"It's Saturday; it has to be a shopping center or a movie theater. There aren't any concert facilities or sports arenas near Bergen," Nate says. "And we don't even know what time it might happen."

"If it's a shopping center, then some time around midday. If it's a movie theater, then at night."

"First thing we need to do is alert security in every possible place," Bradley says. "And we have to call in Wiggins and the FBI. They have the resources, and they can bring in the ATF. Bomb squads will be crucial."

I shake my head. "I agree with all of that, but it's not enough. We'd be depending on luck, and that's way too big a chance to take. And we'd have to get lucky twice; here and in Vegas. Not going to happen."

"You got any better ideas?" Bradley asks; a well-timed question, because I think I do.

"Yeah. Wiggins told me that the explosives that courier would use would be triggered by a cell phone call, that the devices themselves would have cell numbers to be activated remotely with a phone call. So we shut down the cell towers."

"Shut down all the cell towers in North Jersey?" Bradley asks.

"Every one that could provide service to the radius that Bergen Hospital covers. I don't know how many there are, but there must be a lot of them. Shutting them down is our only way to ensure the device doesn't go off."

"Different companies own different towers," Nate says. "We have no way of knowing which provider would be the one on the device."

"That's why we have to get them all," I say, and then I turn to

Bradley. "Wiggins needs to do this, because it has to be a Federal judge, and it needs to be done immediately. Each provider is going to have to be served an order on an emergency basis. It should cover the Bergen County radius, and the service radius for Harriman Hospital in Vegas. If a tower reaches the edge of the radius, they should opt to be overly careful and shut it down."

"This is a huge ask," Bradley says. "We know we're right, but to get a judge to issue an order like this...I don't think we have enough hard evidence."

"You've got to convince Wiggins, and he needs to convince the judge. Make sure they realize that whoever says no is going to have a lot of blood on their hands."

All we can do now is wait.

I REMEMBER ENOUGH ABOUT THE OLD ME TO KNOW THAT I HAVE never been good at waiting. My jaw starts to clench, and then it spreads to the rest of my body, until it feels like I am going to explode. It's not the most pleasant of feelings.

This waiting is going to be in two parts, and that's in a best case. First of all, Bradley has secured a 7:00 A.M. meeting with Wiggins by triggering some kind of Homeland Security emergency alert procedure. He will be trying to get Wiggins to go after a court order to shut down all the cell towers. So we have to wait and see how that goes.

I can't imagine that Wiggins can make the call by himself, but assuming he wants to and can get the needed approvals, then they have to go to a judge to get the order issued. Which means more waiting.

I'd feel better if this approach was likely to succeed, but it isn't. It's going to be a very heavy lift to get Wiggins and the judge to go along; we really don't have that good a case to make.

It's almost eight o'clock, which means that Bradley has been gone for more than two hours. Nate and I have been just sitting and basically doing nothing; we've insulted each other a couple of times, but our heart really hasn't been in it.

Jessie's been on the computer doing whatever it is that Jessie does on the computer. But she's using the computer in my office rather than hers, because she wants to be here when Bradley gets back and gives us the news.

I called Lieutenant Roberts on his cell phone at 3:00 A.M. Vegas time to update him on what was going on. He answered the phone sounding completely awake despite the time, which is very definitely a cop thing, and possibly a Vegas thing as well.

I don't know if he thinks that we're right or not, but he certainly didn't dismiss it out of hand. He's going to wait along with us to find out whether we can get a judge to issue the order, since it would cover Vegas as well.

With Harriman being so close to the Strip, his list of potential targets is considerably larger than ours. Every hotel, every casino, is a potential disaster waiting to happen, triggered by a simple cell phone call.

Bradley finally returns and comes straight to my office, where we've been hanging out. "Good news and bad news," he says, and we just wait to hear it.

"The good news is that the Bureau will seek the court order, and in the meantime they will figure out what to do if they get it, meaning who to deliver it to, and how to do it quickly. He thinks it can all be done electronically."

"And the bad?" Nate asks.

"He thinks we're probably wrong, but doesn't want to take the chance that we might be right. But neither he nor the people he works for thinks we'll get the judge to go along."

"Why?"

"A bunch of reasons. It will cause very significant public disruption, and if the reason for it gets out, a good amount of panic. And except for Lewinsky's brief mention of the sixteenth, there's no solid information that today is the day. They can't keep those towers down forever."

"What else?"

"There's too much hunch involved without any real evidence that this organ thing is happening. They were not terribly impressed with the fact that William Simmons had a driver's license, even if it turns out to be a fake.

"And the last thing, as if all the rest wasn't enough, is that even if we're right about everything . . . the motive and the timing . . . we still have only a small chance of preventing it. Because if we shut down the cell service, then they pull the device, and do it tomorrow. Or next week. Or the week after that."

I don't necessarily agree with all that he is saying, but there's no use arguing the point. All he is doing is quoting Wiggins, so convincing him won't accomplish anything. Now if I could talk to the judge, that might be a different story. But that's not going to happen.

"We need to come up with a plan in case we get shot down," I say.

Bradley nods and says, as he's leaving the room, "Let me know when you have one."

I come up with a couple of ideas, both pretty weak.

IF THE JUDGE REFUSES TO ISSUE THE ORDER, I CAN TAKE ADVAN- tage of the celebrity and credibility I have and go public. I can warn people about what I think might happen, and warn them to stay away from the areas that are possible targets.

I can even berate the justice system for not intervening to protect the public, and hopefully shame them into doing something. I have no doubt that the TV networks would cover whatever I had to say about this. I'm a citizen, and as such I have the right to speak out, and the platform to do it from.

Of course, as a member of the police department, I have no such right. I'd probably get fired, especially if my dire warning turns out to be a false alarm.

The greater negative is similar to the one Wiggins voiced; all it would do is make the bad guys retrench and delay their attack. They don't have any time pressure, or at least none that I know of. So it would appear that I was wrong, and if I tried to go back to the well when the threat once again became imminent, no one would listen.

The other possible strategy I've come up with would be to find Philly DeSimone, take him into a room, and pound the shit out of him until he talked. I could find him easily, since we have had a tail on him for a while. The "pounding the shit" part is more problematic; I would be fired, arrested, and probably imprisoned. And it might not even work.

But it would be fun.

I'm alone in my office having these fantasies, when the door opens. I'm hoping it's Bradley with news, but it's not: it's Nate. "I just thought of something that makes me even surer that we're right," he says.

"Let's hear it."

"It's pretty disgusting."

"Nate . . ."

"Okay. We thought that Shawn and Tony Silva got their heads cut off because the killers were sending a message. But . . ."

I interrupt, because I've realized where he's going. "They were using the organs. If they were going to kill reasonably young, healthy people, why let the organs go to waste?"

"I told you it was disgusting," Nate says.

I nod. "And remember that the coroner admired the cut? He said it was clean, almost surgical. Said he couldn't have done a better job himself."

"Dr. Cassel," Nate says. Then, "Can you imagine that somebody might have paid money for Tony Silva's heart? I didn't even know he had one, but if he did, then whoever got it was ripped off."

It's almost nine thirty, and we still haven't heard a decision. Wiggins called Bradley a while ago to tell him that the petition was filed with the court, and it was now out of his hands. According to Bradley, he didn't sound optimistic.

It's been six and a half hours since I woke up in bed with the realization of what I think has been going on. It feels like a month.

And still we wait.

Ever since Joey Silva went to jail, Philly DeSimone has been heavily guarded.

PART OF IT IS JUST BEING SMART AND CAREFUL; A PERSON IN Philly's new position never knows when someone might take a shot at him. Certainly there are enough people Philly has wronged in his life. And while Joey doesn't seem to realize that Philly is responsible for his current plight, Philly can't be quite sure of that.

The other part is that Philly has an interest in it appearing that he is in danger, since from the beginning he's wanted the appearance of a possible war between Tartaro and Joey Silva. Might as well continue that deception.

But on this morning, Philly left without his guards, because he did not want anyone to know where he was going. He was meeting Nick Saulter at a storage facility in Lyndhurst, where he had been storing the explosive device since getting it from the courier.

Philly would have preferred not to be so directly involved, but he'd had no choice. He was the only one who had met with the courier, and who had received instructions on how to set the device. He hadn't trusted that to anyone else, mainly because no one else in his organization besides Nick knew about this.

He hadn't regretted that decision. This way no one other than

Nick could ever talk to the cops about him, and that would be dealt with after this was over. He knew that Nick believed his pay for doing this job would make him wealthy for the rest of his life, and that was actually true.

What Nick didn't know was that his life was going to end before the day was out. Philly did not come this far to leave any loose ends.

Nick was waiting for Philly at the storage facility, and they went inside. Nick was already wearing the beard and glasses that would serve as enough of a disguise to make him impossible to identify if the security cameras successfully photographed him. He brought with him the shopping bag from Cara's Village, a toy store inside Paramus Park, that he had gotten during the last rehearsal.

Having the device in that bag would make it even less likely to attract attention, since many shoppers would have similar bags. It was made of a heavy plastic, strong enough to carry the device, but not quite strong enough to withstand the impact of the explosion. A bag made out of steel wouldn't be nearly strong enough for that.

Philly didn't need to teach him how to set the device, because he was going to do that himself. That presented the tiniest of risks; the device had a cell phone number, and only Philly knew that number. But if someone, anyone, happened to dial a wrong number in the next few hours and reached that device, it would not go well for whoever was standing nearby.

But the odds against that wrong number were worth bucking, if the alternative was Nick having to set the device. Nick was not the brightest guy in the world, although there was no one other than himself that Philly would have trusted to do the job.

Philly put the device in the bag, and again went over the instructions. The restating of the plan was probably unnecessary, since it was to be done exactly the same as the rehearsals. But Philly wasn't taking any chances.

Nick was to arrive at twelve thirty, go up to the food court and order two hamburgers, fries, and soda at the counter, and take it all to a table near the center. He would put the bag under the table, and at twelve fifty he would leave.

The bag would remain under the table, and Philly would leave his jacket draped on the seat. He would also leave one uneaten hamburger on the table, as well as half of the drink. It would appear to anyone that he had gone off, probably to the bathroom, and was coming right back.

The chances of anyone thinking otherwise and reacting within those ten minutes in a manner to avoid the explosion were infinitesimal.

The whole process at the storage facility took about fifteen minutes, and Philly and Nick left and drove off in their separate cars. Nick carried the bag very carefully, and laid it gently on the seat on some pillows. He knew that it would take the phone call to set it off, but why take chances?

Bradley comes in to give us the news:
the judge said no.

ACCORDING TO WIGGINS, THE FBI LAWYERS GOT THE IMPRES-
sion that it wasn't a close call, that there wasn't nearly enough evidence to warrant the kind of action we are asking for.

Nobody is surprised; everyone is disappointed.

I float my idea about going on CNN and scaring the shit out of
everyone in New Jersey, but Bradley kills it for all the obvious reasons. I could do it anyway, but I think he's right. Jessie and Nate
don't like the idea, either.

Then I suggest my getting Philly in a room and pounding on
him until he confesses. Nate thinks it's great and offers to be the
pounder, as long as Philly is the poundee. But Jessie is opposed, and
Bradley says no. I can say this; if a bomb really goes off today, I'm
going to find Philly, and no one is going to stop me.

There is very little we can do proactively to stop whatever
might happen. Bradley calls in every cop on the force, and they
are directed to the various shopping malls that are potential targets.
Security personnel at these places have been alerted as well, but
none of us have any confidence that these moves will make a difference. It is truly needle-in-a-haystack time.

"Where is Philly now?" I ask.

Jessie, who is in charge of the surveillance, heads to her office to find out. Whenever a cop is tailing a subject, he or she files frequent reports to update where the subject is and what he's doing.

"Where do you want to go?" Nate asks. We're going to be part of the team watching for something suspicious, but we don't have a specific assignment, so as to maintain flexibility.

I shrug. "I don't know. Maybe Paramus Park or Garden State Plaza. They get younger demographics than The Shops at Riverside."

He doesn't ask why younger is important, because he knows. Younger victims mean younger, healthier organs.

I call Roberts in Vegas and brief him on our total lack of success. He's going to make an effort to get a local judge to issue the order for Vegas, but he and I know he has no chance of prevailing. As little evidence as we had here, at least it was New Jersey based. Roberts essentially has nothing.

"Take a look at this," Jesse says, coming into the office holding a piece of paper. The tone in her voice and look in her eyes convinces me to cut the call with Roberts short.

"What have you got?" Nate asks.

"Mulcahy reported in a half hour ago," she says, meaning Neil Mulcahy, the cop assigned to tail Philly. "I didn't see it because I was in here."

"And?"

"He followed Philly to a storage facility in Lyndhurst. He met a guy there and they went inside for about fifteen minutes. He had no way of knowing what was going on in there. He was looking for guidance on what to do, but I wasn't there to tell him."

I can tell she's beating herself up over that fact, but she shouldn't be, and I tell her so.

She continues, "They left and Mulcahy followed Philly, like he was supposed to, so he doesn't know where the other guy went. But he got a picture of him with a zoom lens."

She hands me the picture. It's of Philly and some bearded guy who none of us recognize, leaving the storage facility and walking toward their cars. The bearded guy is holding a large plastic bag, and by the way it is hanging, it looks like it's pretty heavy.

I know what must be in there, and it sickens me.

But I also know what is on there, and it gives me an idea.

"Can you guys make out the writing on that bag?" I ask.

Nate, Jessie, and I stare at it, all squinting, but none of us can make it out.

"Can you blow it up?" I ask.

"Of course; it's on my computer. Let's go."

We follow her into her office, passing by Bradley's on the way. "We got something," I yell to him, and he's out of his chair like it was an ejector seat. He follows us to Jessie's office and to her computer.

While Jessie presses keys on her computer, I fill Bradley in. I'm annoyed with myself; I should have told Mulcahy what was going on. If I had, he could have guessed what was in the bag and followed it, rather than Philly.

We're all looking at the computer screen as the image gets larger, and the focus centers on the shopping bag. Each time it gets larger, it gets blurry, and then Jessie brings it into better focus. But the larger it gets, the less focused it is.

Finally she stops, apparently having done the best she could. The letters are there; it looks like two words, but most of the second word is obscured by the man's body.

Even the first word is very hard to make out. Nate looks at it and says, "Carls?"

I was going to say the same thing, but I have no confidence in it.

Jessie smacks her hand on the desk. "No! It's Cara's. It's got to be Cara's Village."

"What is Cara's Village?" Bradley asks.

"It's a toy store; I bought a set of blocks there for my nephew a few months ago. Let me go to the website."

Within seconds the Cara's Village website is on the screen, and at the top is their logo. "It's the same style lettering," I say. "No doubt."

"Please tell me it's within the hospital coverage area," Bradley says.

She nods. "Paramus Park. That's got to be the target."

Like everything else in this case, we are going on educated guesses. Unfortunately, we've been wrong most of the time. After all, we had been thinking that we were dealing with a drug case.

And we can be wrong again now. Just because the guy was carrying a Cara's Village bag doesn't mean that he's going to attack that shopping center. But it makes sense. He probably has done some dry runs, and he would have used a bag to do it. Also, having a bag from a store in the same shopping center would seem completely normal.

Of course, the guy could have nothing whatsoever to do with an attack, and he could just have been buying some toys for his kids. But you take your best guess and you go with it, and our best guess is this guy is going to be carrying a bomb into Paramus Park today.

Bradley decides to direct more manpower to Paramus Park but still keep the other places covered. He sends out the photo of our suspect to every cop in his command, with instructions to detain him on sight, using whatever force is necessary. Niceties are not going to get in the way here; if we find this guy, he's going down.

Nate, Jessie, and I go out to Paramus Park in a van specially equipped for electronic surveillance. Jessie will stay in it, and it will be the communications hub. Bradley has stayed behind to run the whole operation.

This is our one shot.

There are twelve cops already at Paramus Park
when we arrive.

THEY CAME IN UNMARKED VEHICLES, SO OUR TARGET WOULD
not sense the heavy police presence. Jessie parks the van way in the
back, in an empty area of the parking lot.

I come up with a plan for what to do with our guy should we
catch him, and I tell Jessie to prepare for it. She's not happy about it,
but will go along. At least I hope she will; it is the one foolproof way
to make sure that Philly DeSimone goes down.

It's five minutes before noon when we get into the mall, and we
don't see anyone resembling our boy. There's no telling what time
he'll be getting here, if he's coming at all, so we could be in for a long
wait.

We spend our time walking around, looking for him but also
looking for a package that he might have left before we got here.

Nothing.

We have every door covered with personnel, and Nate and I are
sort of playing free safety, roaming and making ourselves available
to get anywhere that we're needed.

We're passing near the South door at twelve thirty when I see
him. I'm positive that it's him, and that feeling is reaffirmed by the

fact that he's carrying a bag that says Cara's Village. I say a silent thank you to Jessie for buying her nephew that set of blocks.

Nate and I make contact with the two other cops watching that entrance, but they've already seen the suspect. I make a slight motion for them to come toward him from the sides, and they start to do so. I am going to meet him head-on, and Nate is going to go around and block off the exit, should he try to run. Nate is a really good exit blocker.

We converge on him, and it takes a few seconds for him to register what is happening. Once he gets it, he quickly looks around and sees that he's surrounded on all sides. None of us have drawn weapons, since the last thing we want to do is start firing in a crowded area, especially with an unexploded bomb in the potential cross fire. If he goes for a weapon, we are close enough to stop him before he can reach it.

He decides that his best chance is to run back toward the open door, but there is no way he is going to get by Nate. Nate gives him what looks like a left jab to the throat . . . the punch doesn't travel more than six inches. But it sends the guy to his knees, gasping.

We all move in on him, and I yell out to the shoppers that have seen the punch, "Police. We have this under control." Within seconds we have him on his feet and handcuffed, and I have the shopping bag. It's fairly heavy, and whatever is inside is gift wrapped. I sure as hell hope it's not another set of blocks.

I have a communications wire attached to my wrist, and I talk into it to Jessie, who is on the other end. "We have our man. You know what to do."

"Bomb squad is on the way. How about letting them handle this?" she asks.

"Jessie, you know what to do."

"Yeah," she says, clearly not pleased. If by some chance I'm still alive, I suspect I'll be sleeping in my apartment tonight.

We go out the back, and the parking lot is still empty. Jessie pulls up in the van, and I get in with the suspect and the shopping bag. I turn to Nate and say, "See you in a little while."

"What are you doing?" he asks, but I don't answer. Instead Jessie gets out. She's staring daggers at me, but manages to murmur, "Please be careful, Doug."

I hear Nate asking Jessie what is going on, but I don't wait around to hear her answer; I already know what it will be. I also know what his reaction to it will be, and it will include some choice obscenities.

I secure the suspect in a chair in the back and drive out to an area in the back of the parking lot that is completely empty; there are no cars or people for at least a hundred yards, and behind us are woods. I park the van and shut it off.

The package is on a chair next to the suspect, and I take the chair across from him. The clock on the console says twelve forty-five, and the suspect is already nervously staring at the package and the clock.

"What's your name?" I ask.

"I'm not talking to you," he says.

"Why are you here?"

He doesn't say anything, but he keeps looking at the clock.

Twelve forty-six.

"You were seen with Philly DeSimone today. We want to know why."

No answer.

I pretend to dial my phone, and then I talk into it. "The suspect is not responding to questions. Send somebody out to get him and bring him in." Then I pause, as if listening to a response, and say, "No rush; we'll wait. We have nowhere to go. An hour is fine."

There is a flash of panic in the guy's eyes, as he comes to believe that I don't know what's in the package, and that we're going to be sitting with it for a while. I don't know what time the detonating phone call is set for, but he does, and he's worried about it.

What he doesn't know is that everything said in the van is being taped.

Twelve forty-nine.

"You sure you don't want to talk to me? Once they come to get you, it'll be too late."

He finally speaks. "I didn't do anything wrong."

"Ah, the verbal communication is established. What's your name?"

"Nick Saulter. Can we get out of the van? I have claustrophobia."

Nice try, Nick, is what I'm thinking. "I don't give a shit what you have, Nick" is what I actually say. "Tell me about Philly DeSimone."

"What about him?"

"What does he want you to do?"

"I've got nothing to say about that."

"Up to you, Nick."

Twelve fifty-two.

Nick hasn't taken his eyes off the clock; it's digital, and I swear, the last time it advanced by a minute he cringed. But he doesn't say anything. His mind must be racing to come up with some solution, but there's no good outcome.

If he does nothing, then someone will be calling the device, and he will be blown to bits. If he tells me what I want to hear, then he will be sent to prison for attempting a terrorist act. It will be an attempted mass murder, which will not go well for him.

Twelve fifty-four.

If he was smart, he'd know that even if I took him out of the van, when the device eventually blew up, he'd get chewed up in the justice system in the same fashion as if he talked. Staying silent has no upside whatsoever.

My guess is that it would be called at a round number time, probably one o'clock. There would be no reason to have told him that it will go off at twelve fifty-seven, or one oh three. That's just not human nature.

Twelve fifty-six.

"All right! There's a bomb in that bag! It's going to go off in four goddamn minutes."

"Who gave you the device?"

"Philly DeSimone."

"When and where?"

"This morning, at a storage facility in Lyndhurst."

"How long has this been planned?" I ask.

"For months. Let me out of this van!"

Twelve fifty-eight.

He's panicked; it must be set for one o'clock.

"Why did Philly want to kill people?"

"I don't know; I swear. He never told me."

"The same thing is happening in Las Vegas. What is the target out there?"

"I heard him say a casino, but not which one. Please, it's going to go off."

"At one o'clock."

"Yeah, one o'clock!" The digital clock advances to twelve fifty-nine. "In one minute!"

I open the bag and rip open the package. "I had bomb squad training at the police academy, which fortunately predates my memory loss. If it isn't obvious how to disable it, then I will leave it outside and drive away."

The clock moves to one o'clock. "Shit!" Nick screams. "It's going to blow."

"I forgot to tell you," I say. "We set that clock five minutes ahead."

Fortunately, I recognize the type of connection on the device, and I am able to cut the appropriate wires. I'm not sure why I haven't been nervous this whole time; maybe I better start seeing Pamela again to find out.

"Safe to come in," I say to everyone outside who has been hearing all of this. "The device is disabled."

I hear cars screeching up, and Nate and Jessie are the first ones into the van. Jessie's first move is to hug me, which as first moves go is a pretty good one. Fortunately Nate does not do the same.

"You might want to read Nick his rights," I say to Nate.

He nods. "I will. Then, after I strangle you, Jessie can read me my rights."

I call Roberts in Vegas as soon as
I get out of the van.

I TELL HIM WHAT HAS HAPPENED HERE, AS WELL AS NICK'S SAY-
ing that the target in Vegas is a casino. I also tell him that Bradley, who has arrived on the scene, is calling Wiggins. My guess is that after the day's developments, this time they will be able to get the order to turn the cell phone towers off in Vegas.

Bradley comes over and says, "You do nice work for a psychopath."

"You're making me blush, but I cherish your approval."

"That was a stupid stunt," he says. "First-class, grade-A stupid."

"That's not quite the approval I cherish. What did Wiggins say?"

"That he'll get the judge to issue the order if he has to water-board him."

"Good."

"You want to do the honors and arrest Philly?" Bradley asks.

"I don't care about Philly, but Nate would love doing it. It's the renowned Dr. Cassel that I want the pleasure of arresting."

"You know where he is?"

"I'm sure he'll be at the hospital today, even though it's Saturday. He's expecting a lot of casualties."

Bradley and Nate go off to arrest Philly, while I take Jessie with me to deal with Cassel. He's someone I can handle on my own, but it'll be nice to spend time with Jessie, and will give her plenty of time to yell at me for taking stupid chances.

"That was the old you," she says, once we get in the car.

"Thank you."

"It wasn't a compliment."

"Oh."

This could be a really long ride.

The judge gave the order to shut down
cell service in Vegas.

ROBERTS WAS CONCERNED THAT IT WOULD NOT BE ENOUGH,
that the casinos should also be evacuated. But it didn't matter what
Roberts thought, because the FBI and ATF came in and completely
took over the operation.

And they took a rather aggressive approach, detaining everyone who could possibly be involved. Included in that were Dominic
Romano and three of his soldiers, two of whom were the men who
helped him get rid of Salvatore Tartaro. One of them has already
confessed to being part of his murder.

Also detained was Daniel Lewinsky's counterpart at Harriman Hospital, Louis Aldridge, and not surprisingly, he was the one
to crack under the pressure. Aldridge confirmed an operation similar to the one at Bergen, and was also able to identify Lucky Linda's
Casino as the target.

Aldridge's statement was more than enough to get Dominic
Romano arrested, and no doubt will help lead to his conviction.
Both of them are going down, though Romano has further to fall.
If Aldridge is lucky, he and Romano won't wind up sharing a cell.

The FBI and Vegas cops caught an incredible break when the

guy tasked with delivering the device to Lucky Linda's went ahead and did so. He had heard about the cell phone outage, but assumed it was temporary. He couldn't get Romano on the phone to possibly get different instructions, because, of course, his cell phone didn't work.

So he went ahead and left the package, thinking he could always go back and get it, as he had done in the rehearsals. He wound up running into eleven waiting FBI agents, a confrontation which did not go well for him. The device was retrieved and disabled.

Roberts called me when it was over, and thanked me. "Great work," he said. "When word about what you did gets out, they'll comp you the Presidential Suite at the Excalibur."

When it comes to public relations,
Bradley is no dope.

ONCE THE ARRESTS ARE MADE ON THIS END, HE CALLS A PRESS
conference to run his victory lap. He knows that Wiggins and the
Bureau will not be far behind, and their track record for crediting
local cops with successes is not stellar.

Bradley goes much further than I would have in revealing the
details of what happened. There is no harm in discussing the plot to
blow up Paramus Park, since the media had already latched on to
that. But he also ties it into Bergen Hospital and Rita Carlisle, and
I don't think we have that buttoned down enough yet to have gone
public.

Fortunately, he just refers to "fraudulent activity" at the hospital, rather than discuss the organ harvesting. But with the murder
of Daniel Lewinsky in the public record, and the arrest of Dr. Steven Cassel, the press will grab on to the story like a dog with a bone,
and will no doubt uncover everything.

Bradley is pretty gracious in crediting Nate, Jessie, and me with
breaking the case. Of course, because of my existing celebrity status,
I am elevated into the number one slot in the subsequent stories.

I'm aware that nothing I can say will be able to change that, so this time I take a different approach; I don't say anything. I decline all interviews and encourage Jessie and Nate to do them.

Jessie does a couple and finds them unpleasant and uncomfortable. Nate does many and eats it up. Every time he does a television interview, he asks us if he had looked fat. Jessie says no and I say yes. But Nate loves doing the interviews, although he's not thrilled with the food they have in the greenrooms.

Unfortunately, Wiggins has moved in and cut us out of the legal process; all the arrested parties are under Federal control because it has become a Homeland Security case. Even the implicated hospital employees here and in Vegas are folded into that, and it's being treated as one large conspiracy.

That's all fine as far as ultimately attaining convictions; it's fair to say that the Feds will be better at that than us, although these are not tough cases to make. The problem from our point of view is that we don't have the ability to question any of the accused, so as to find out all the details of what went on.

Bradley asked for and was given an audience with Wiggins to get an update. It's a courtesy that Wiggins did not have to extend, but he is apparently respectful and appreciative of our efforts. Maybe because he knows that without us, they'd still be shoveling up bodies in Paramus Park and Lucky Linda's.

Bradley comes back from his meeting with Wiggins and updates us on what he was told. A number of people have clammed up, but others have talked, and while they haven't learned everything, they've learned a lot. The FBI has their theories about the rest of it, and Bradley wasn't completely clear on which parts were known to be true, and which were those theories.

The basic conspiracy was as we believed; organs were being harvested on the black market, at ridiculously high prices. In some cases, like William Simmons, murders were being committed. But in many of the situations, the deaths were either from natural causes or accidental. In some instances, driver's licenses were being forged after the fact to make it seem as if the deceased was a voluntary organ donor.

Then, when the organs did not make it to the legitimate channels, it was covered up in hospital paperwork. Since hospital policy was to not tell surviving family members where their loved one's organs went, those people would have no way of knowing what really happened.

"Was Galvis involved?" I ask.

Bradley shakes his head. "It doesn't seem so. Cassel fed him all that information about the drug operation, claiming he had uncovered it himself but as a doctor didn't think it was his place to get involved. Galvis was happy to convey the information, because if it got Lewinsky fired, then Galvis would get promoted into his job."

"So Philly was the ringleader?" Nate asks.

"That much is clear," Bradley says. "And get this. It appears that Joey Silva didn't know about the planned attack on Paramus Park at all. He thought the reference to the 'sixteenth' meant that a couple of murders were to be committed, not that the world would blow up."

"Joey won't walk, will he?" Jessie asks.

Bradley shakes his head. "No chance. They've got him on way more than enough; they don't need the Paramus Park attack."

"What about Vegas?" I ask. "Was Dominic Romano taking over the way Philly did here?"

"Yes. He and Philly were in on it together to get rid of their bosses, and make this their big killing. Pardon the pun. Wiggins doesn't think that Salvatore Tartaro knew about the casino attack, either. But it doesn't matter now, because they have confirmation from one of the soldiers that Tartaro is history."

"So why did Shawn come up to Doug at the meeting with the scrapbook story?" Jessie asks.

"Let me take a shot at that," I say. "Dominic and Philly conspired to send him. He and Philly wanted their bosses out of the way, and they were hoping that we would nail Joey Silva on the Carlisle kidnapping. Then, they'd have killed Tony, so Philly would be in charge.

"When that wasn't working as fast as they needed it to, they used Lewinsky to implicate Joey, and Wiggins did their work for them by arresting Joey. I'm sure Philly had Shawn killed, with Dominic's approval. He had done what he was supposed to by getting me involved, and they knew that his head showing up in Eastside Park would motivate us even more."

Bradley nods. "That pretty much sums it up."

"And at Bergen Hospital, Dr. Cassel was pushing out Lewinsky at the same time that Dominic and Philly were pushing out their bosses."

"Do we know who received all these organs?" Jessie asks, and Bradley says that we don't, and probably never will.

"But the ironic thing is that whoever got them, it probably saved their lives."

I nod. "Now we know what Joey meant by 'giveth and taketh away.'"

John Nicholson was released from prison today.

I'M GLAD ABOUT THAT, BUT VERY SORRY ABOUT CONTRIBUTING to a process that wrongly took away three years of his life. I apologize for that when he calls me, even though he's calling to thank me for getting him freed.

"I had some wild fantasies about how I might someday get out," he says. "You weren't in any of them."

I laugh. "I'm not surprised."

"Yeah. But you were the one who came through."

I'm moving into Jessie's house, at least part way. I'm keeping my apartment and half my clothes there, while bringing the other half to Jessie's. I'm not sure if she told Bobo about the new arrangement yet. He still looks at me as if I'm lunch.

"I think this will work out great," she says. "Unless it doesn't."

"Are you ready to set a date?" I ask.

"No, but I'm almost ready to set a date to set a date."

"Well, now we're getting somewhere."